DOUBLE YOUR PLEASURE . . .

"Just one thing, ladies," I said. "Uh . . . could we do it one at a time, perhaps?"

"One at a time?" Vinnie said.

"Separately?" Winnie said.

"Yes," I said. "Separately. Just for a change. Call it an experiment."

"Oh, we couldn't do that," Vinnie said.

"We would never do that," Winnie said.

"We do everything together," Vinnie said.

"We're sisters, you know," Winnie said.

"Twins," Vinnie said.

"Identical," Winnie said.

"Yes," I said. "I get the picture."

→ → →

26 NIGHTS

OTHER BOOKS IN THE SERIES

THE EDITORS OF
PENTHOUSE MAGAZINE
PRESENT...

26

Can
one man
sleep
his way
through the
alphabet?

NIGHTS

A SEXUAL ADVENTURE

WARNER BOOKS

A Time Warner Company

WARNER BOOKS EDITION

Cover design by Tony Russo

Warner Books, Inc.
1271 Avenue of the Americas
New York, NY 10020

Visit our Web site at
www.twbookmark.com

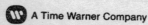 A Time Warner Company

Printed in the United States of America

First Printing: February 2001

10 9 8 7 6 5 4 3 2 1

26
NIGHTS

Chapter I

AMBROSIAL IS THE SCENT OF WOMAN. As
always, even before I was fully awake, I knew
by the scent that she was there beside me. It is
indescribable and, to some, undetectable—too
many men of my acquaintance have told me
they are unaware of it, except under obvious circumstances, which seems to me very sad—but it is the scent
of heaven, and on those rare mornings when I awaken to
its absence, I am possessed by a terrible depression, combined with the need to experience it again as soon as possible.

This morning, however, it was not absent. Gratefully I
reached out for the sweetness beside me, not yet awake
enough to recall who it was. It didn't matter. The scent
told me it was female, and my hands soon confirmed that
conclusion. Soft it was, and warm, with smooth skin, with
yielding breasts, round behind, sweet tender thighs . . .

"Good morning," came a throaty voice, and then I remembered. Phyllis. Blond, pretty, kittenish . . . and married. But with a husband who traveled. Very convenient.

The trip that had taken him away this time was not the first one of which Phyllis and I had taken advantage. There was something else about Phyllis—something I strove to remember. I pride myself on my memory of these things, somewhat encyclopedic, if I do say so. Ah yes—it came to me. Phyllis liked to be touched in a certain way. High up between her thighs . . . just at the lower end of the vaginal opening . . . just . . . there . . . like this . . .

"Ohhh!" Phyllis gasped. "Oh Jesus . . . Oh Steven . . ." And she slithered across the bed to me and pressed her estimable body hard against mine. And wiggled. My fingers did that thing again, and then explored a bit further. "Jesus . . ." she said again, and her leg came across me, and then she was pulling herself on top of me, straddling me and grasping my cock (which had been hard since before I was awake) and sliding herself down over it.

My appreciative groan and the ring of the telephone came simultaneously.

"Oh God . . ." Phyllis said breathlessly. "Oh no . . ."

"It's only Miss Greenglass," I said. "Not to worry." Without moving enough to dislodge her, I reached for the phone on the bedside table.

"Don't answer it," Phyllis said, but I merely winked at her.

"Yes?" I said to the phone.

"I'm here, Mr. Walling." It was indeed Miss Greenglass, my secretary, who came to my house every weekday morning at a ridiculously uncivilized hour, a practice from which neither pleas nor threats could dissuade her.

"I'm busy, Miss Greenglass," I said. Which was true only in a sense, for I wasn't doing a thing other than lying there while Phyllis of the bouncing breasts and sweetly flexing legs was moving rhythmically up and down.

"I'm sure you are," Miss Greenglass said, with just a hint of sarcasm. Perhaps Phyllis's rather heavy breathing had made itself heard through the phone; or perhaps it was just that Miss Greenglass was accustomed to my being busy at that hour. "I'll make a start on those contract figures, Mr. Walling, shall I? Until you are . . . free."

"Fine," I said. "Thank you, Miss Greenglass." I hung up just in time to prevent Miss Greenglass from hearing a series of cries from the ever-orgasmic Phyllis, which would surely have confirmed what she already knew. Phyllis threw back her head, spasmed her way through a splendid climax, and then collapsed on top of me.

"Don't worry about Miss Greenglass," I said. "She's used to waiting." And rolling her over—very carefully, so as not to break our pleasurable connection—I proceeded to partake further of the matchless joys of the female body.

"Have you *quite* finished, Mr. Walling?" Miss Greenglass asked as I joined her in the room that serves as my office.

"For now, Miss Greenglass. For now. Mrs. Dilsey is rather tuckered out, and as there don't seem to be any other females around at the moment . . . Unless, of course, *you* would unbend enough . . ."

Miss Greenglass just looked at me in that particularly bleak manner of which only she is capable. My proposition was not new to her; indeed it was broached, with increasing hopelessness, virtually every day, invariably followed by her rather disdainful refusal. "I am sure," she said now, "that you will have no trouble finding adequate prey before the day is out. Shall we get to those figures now?"

The figure I was most desirous of getting to was hers,

as she well knew. That figure was as tantalizing as any I have seen, and her severe and businesslike manner of dress only made it seem more alluring. Her dark hair was generally gathered and pinned neatly behind her head; I longed to see it loose and swinging about her very attractive face. But alas, after six months in my employ, working in my house five days a week, I had not even been allowed to address her by her first name.

"Prey?" I said, assuming a wounded air. "I assure you I do not think of the ladies I am fortunate enough sometimes to . . . let us say . . ."

"Dally with?" Miss Greenglass quickly supplied.

"Thank you. I do not think of them as prey. I may hunt them, in a sense, but I don't shoot them, I don't wound them, I don't cause them distress in any way. I merely give them pleasure, and they return the favor."

"How generous," Miss Greenglass murmured. "Shall we get to work now?"

"As a matter of fact," I said, "I am going out. I have an appointment at Brooks Brothers to be measured for a new suit. I happened to stop in there yesterday, and there is a lovely young woman working there as an assistant. You know, I can remember when there were no ladies at Brooks Brothers. Sometimes the times change for the better."

"The designated target for the day, I take it," Miss Greenglass said.

"You insist on using such sinister imagery. But the thought has crossed my mind. Her name is Abigail. I've always liked that name. There's something prim and old-fashioned about it, but at the same time it's got a kind of little-girl quality. Abigail. I'm partial to names beginning with A, you know." Miss Greenglass's first name is Anne.

"You are fond of names beginning with any letter of the alphabet from A to Z," she said sweetly. "Providing they are female."

"Come to think of it, that's true," I said. "And I suppose I must have gone through all the letters at one time or another. Well, perhaps not X . . . no wait, there was a rather luscious lady a couple of years ago whose given name, I believe, was Xanthippe—she was the daughter of a classical scholar. Didn't really use it, though. Called herself Tiffany, actually. It was only by accident that I found out . . ."

"What you should do," Miss Greenglass said, in that Greenglassian tone of hers, "is go through the alphabet in order. It would provide more of a challenge, I should think, than mowing them down indiscriminately."

I thought a moment. "Actually," I said, "you may have something there. It *would* be a challenge. Beginning with Abigail—assuming she is amenable, of course—I could then go on to, say, a Barbara or a Betty, then a Carolyn or a Christine, or . . . You know, if I managed one a week, I could get through the entire alphabet in six months!"

"How in the world," Miss Greenglass inquired, "would you ever limit yourself to one a week?"

"Oh, well I could have others in between, of course . . ."

"No, you could not," Miss Greenglass said. "That would be part of the challenge, you see. You must limit yourself to the alphabetical succession until it is completed. And if you haven't completed it within the six months, you should consider that you have failed."

I looked at her curiously. "I didn't realize you were making the rules here," I said. "Do you by any chance think I couldn't do it?"

Miss Greenglass favored me with her inscrutable gaze. "I do think it would be rather difficult," she said finally. "Even for you."

"Would you," I said slowly, "like to make a little wager on the matter?"

"A wager, Mr. Walling?"

"A wager. That I can sleep with twenty-six women whose first names begin with each letter of the alphabet, in succession, within six months."

"And no others in that time?"

I shrugged. "If you insist. That will inspire me to proceed more ardently."

"And what would be the stakes in this wager?" Miss Greenglass inquired. Her voice was cool as ever, but I thought I saw a very slight flush on her cheek, indicating that she had an idea of what my answer would be—or at least part of it.

"Well," I said, "if by some chance I should lose—as you obviously think I am bound to do—I will, let us say, double your salary. Hell, I'll do better than that—I'll triple it. How's that?"

"That is certainly tempting," she murmured. "Extremely tempting, Mr. Walling. And if you win?"

I looked straight into her eyes, and I must give her credit for returning my gaze in kind. "If I win, Miss Greenglass," I said deliberately, "I will then expect to start the alphabet all over again—with Anne Greenglass."

"I see," she said. And still she didn't look away from me. I didn't really expect her to accept. Which shows that although in some ways I may know more about women (I say immodestly) than any man alive, in other ways I know nothing about them, and neither does anyone else. "All right," Miss Greenglass said. "I accept the wager."

I nearly fell over. "You do?" I said stupidly.

"Yes," she said. "I do. Now are you leaving immediately, or can we do some work on these figures first?"

"It has long been a fantasy of mine," I said to Abigail, "to make love to a woman in one of the little dressing rooms at Brooks Brothers."

"Really, Mr. Walling!" Abigail blushed prettily and turned away to straighten a stack of pin-striped shirts on a display table beside her. In spite of the blush, I had the feeling that the lady was not quite as shocked as she pretended to be. Young ladies (and the winsome Abigail was surely still in her early twenties) are seldom sheltered maidens these days. A woman who earns her own living—even in a staid environment like Brooks Brothers—is hardly sheltered; and sweet-looking and diffident though she was, Abigail, I was sure, was no maiden.

But she was obviously not to be had at the drop of a fantasy. "Oh well," I said cheerfully. "If the dressing room is out, I'll have to settle for taking you to lunch. What do you say?"

"Oh, thank you, Mr. Walling, but I don't think—"

"Just lunch," I said, putting up my hands to show my innocent intentions. "A friendly lunch, in a public place. Anywhere you say."

Her fetching brown eyes turned to me. They went beautifully with her soft shoulder-length hair. "Anyplace?"

"Name it."

Was there a hint of mischief in those wide eyes? "I've always wanted to eat at Lutèce," she said.

Lutèce! The girl had expensive tastes. But then it has

always seemed to me that money has no better use than to be put to the service of love. Or lust.

"I like a lady who knows what she wants," I said. "Lutèce it is. Shall we go now?"

Her eyes widened further. "But—but don't you need a reservation? How will we get in?"

"For me," I said, "they'll make room."

Which, of course, they did, thus further impressing my lovely companion, who appeared a bit awed by the elegance of the surroundings, the smooth solicitude of the waiters, and the superb delights of the meal itself. A perfect situation for a seduction, one would think; and yet despite my best efforts, I could see that I was not making any noticeable progress in the direction of that dressing room. Abigail was friendly and, after several glasses of wine, even a bit flirtatious, but though I was sure I could get to her eventually, a protracted wooing was not in the cards at this point. If I were to win my bet with Miss Greenglass, I had to get the show on the road, so to speak. I wondered what would happen if I were to tell her about the bet—lay the aforementioned cards, as it were, on the table. I decided it was worth a shot; if it didn't work I would be no worse off, and I could get back to Abigail sometime in the future.

"Abigail," I said. "I want to tell you about a wager I made recently."

I told her everything. Well, almost everything. Of course I was wise enough to hasten to assure her truthfully that I had been attracted to her long before the wager was even thought of—indeed that my attraction to her (first name and all) had been the genesis of the wager, and not its result. But I did prevaricate a bit about the stakes—and also about the other party to the bet. I implied that it was with a business acquaintance, and purely for money. Less colorfully romantic than the truth, perhaps, but, as calculated, safer. Abigail was shocked again—or pretended to be. "You actually . . . You said you would . . . You intend to . . ."

"Yes," I said. "I did, I said, I do. And it's all your doing, Abigail. If you weren't so lovely . . . or if your name didn't begin with A . . ."

"Really, Mr. Walling." She drank some more wine. "You can't believe I would—just like that—"

"I was hoping you would," I said softly. "After all, when a man sets himself an arduous task, he likes to start it off as pleasantly as possible. My future labors in this endeavor would be made so much easier if only I had you to look back on. And," I added shrewdly, "to look forward to again when it's over."

"You are a terrible man!" Abigail said. She finished her wine. And then she said, "Right there in the dressing room?"

The dressing rooms at Brooks Brothers are larger than those in many other establishments, but still not what you might call capacious. Fortunately, the doors lock from the inside, and though for two people to lie on the floor, let alone conduct any strenuous activity there, might be somewhat impractical, the rooms are furnished with narrow wooden benches on which one may place one's clothing. Abigail and I did not use ours for that purpose; the clothes we discarded lay on the floor, while we occupied the diminutive bench ourselves, I seated on the hard wood, with Abigail seated on me, with her back to me, bent slightly forward and clutching at my legs for support, with my arms around her, my hands covering her fine round breasts and my rampant cock deep inside her sweet, pulsing vagina.

In this position we could both see ourselves in the full-length mirror opposite the bench, and I must say that the sight of Abigail's delectable body slowly rising and falling against me did nothing to diminish my ardor. Abigail enjoyed it too, and the first time she came I had to put my hand over her mouth to stifle her cry. By the second time she had turned around to face me and we were kissing passionately, so that the sound of her climax was muffled against my mouth. As was mine against hers.

Afterwards Abigail, anxious about getting back to work, and I think a little scandalized at herself for what she had done, dressed herself swiftly and left with hardly a word. I resumed dressing—more leisurely, feeling quite contented and trying to recall the women I knew whose names begin with B.

Chapter 2

BECAUSE MY DELICIOUS (IF UNUSUAL) WAGER
with Miss Greenglass, which I was determined
to win at all costs, stipulated that I limit myself
to the alphabetical succession, thus prohibiting
me from pursuing my normal habit of finding
pleasure with any agreeable female who crossed my path,
my search for the next lady in line (or as I humorously
thought of her, my B-girl) was to my mind quite urgent;
not because I had only an average time of one week per
woman if I were to fulfill the terms within the allotted six
months, but because I was accustomed to experiencing
the joys of copulation nearly every day of my life. To me
it was as necessary as the drink to the alcoholic, the drug
to the heroin addict—with the difference that my addic-
tion did no harm to my body, but on the contrary was
most beneficial, perhaps even essential, to my physical
and spiritual well-being.

Thus, as I said, even as I was donning my clothing in the
Brooks Brothers dressing room after my pleasant en-

counter with the winsome Abigail, I was searching my mental Rolodex for ladies I knew whose first names started with B. I had a quite fond and not too distant memory of Belinda Reynolds, the socialite and former editor of one of the high-fashion magazines (I can never keep them straight); but alas, she had recently gone with her husband to live in Monte Carlo. I could, of course, simply have hopped on a plane, but surely there were more convenient alternatives. I thought of Bonnie Packard, a slender and pleasingly passionate gallery owner with whom I had spent a night six months ago; but though I had enjoyed her pliant and eager body, her incessant chatter before, during and after our lovemaking had gotten on my nerves to the point of giving me a headache. No . . . I would think of someone else—or even better, find someone new, as a fresh experience is always more intriguing and stimulating for me than a repetition of past pleasures.

As it turned out, my need was resolved (or so I thought) in a very simple and unexpected way. As I emerged from the dressing room and was making my way to the front door, Abigail came up to me, blushing quite noticeably, but smiling in a way that did wonderful things for my ego. "Mr. Walling," she whispered. "I was just—"

"My dear Abigail," I said. "Surely after the past hour you might call me Steven, don't you think?"

She blushed harder. "Steven . . . I was thinking . . . about your bet . . . and how I might help, maybe . . ."

"You already have, Abigail," I said. "And most enjoyably, too."

"Well . . ." she said, looking away from me. "I—I have this friend . . ."

"Oh?" I said. "Have you indeed?"

"She—she's very pretty," Abigail murmured. "And she likes . . . well . . . she likes men . . ."

"Excellent qualifications," I said. "And her name is . . ."

"Her name is Betty," Abigail said.

"Betty!" My luck was holding. "What a fine, sweet lady you are, Abigail. And how can I get in touch with this Betty?"

Abigail handed me a slip of paper. "This is her number. I just talked to her. She's expecting your call."

What a girl!

"Not that she—" Abigail said hastily. "I mean, she didn't say she'd—I mean, I don't know if—"

I smiled benignly. "I understand," I said. "Don't you worry, Abigail. You just leave that to me."

As it turned out, what had caused Betty—who was not, as she told me, generally fond of blind dates—to be receptive to the idea of meeting me was Abigail's mention of the lunch she and I had had at Lutèce. During our phone conversation she mentioned it twice, making it quite obvious that she would not be averse to beginning our proposed evening together by dining on those elegant premises. I, however, avoided making a definite commitment on that score, as I find eating at the same restaurant twice in a row to be an even less exciting prospect than sleeping with the same woman on successive nights.

Thus, despite the fact that Lutèce might have had the same salubrious effect on Betty as it had had on Abigail, I decided to take a chance and surprise her with the unexpected. Accordingly, I showed up at her door that evening attired in impeccable evening dress—and bearing a large brown paper sack filled with cartons from a local Chinese take-out establishment.

Betty turned out to be an attractive redhead, perhaps a few years older than Abigail, with a friendly smile and a pleasingly voluptuous figure. If she was a bit taken aback at first by the unorthodoxy of my dinner plans, she was also, as I had hoped, at least as intrigued as she was disappointed. Soon we were sitting side by side on her sofa, the little white boxes scattered before us on her coffee table.

Romancing a woman is second nature to me, and while I will not go so far as to say that my charm is invariably successful, long experience, steady application and beneficent gifts of nature have given me a certain confidence not unwarranted by my track record, as it were. It was not long before Betty and I were feeding each other tidbits with the cheap wooden chopsticks that had come with the meal; and it was but a short step from there to the nibbling of choice morsels from each other's lips. This type of gourmandizing being conducive to a certain amount of dripping and spilling, we naturally found it expedient to remove our clothing.

I am always open to new experiences, and there on Betty's sofa I discovered some quite pleasant ones. Never before, for example, had I had my erect phallus wrapped tightly in Chinese sesame noodles, which were then eaten away by soft lips, sweetly nibbling teeth and hungrily slurping tongue. I also discovered how spicy a woman's nipples taste under a thin coating of hot Oriental mustard, as well as the tangy flavor imparted to female flesh by a bit of soy sauce on the torso as one licks one's way down. I needed no condiments, however, to enhance the essence of the lady when my mouth reached the juncture of her beautiful thighs. Nothing on earth can improve the taste of woman herself . . . nothing on earth or, I am certain, in heaven either. After some time we repaired to Betty's bedroom, where without further benefit of Oriental viands we spent a long delicious night feasting only on each other's flesh . . .

Miss Greenglass was already hard at work when I arrived home the following morning. As I looked into the office with a cheerful (if somewhat sleepy) greeting, she regarded me with faint disapproval in her fine, dark eyes. Those eyes may also have held a tiny glint of amusement, but with Miss Greenglass it was difficult to tell.

"Good morning, Mr. Walling," she replied, and in her voice there was no trace of amusement at all. But she could not refrain from referring to our wager, in which, after all, she was both a party and a part of the pot, so to speak. "I take it," she said, noting my attire and my unshaven condition, "that your pursuit of Abigail has been a successful one."

I smiled broadly at her. "Ah, Miss Greenglass," I said expansively. "As usual, you underestimate me." Sitting down at my desk, I leaned back and put my feet up, feeling quite smug indeed. "My dear lady, you do not—literally—know the half of it. Not only did I spend a most pleasant—and yes, successful—afternoon with sweet Abigail, but not being one to waste time, I used the evening to complete the second step in our most interesting wager. I have taken care not only of A, but of B as well."

Miss Greenglass's eyebrows rose, the only sign of surprise visible upon her placid, but lovely, countenance.

"Really, Mr. Walling?" she said. "That seems quite enterprising, even for you."

I looked at her sharply. "You aren't doubting me, are you? I hope you know that I would never stoop to lying, even to win such a wager as this one. I suppose I could bring some kind of proof of each success, but . . ."

"You misunderstand me, Mr. Walling," Miss Greenglass protested. "Of course I have absolute confidence in your word. You do have many failings, but untruthfulness is not among them. I will trust to your honor in this matter."

"Good," I said. "Because I assure you that I intend to go all out, and accomplish superhuman feats in order to win access to that splendid body of yours. Not to mention to avoid tripling your salary. Now that Abigail and Betty are behind me, I shall start this very day to search for a C. Why, at this rate, I could accomplish the whole thing in less than two weeks!"

"I beg your pardon," Miss Greenglass said, raising those eyebrows again, "Did you say 'Betty'?"

"Yes," I said. "Beautiful Betty. But you don't know her, Miss Greenglass. She is a friend of Abigail's, and—"

"But Mr. Walling," Miss Greenglass broke in, "Betty is not a B name."

I stared at her blankly. "What?"

"Betty," Miss Greenglass said slowly, as if explaining something to a small child, "is not a real name, Mr. Walling. It is generally a diminutive for Elizabeth. So if indeed the lady's name, as seems likely, is Elizabeth, you have already abrogated the terms of the wager by violating the alphabetical succession. I shall expect my raise as of the first of the month."

"Now wait a minute," I said. "Wait just a minute here.

This is crazy. Betty is the woman's name. She calls herself Betty, everybody else calls her Betty, that's the name she uses. Betty. It's a legitimate name, and it's a legitimate B. The bet is still on!"

"I'm afraid not," Miss Greenglass murmured. "Nicknames or diminutives are too easily come by, Mr. Walling. We were referring to true proper names, and I must insist on those terms."

"It's a damned technicality!" I protested hotly.

"A technical knockout," Miss Greenglass said, "is still a knockout."

I reached for the phone. "First let's find out if this is true." Quickly I dialed Betty's number, but received no answer. Then I called Abigail. Oh yes, Abigail told me, her friend's actual name was indeed Elizabeth, but she hated it, so . . . With a sinking heart, I thanked her and hung up.

"Look," I said, somewhat desperately. "This is really not fair, Miss Greenglass, is it? We didn't really set the rules about names that firmly, and I had no idea whatever that Betty would not count as a B. I'm sure if we put this to an objective arbiter, it would be seen as a case of—"

"I hardly think that doing so is either necessary or desirable," Miss Greenglass said. She paused a moment, deliberating, though her face showed nothing of her thoughts. At last she sighed gently. "Very well," she said. "Perhaps there is reason for compromise here. Let us consider the wager still in force. However—" she added swiftly, "I must insist that Betty does not count, and that a legitimate B is still to be accomplished."

"But—" I began, but I could see that Miss Greenglass was not about to compromise further. I was relieved that our bet was still on, but nevertheless disgruntled at the invalidation of my two-in-one-day triumph. In my frustration, I felt that I had to get that pesky B out of the way as quickly as possible. Accordingly, I again thought of Belinda the social butterfly and of the lovely, but loquacious, Bonnie. As Monte Carlo was less convenient than the West Side, I immediately picked up the phone to call Miss Packard.

"Steven!" Bonnie said. "How wonderful to hear from you. You know I was thinking about you only this morning, wondering when you were going to call me. You know, we had such a good time together, when was it, not that long ago, and I would just love to see you again. Oh, do you remember that night when we went to Mortimer's and we ran into those awful people who invited us to their party, and then we went back to my place, oh Steven, wasn't it wonderful, you are such a wonderful man. I was saying just the other day to Sheila, you remember Sheila don't you? Well she's getting divorced again if you can believe that, but anyway I said to her—"

"Bonnie," I said, "I'll call you back." I hung up. "Miss Greenglass," I said, "book me on the first plane to Monte Carlo."

"What in the world brings you here, Steven?" Belinda asked when I called her from the airport.

"I came to gamble, of course," I said, which in a sense was true. "And I can't wait to see you, Belinda. I can be there in—"

"Oh, but I'm giving a dinner party this evening," Belinda said. "Perhaps we could get together tomorrow night instead?"

"I have to go back tomorrow."

"What? But—"

"But I'm dying to see you, Belinda," I said. "I'm longing to see you. To touch you, to kiss you, to—"

"Steven! Really! Just because we once . . . well . . ."

"And it was lovely. Wasn't it?"

"Oh . . . yes . . . yes, it was . . ."

"I can be there in half an hour," I said.

"But my guests will . . . Oh dear . . . Well . . . I'll leave instructions for you to be taken upstairs, and I'll slip away when I can. But it will have to be quick, Steven. You understand . . ."

"Even a moment with you, my sweet, is worth crossing an ocean for," I said. "See you soon."

Sure enough, when I gave my name at the door of Belinda's imposing residence, I was immediately taken upstairs to a bedroom and asked to wait. Within fifteen minutes Belinda came in. Though somewhere close to forty, Belinda was still a remarkably attractive woman, with an ample but well-kept body now shown to advantage in her formal dinner gown. Her blond hair was not, I knew, completely natural, but it complemented her still-youthful face, with cool blue eyes that could warm up very quickly under the right circumstances. Those eyes had a certain sparkle as they regarded me lying comfortably on the bed where I had been waiting.

"It's so good to see you, Steven," she said. "But I've just managed to slip away for a moment. Even a hostess must go to the bathroom . . . but I can't leave my guests for long."

"Then let's not waste time," I replied, and pulled down my zipper.

"You are so wicked!" Belinda murmured. "But you're right." Lifting her dress, she reached beneath it to pull off her panties. "This will have to do," she said; then, "Oh,

Steven!" as I released my already stiff, but still growing, penis. "God, I hope Geoffrey doesn't come looking for me!" Pulling the dress high over her shapely legs, she climbed onto the bed and onto me. "How is Geoffrey these days?" I asked somewhat hoarsely, as Belinda lowered herself slowly, taking me into her. "He's fine," she gasped. "Now be quiet, Steven."

I was happy to obey. After all, it could have been Bonnie . . .

Chapter 3

COMING BACK ON THE PLANE FROM MONTE CARLO, I must confess that I was feeling rather pleased with myself. In spite of the false step I had taken with Betty, and how close I had come to losing my wager with the lovely Miss Greenglass before I had fairly gotten started, I had managed to extricate myself from that danger, and to accomplish the first two stages of my progress within an equal number of days. If I continued to be so fortunate I would be able to conclude the whole thing in less than one month, rather than the allotted six; and with this pleasant idea in mind I allowed myself to envision, as I had so often before, just how that Greenglassian body would look when those severely proper garments were removed, and how that coldly forbidding exterior—which to my mind held the promise of such inner heat—would melt, and then burn, under my hands, my lips, the ardent passion of my lovemaking . . .

This stimulating reverie soon produced a familiar stiffening in my trousers, which in turn brought me back to the business at hand—the necessity of locating the next lucky lady to act as the instrument of my advancement toward the prize. Viewing the situation in the light of reality, I admitted to myself that it was unlikely that this initial rate of progress would continue, and that I must make what hay I could against leaner times. So once again I began leafing through my mental card file, this time for females of the C persuasion, at the same time keeping myself alert, as always, to the presence of whatever comely companions might come my way.

Naturally I was flying first class. I do this not only for reasons of comfort and convenience, but because it is in that section that the youngest and prettiest of the available stewardesses—pardon me, flight attendants—are to be found. The airlines, of course, will not admit to this, indeed will deny it strenuously; but facts are facts, and one has only to use one's eyes.

I used mine to single out two particularly attractive prospects among the several attendants as they performed their various duties. I did this out of habit, but whereas ordinarily such attractiveness would have been my first priority, now the primary consideration must be first names; and so I set about exerting myself to learn them.

Why was it, I wondered with some irritation, that flight attendants no longer wore name tags? Was this another supposedly praiseworthy result of the feminist movement? One would have thought that the absence of such identification would increase rather than mitigate the objectification of these women. In any case, I missed them. Not only was it easier to get acquainted when you already knew the name of the lady fluffing your pillow or serving you lunch, but they also provided a good excuse for examining the shape of her bosom while pretending to peer nearsightedly at the little pin on her chest.

This was not, however, an insuperable difficulty; all the ladies were gracious, and though some responded more obviously than others to my easy charm (I have explained that said charm was a combination of natural endowment and long practice, and at the risk of appearing boastful, I shall, for purposes of truth, abandon any further attempt to be modest about it) I had no difficulty in obtaining the necessary information. There was Patricia, Samantha and Meredith (the latter, alas, one of the two I had picked out for their particular comeliness), and there was a brief appearance by a lady co-pilot named Bridget. There was one other, the second of my two initial choices, whose duties kept me from engaging her in conversation for some time.

Nor did I neglect my fellow passengers. Gazing around the cabin, I spied several young women who piqued my interest—but unfortunately they weren't wearing name tags either. I solved this problem rather cleverly, however. In the course of a trip to the bathroom I stopped by the stewardess' lounge, where Meredith was attending to something or other, and while engaging her in further conversation I managed to get a glance at the passenger manifest on a clipboard hanging from the wall. A quick perusal yielded just one female name beginning with C—Carolyn McGrath, seat L-13. On my way back I checked it out—but alas, Carolyn turned out to be a plump, silver-haired lady of at least sixty-five. I decided to continue the search.

When finally I was able to make the acquaintance of the remaining attendant, however, my spirits rose again. Encountering her alone in that same lounge area, I was pleased to find that she was extremely pleasant and outgoing, and indeed that she appeared to be at least as attracted to me as I was to her. She had lively dark eyes and a mischievous smile; her dark brown hair was pinned up under her blue stewardess cap, but her uniform did not conceal the ample beauty of her figure. After a few minutes' conversation I had no doubt of her availability; but of course I knew it was unlikely that I would be able to take advantage of it. I held my breath as I waited to hear her tell me her name in reply to my casual query—and could hardly keep from grinning when she answered, "Catherine. What's yours?"

At least that's what I thought she said. That's what I wanted her to have said. But of course after a moment it occurred to me, as it will have occurred to you, I'm sure, that I might be wrong. That she could have said not "Catherine," but "Katherine."

Inwardly, I prayed (I don't know to whom or to what, but pray I did). "Pretty name," I said, smiling at her. "One of my favorites. Is that Catherine with a C or with a K?" And again I held my breath.

"A K," she said, smiling back. "My mother was a Hepburn fan."

I cursed her mother silently. I cursed her father too, for allowing her mother to make such a nonsensical decision. I cursed Katharine Hepburn, and I cursed Spencer Tracy as well, just for good measure. "Ah," I said. "What a shame. I mean—" I added hastily as she raised an eyebrow at me, "I mean it's a shame that we don't have more time to get to know each other."

She gave me a slow smile that went straight to my groin. "We have the rest of the flight," she said softly.

Turning away an available woman is one skill I am not practiced at, nor had I any wish to develop much expertise in that area. Certainly not with this woman. But I had no choice. "Not the best of circumstances," I said rue-fully. "Not much privacy on a plane, is there?"

She smiled again. "Oh," she murmured. "I'll bet we could arrange something." She took a step toward me until the tips of her breasts just grazed the front of my shirt, and gazed up into my eyes. "Don't you think so?"

I knew damn well so, and I won't pretend that I wasn't seriously tempted, bet or no bet. I admit the thought was in my mind that I could have a brief airborne fling with this lovely morsel, and Miss Greenglass need never know.

Katharine glanced at her watch. "I have a break right now," she whispered. "Come with me." And she brushed past me, the movement setting my loins throbbing, and walked up the aisle toward the section where the lavatories were.

Now in spite of my disingenuous protestations, I had shared airplane lavatories with females before, and I knew it was quite possible to conduct amorous activities in such quarters; and further, that the ingenuity required to maneuver in that cramped space could even intensify the pleasure. And watching the movement of Katharine's hips and buttocks as she glided up the aisle, I was sure her ingenuity would match mine. Damn! Why had I ever agreed to limit myself to the alphabetical succession? What did it matter if I sampled one or two others in be-tween, as long as I accomplished the primary goal? But rules were rules . . . and I was following Katharine up the aisle just so that I could explain to her that I couldn't . . .

But before I could catch up with her she had popped into one of the lavatories. Of course the "Occupied" sign did not come on; she was waiting for me to join her. Well, perhaps it would be better if I could make my apologies in the privacy the bathroom afforded. Being careful that no one was watching, I slipped in also, sliding the lock after me.

The lack of space in the tiny cubicle of course thrust us together, and Katharine cooperated. Her arms went around me and her body molded itself to mine from shoulders to knees. "Hi," she murmured. And then she kissed me, thrusting her tongue immediately into my mouth.

This woman had the longest and most agile tongue I have ever had the pleasure of experiencing. Before I knew what was happening, it was so far down my throat that I almost felt I could swallow it, and what she was doing with it made me weak in the knees. For several long moments I could do nothing but enjoy the sensation, and of course attempt to reciprocate that enjoyment.

When our mouths finally parted I was nearly breathless, and my stiffness was making a sizable dent in Katharine's belly. But the thought of that damn wager had not entirely deserted my spinning head; although every nerve, every cell in my body was telling me again that it wouldn't make the slightest bit of difference, and Miss Greenglass need never know about this.

But I could hear her voice in my mind, that cool, steady, disturbing voice. "Of course I have absolute confidence in your word. You do have many failings, but untruthfulness is not among them. I will trust to your honor in this matter."

Damn the woman!

With what strength I had left I attempted to push Katharine away from me, an action which neither the tight space nor her clinging arms made very easy. But I managed to get an inch of space between our bodies, and to recover enough breath to say, "Katharine . . . I'm sorry . . . I can't."

"What!?" She stared at me for a moment, but she must have decided I was joking, for with a grin she pushed her hips up against me again, twisting herself against my all-too-obvious arousal. "Oh, I think you can, all right," she whispered. "Oh yes, indeed."

"Don't." I tried to push her away again, but now my back was pressed against the wall of the cubicle, and I couldn't separate us without actually hurting her. Besides, I didn't have the strength. And now Katharine began to slide down my body, lowering herself slowly, letting her breasts rub against me all the way down, until she was on her knees. "Let's just see," she murmured, and her hands were tugging at my zipper.

Oh dear Lord, I thought. Maybe . . . if I just let her . . . if there was no actual intercourse, would that really count? I tried desperately to convince myself that it wouldn't. Her fingers opened my fly and found my erection and pulled it out, and her head bent to me, and . . .

"No!" And somehow I managed to turn away from her, putting my hands down to shield myself, using them to tuck myself back in and zip up. "I'm sorry," I muttered, fumbling for the door lock. "Really, I'm . . . I'm really . . ." With my head swimming, and stammering as I had not done with a woman since I was twelve years old, I got the door open and lurched through it, leaving Katharine there on her knees, astonished and, I was sure, furious. As well she might be.

I slumped against the wall by the lavatory door, trying to catch my breath, and feeling that everyone on the plane was staring at the red-faced, panting man with the very obvious bulge in his trousers. Oh, Miss Greenglass, I thought. Look what you've brought me to. Lord, I hope you're worth it!

I was still waiting for my erection to subside when Katharine emerged from the bathroom. She did not look happy. "Katharine—" I started to say. "Let me explain . . ." But she swept by me without even looking at me, and I didn't have the heart to go after her, even if in my condition it had been practical.

I had known my initial luck was unlikely to hold, but this seemed to be rubbing it in a bit. When I returned to my seat I was feeling so low I even considered the matronly Carolyn in seat L-13. After all, older women could sometimes be extremely passionate. But no. No . . .

When I arrived home, still feeling frustrated and morose, I reported to Miss Greenglass not only my success with Belinda, but also my aborted encounter with Katharine—adding that I hoped she appreciated the honesty, restraint and strength of character I was displaying in this matter.

Her only reaction was a ladylike shrug. "But of course, Mr. Walling," she said coolly. "I hardly expected anything else."

I didn't know whether to kiss her or strangle her.

"Now hear this, Miss Greenglass," I growled. "Tomorrow I intend to call Christine Dunmore—you may remember her, I did some business with her father."

"I recall her vividly," Miss Greenglass said. "As do you, I'm sure. A quite pretty young lady, who had a very obvious crush on you. Her father's presence precluded you from taking advantage of her youth, I believe. But by now she will be of age, will she not?"

"Indeed," I said. "I intend to ask her to come here, and I intend to make love to her here in this office. In fact, right here on this desk. Now you may perhaps wish to absent yourself from the office at that time, Miss Greenglass. That is entirely up to you. But by God, it's going to happen!"

Miss Greenglass did, of course, choose to be elsewhere at the time of Christine Dunmore's visit; and I did make love to Christine, though out of some perverse impulse I did so on Miss Greenglass's desk rather than my own. But though Christine was as passionate, sensuous and inventive as a man could wish, I must admit that even as I bared her lovely young body, and kissed her breasts, and reveled in the clutch of her legs and the warmth of her eager pussy, my concentration was less intense than is usual for me in such situations; my body brought her almost automatically to ecstasy, as hers did for me, but my thoughts were elsewhere—with Katharine, who had gotten away . . . and even more, with Miss Greenglass, who, I desperately hoped, would not.

I decided it would be best to keep these activities outside the office in the future . . .

Chapter 4

DESPITE THE FACT THAT, SINCE ATTAINING maturity, I have never felt the desire personally to participate in those strenuous athletic endeavors which so delight the boyish hearts of many of my colleagues—believing as I do that regular and frequent amorous activity is exercise enough for any man—I do nonetheless occasionally enjoy watching professional athletes at work. My preference is for individual rather than team sports—being something of an individual type myself—and of these, perhaps my favorite is tennis, an activity that provides the viewer with the spectacle of physical grace and skill, while avoiding, on the one hand, the sanguinary violence of boxing, and on the other the soporific longueurs of golf.

I was reminded of this occasional indulgence of mine by two circumstances. The first was that it was nearly Labor Day, which meant that our city was about to be graced by one of the premier tennis tournaments of the season, the United States Open—an event which I had an invitation to attend as the guest of one Mrs. Mergandahl, a prominent socialite whose very wealthy husband reserved a block of seats courtside each year, and who, with admirable civility, had shared both his seats and his wife with me on several occasions. And the second was that Mrs. Mergandahl's first name was Deborah.

Nearly a week had elapsed since my enjoyable if somewhat distracted session with young Christine in my office. As I had accomplished the first three stages of my wager with Miss Greenglass in nearly as many days, I was not overly anxious on that score, and the sad fact was that my aborted encounter on the plane with Katharine had left me so bemused that for several days my libido sagged. This shocking state of affairs could not last long, of course, and the thought of Deborah's bountiful charms was just the thing to turn it around.

"Miss Greenglass," I said, looking up from a report my lovely assistant had just typed for me with her usual impeccability, "could you please check my calendar and tell me when I'm scheduled to attend the U.S. Open with the Mergandahls."

"Thursday, Mr. Walling," this amazing lady said, without looking up from her keyboard. "Mrs. Mergandahl called this morning to remind you. There will be a seat for you in her box at the Open—no doubt at her side."

"You know, Miss Greenglass," I said slyly, "I just thought of an amazing coincidence. I'm up to D in our little wager, and Mrs. Mergandahl's first name happens to be Deborah."

She shot me a glance of such disdain that a weaker man would have been knocked over. "I deem it rather unfortunate, though inescapable," she said, her voice matching her look, "that you have such a backlog of women to utilize when necessary. I see now that I should have limited our wager to new conquests only."

"But you didn't," I said smugly. "Even the terrifyingly efficient Miss Greenglass slips up once in a while, doesn't she? Which means that the irresistibly alluring Miss Greenglass will soon be slipping into bed with the overwhelmingly charming Mr. Walling, who—"

Miss Greenglass never stopped typing. "There is still a very long way to go, Mr. Walling," she said.

Sure enough, my VIP pass was awaiting me when I paid a visit to the USTA National Tennis Center a few days later. It was now over a week since I had been with a woman, and I fully intended to join Deborah (and to be joined to her) as swiftly as possible. However, while strolling toward the stadium, I stopped to look at a posted listing of the day's matches.

Since it was still early rounds, there were no really exciting matchups. I was about to pass on, when another name caught my eye, though I had never seen it before. A Ms. Dolorosa LaPensa, of Chile, was playing another unknown, one Peggy Rinehart, an American, on one of the outer courts.

Dolorosa, eh? A female tennis player, who would doubtless have a finely toned, wonderfully supple body and a great deal of stamina . . . as well as a name beginning with D.

I felt my libido perking up already. Perhaps this line of thinking wasn't very loyal to Deborah, but a fresh conquest is always more stimulating than a repeat performance. Of course this Dolorosa could turn out to be a disappointment; but what the hell, it was worth taking a look, and I began the long trudge out to Court Sixteen.

I had to assume that Ms. LaPensa was the dark-haired one, and if so she was most definitely not a disappointment. Small but solidly built, she flung her impressive body about on legs that improbably combined the muscularity of an athlete with the sleekness of a model. Those short, bouncy tennis skirts are one of the blessings of civilization, but lamentably few players have legs worthy of such a showcase. Dolorosa did.

She was winning her match handily, and enjoying the hell out of it too. With each winning shot against her hapless opponent she jumped up and down with excitement, looking around to make sure the spectators appreciated it as much as she did. Unfortunately there wasn't much of a crowd out there, and those who were watching didn't evince much enthusiasm for this unimportant contest. So I began to cheer and applaud for her each time she hit a winner, with the idea of trying to ingratiate myself with her.

When she won she practically turned a cartwheel on the court before running to the net to shake hands with the blonde. I watched carefully for signs of anyone who might deflect my approach, but after receiving a few desultory congratulations from dispersing spectators, she picked up her things and started off alone.

Luck was with me, but I didn't yet know how much. I approached her as she started out of the court.

"Nice match," I said.

She gave me a grin that could have lit up all of her native country. "Ah! I am win, yes?" she said with a heavy (but charming) accent. "I see you watch me. You cheer for me. I am good, no?"

"You are good, yes," I said. "I wonder if I could—"

But this happy, bubbly and very sexy young lady was too high on victory to listen. "Yes, I am good player," she burbled. "I be number-one player some day. I am win good. I am love to win always."

"I can see that," I said. We were walking toward the building that housed the locker rooms. Not the ones reserved for the top seeds, but those for the lesser lights, though I suspected it wouldn't be long before Dolorosa would be moving up. "Maybe after you change," I began, "we could—"

"I am feel good," Dolorosa said. "When I am win I am feel like—it make me feel—how to say—excite?"

"Excited," I said. "Of course." But I thought she meant something more, and I decided to take a chance. "You mean passionate? Aroused? Hot?"

"*Pasión,*" she said, giving it a Spanish inflection. "*Sí.* Yes. I am want to—" She stopped then, and looked at me. And I mean looked at me. "You like me?" she asked suddenly. "No?"

"Yes," I said. "Yes I do."

By now we had reached the building. "You come," she said, and entered. I followed her until we were outside the locker room door. "I'll wait right here," I said. "Don't take—"

"No. You come." She opened the door.

"No, no," I said. "I can't go in there, Dolorosa." I wondered what people called her for short. Dolo? "That's the women's locker room."

"Wait," she said, and went inside, but she was back in a moment. "Is okay. Nobody here. Come." And grabbing my hand, she pulled me into the locker room after her.

"But someone else might come in," I protested. "Why don't I—"

"I no care," she said. "I am win, I feel good. Someone come, I chase them out. Or if they stay, is no matter."

"Well, that's a very enlightened attitude," I said. "But—" And then I stopped myself realizing that once again, as with Katharine on the plane, I was ruining a perfectly good opportunity—and this time with no real reason. What was wrong with me? What was wrong with a little risk? Nothing. I throve on risk. I welcomed risk, damn it. I may have been stimulated to this realization by the fact that Dolo had started to unbutton her shirt.

"I am take shower," she said, pulling the shirt off. "All sweat, yes? I play hard, I sweat. I am good."

"Oh yes, you are," I said fervently, as her bra came off. I would have taken her, sweat or no sweat. She grinned at me now, posing for a moment, sticking her high, full breasts out.

"You like? I am sexy, no? You come with me in shower."

I envisioned being discovered and barred from the tennis center for life. But as Dolo slipped off the rest of her things, I began to strip also, and in a moment we were both in the shower area, with warm water cascading over our naked bodies.

Dolorosa grinned hugely as she looked down at my growing erection. "You liking me, yes?" she gurgled. "You like me for good tennis player?"

"I like you because you're a gorgeous and sexy woman," I said, and reached for her. She came up against me and we kissed. Her mouth was hot and open, and she purred into my throat as our bodies slithered against each other.

We were both panting when we broke apart. "Is so good when I win," she breathed. "I am not care, me. We do big fuck, yes? Now, yes?"

"It does look that way," I said, and grabbed her again. I meant to pull her down to the tiled floor, but she backed up against the wall, out of the direct spray of the shower, taking me with her. With her arms tight around my neck, she raised her legs and wrapped them around me, as though trying to climb up my body. I clutched at her tight buttocks, helping her, lifting her up, until I was able to join our bodies, and she sank down over my stiffness with a shout of joy, those marvelous legs squeezing me harder than ever.

She cried out a stream of Spanish as we began to move together. I was overwhelmed by the sensations of her breasts sliding on my chest, the clutch of her legs and the springy sinuosity of her writhing body. As we settled into a strong, steady rhythm she fell back into her strongly accented broken English.

"Is good, yes? . . . Is good fuck when I win . . . I be number one . . . Ah, hard now, yes . . . you like it, no?"

I liked it. We both liked it a hell of a lot, and we were moving faster. Dolo's breathless monologue was reverting to Spanish again, when over the sound of the still-running shower we heard feminine voices, feminine laughter. Someone had come into the locker room.

Well, it was too late. At that point I couldn't have stopped if I'd wanted to, and I had resigned myself to discovery; but Dolorosa (without missing a beat) called loudly: "No! Go away, you! Is busy here! Yes?"

The voices went silent. Then after a moment one female voice spoke clearly. "Oh, Christ," it said. "LaPensa must have won again." There were giggles, and then another voice said, "Well, hurry up, okay?" And then they were gone.

"What happened?" I asked.

Dolo laughed triumphantly. "I win them too," she gasped out, still moving. "They know I best . . . Dolorosa

one day . . . champion . . . all know this . . . good play . . .
good fuck . . . yes I win . . . I win . . . I *win*!"

Actually we both won.

After which we collapsed to the floor, and after a few
minutes managed to crawl under the shower again. As
soon as I could I began to get up, but Dolorosa protested.

"I have to get out of here," I said weakly. "Your
friends want to get in."

"They wait," she said firmly. "First I am show you
what else I good at."

And she did.

When I finally emerged from the locker room there
were several women waiting. I felt myself flushing as I
started past them.

"She's good when she wins, right?" one of them said,
and the others laughed raucously.

I tried to grin back at them through my embarrassment. "What happens when she loses?"

"You don't want to know," the woman answered.

"Miss Greenglass," I said. "Please send a note to Mrs.
Mergandahl expressing my regret that I wasn't able to
join her at the Open this afternoon."

"Of course, Mr. Walling," Miss Greenglass said.

The woman was maddening. "Don't you want to know
why?" I demanded.

"I'm sure you will tell me," the lady said calmly. "In
fact, Mr. Walling, I'm sure you will be unable not to tell
me." And, as always, she was right.

Chapter 5

EVEN YOU," I SAID TO MISS GREENGLASS, "CANnot say that I am not being punctilious about this. Although it seems perfectly valid to me, I don't wish to run afoul of any more hidden conditions, such as with Betty. So I would just like to establish beforehand—"

"I must object to your reference to 'hidden conditions,' Mr. Walling," Miss Greenglass said sharply. "The conditions were, and are, entirely plain and aboveboard. The fact that Betty is not a proper name can hardly be—"

"All right," I said, putting up my hands. "All right. Fine. I'm just trying to forestall any further problems of that sort by checking with you up front, as they say. This has to do with Betty, as a matter of fact. When I spent that night with her—"

"In violation of the rules—"

"*Inadvertent* violation—"

"Which, I might add, I very generously overlooked—"

"Which was only fair," I said. "However, as you so quickly pointed out, Betty's proper name—technically speaking—is Elizabeth. And now that I have progressed to E . . ."

"You plan to take advantage of that circumstance by sleeping with her again," Miss Greenglass said. If Miss Greenglass had been in the habit of sniffing, this would certainly have been an occasion for it.

"It seems only logical," I said. "And not only would it take me on to F, but it would be a nice gesture to Betty—ah, Elizabeth. The woman keeps calling me for a repeat performance. It would be simply common decency."

"Your altruism is overwhelming," Miss Greenglass said dryly.

"But, as I say, I want to prevent any future problems; so if there are any technical objections to this plan . . ."

Miss Greenglass was silent for a moment. "No," she said finally. "I suppose there are none. Technically. However, Mr. Walling, as I have said before, the fact that you have a virtually endless list of previous conquests does rather ease your task, does it not?"

"Now wait a minute," I protested. "That's not really fair, Miss Greenglass. After all, of the four ladies who have—ah—contributed to my progress in our wager so far, only one of them—Belinda—has been what you are pleased to call a previous conquest. And that was only because of the Betty business."

Miss Greenglass pointedly did not sniff again.

"However," I went on, "I must say I rather resent the implication that I could not accomplish the same task if quote, previous conquests, unquote, were eliminated. Now, since we did *not* establish that rule, I won't say that I will definitely add that burden to my challenge—after all, when I get to X, it may be quite helpful to be able to look up that Xanthippe I once mentioned—but I will, for my own pride, attempt to limit myself, as much as practical, to ladies not formerly enjoyed by me. Does that meet with your approval, Miss Greenglass?"

"To quote you, Mr. Walling, it seems only fair."

"But please remember that it is not a hard and fast rule," I said. "I wonder what happened to Xanthippe, anyway? But I shall start by finding myself another E, which should not be too difficult. Poor Elizabeth."

I think Miss Greenglass actually *did* sniff that time. I wouldn't swear to it.

It was true that Betty had been calling me rather persistently; our amorous experiment with the Chinese food, and its aftermath, was evidently a most pleasant memory to her. It was to me also, I hasten to add, and actually I regretted giving up the idea of another encounter with that deliciously voluptuous and inventive body. But Miss Greenglass had piqued my pride, and I determined to tell Betty the whole story as soon as possible, as a way, I hoped, of letting her down easy.

With this in mind, I invited her to lunch—at Lutèce, where she had wanted to go at our first meeting.

But she was ahead of me. "I know why you've been avoiding me," she told me when we had ordered. "I got it out of Abigail." (Abigail, as faithful readers will remember, had been the initial step in my current project, and had actually recommended Betty to me.) "I've been complaining to her about your neglect after our night together," Betty went on, "so finally she told me about that silly bet. Honestly, you men! But that's all right. Did you get to E yet? Do you know that my real name is Elizabeth?"

"Actually yes, I do," I said, and then told her about the

complications that fact had caused—and also, rather apologetically, about my need now to find a different E lady.

Betty's face darkened. "Oh," she said. "I see."

There was a long pause.

"I'm sorry, Betty," I said finally. "I know it seems silly, but—"

"Wait," Betty said. "I'm thinking."

I waited.

"I have an idea," Betty said.

"You do?" I said. "What kind of idea?"

"I know somebody," Betty said.

"Really?" I said. "Somebody named Elaine, perhaps? Eloise? Euphronia?"

"Edna," she said.

"Edna?" I was dubious. Edna sounded like someone in a gingham apron on a farm in Iowa, picking preserves or whatever they do.

Betty smiled faintly. She fished in her pocketbook, found a small leather folder and pulled out a photograph. "That's Edna," she said, handing it to me.

The girl in that picture never wore gingham in her life.

"You actually carry her picture around with you?" I said, still perusing the photograph.

"Yes," Betty said. "Edna's a good friend of mine. A very good friend."

"Oh?" I said. "How good?"

"*Very* good."

"I see," I said.

"And if I recommend you . . ."

"You ladies seem to have a veritable referral service," I said. "From Abigail to you to Edna."

"No, no," Betty said. "This is different. This is hardly

Abigail's cup of tea. Abigail would be shocked. And there's a condition."

"Uh-oh," I said. "What condition?"

"I want to watch," Betty said.

"You want to *watch*?" I said. "Are you serious?"

"Yes, I am," Betty said. "It should be a kick."

It was my turn to stop and think. Exhibitionism has never had any special appeal to me, but then, I have nothing in particular against it either. And I am certainly open to new experiences. Furthermore, judging from the photograph, Edna would be an experience worth having.

She looked about twenty-five, with a slender but by no means unfeminine figure, very short black hair, piercing dark eyes, and a direct, almost defiant gaze which for some reason struck me as being extremely provocative.

However, tempting as Edna was, there were other factors to consider. "When you say watch," I said carefully, "you do mean just that? I mean, you understand that you and I can't—ah—enjoy each other again. Especially if Edna and I—"

"I understand the rules, Steven," Betty said, with some asperity. "I think I can manage to control myself."

"I didn't mean—"

"It's okay," Betty said. "I think you and Edna should make for an interesting show. I'm sure I'll be quite turned on. But don't worry, Steven—I won't try to participate." She smiled slightly. Then she said, "Not with you, anyway."

Betty was confident that Edna would have no objection to her idea—or to me—and rejected my proposal that we have dinner together, or at least some kind of preliminary meeting, to allow her to make a decision on the matter.

"It'll be fine," Betty insisted. "All you have to do is show up, Steven. If she doesn't like you she can say so then, all right?"

"Or if I don't like her," I suggested.

"Fat chance," Betty said.

We arranged that we would all congregate at Betty's apartment that very evening, provided Edna was free; and later that afternoon Betty called me to tell me that it was arranged. When I hung up the phone I turned to Miss Greenglass, who had been taking dictation from me directly on her keyboard. Without, needless to say, error.

"That was Betty—ah, Elizabeth," I told her. "It appears I am about to pass the E mark, Miss Greenglass—although not with the beauteous Betty herself." I then told her about Betty's plan, watching her carefully for any signs of shock or discomfort. Of course there were none; her face was as calm and unreadable as ever.

"How interesting," she said when I finished. "It sounds like a rather volatile situation, however, Mr. Walling. You know that if you should—"

"I won't touch her," I promised. "I won't lay a finger on her." Then after a moment I said slyly, "Of course, if you would like to assure yourself of that, you might wish to join Elizabeth as part of the audience. I'm sure the ladies wouldn't mind."

Miss Greenglass favored me with her most Greenglassian look. "Thank you so much, Mr. Walling. But I regret I will be unable to take advantage of your gracious invitation."

"What a surprise," I said.

Edna was already there when I arrived at Betty's apartment. In person she was even more attractive than in her picture. She was casually dressed in a kind of one-piece jumpsuit which fit her slim body tightly and emphasized its lissome curviness. As Betty introduced us she looked me up and down with frank appraisal.

"Betty tells me you're quite a stud," were her first words.

I attempted to look modest, something at which I am not overly skilled. "Betty is too kind," I said.

"Well," Edna said. "I guess we'll find out, won't we?"

Betty grinned. "You're not feeling any pressure or anything, are you, Steven? Just because I gave you a really big build-up. And because Edna can be very critical when it comes to men's performances. And because I'm going to be here watching everything all the time. All that's not going to give you any problems, is it?"

I wondered if this was supposed to be some form of revenge on Betty's part for what she saw as my rejection of her. Also, she was dressed very provocatively, in a tight, low-cut blouse and short skirt, as if to tempt me into breaking the rules. I just grinned back at her, then turned back to Edna, running my eyes obviously over her figure.

"No," I said then. "I don't think I'll have any problem at all."

"Well, good," Betty said. "Okay then, let's get started. Edna, why don't you take your clothes off?"

"Hold on," Edna said. "Are you directing this scene?"

"Why not?" Betty said.

"I don't take directions," Edna said.

"Okay," Betty said. "Sorry. I just thought it would be logical for you to take your clothes off."

"If you want my clothes off," Edna said, "why don't you take them off?"

Something changed in Betty's face. "Would you like me to?"

"Sure," Edna said. "But why don't you take yours off first?"

There was a pause.

"Should I?" Betty said then.

"Why not?" Edna said. "You don't mind if Betty goes naked, now do you, Steven?"

"Well, no, I guess not," I said. "But—"

But Betty was already stripping. I remembered that voluptuous body all too well, the bounteous breasts and the fine legs and the beckoning red patch of pubic hair; and I felt myself becoming aroused as it was revealed to me again. Betty took off everything.

"Now mine," Edna said.

Betty approached Edna and reached for the zipper at her throat. But somehow her hands got distracted, and instead she was suddenly caressing Edna's breasts through the smooth material of the jumpsuit. "Oh," Edna said. "That's nice," and put her hands on Betty's body.

Then they kissed.

I felt quite superfluous. "Ah . . . ladies . . ." I said.

"It's all right," Edna said, as Betty now found the zipper and pulled it down. "Everything's cool. Go with the flow, okay?"

I was willing to go with the flow, but the flow seemed to be going away from me. I began to feel foolish standing around, so I sat down in a convenient chair and watched Betty pry Edna out of her suit. Edna wasn't wearing a bra. Her breasts were not large, but were firm and flawless, with unusually long nipples. Betty kissed them, first one and then the other. Then Edna kissed Betty's nipples, more lingeringly. Sucking and licking them. Until Betty was panting. And then they were both sinking to the floor.

"Ladies . . ." I said again.

"It's okay," Edna said. "Join in any time."

"Absolutely. By all means," Betty said breathlessly.

I would have loved to join in. A three-way free-for-all with two passionate ladies, both delicious and yet so different from each other, was a prospect few men would choose to pass up. As my loins were telling me in no uncertain terms. But then few men would have gotten themselves into my peculiar predicament. I was only allowed one lady, and it might be difficult, in the present circumstances, to limit myself to that number.

Betty was now lying on her back on the floor, with Edna crouched above her, kissing her way slowly down Betty's body. Kissing and licking. From her breasts down over her stomach, and on down to that flaming red triangle. And on down. Betty was moaning. She bent her gorgeous legs to give herself leverage to lift her lower body toward Edna's searching mouth.

Both my head and my crotch were shouting at me that I had to do something, and soon. After all, with some care and a little restraint I should be able to fulfill both the requirements of my wager and the importunity of my passion.

I stood up and quickly took my clothes off. Betty was looking up at me from her supine position, but her eyes were somewhat glazed, and I wasn't sure how much she was aware of. Edna was bent over with her back to me, her face buried between Betty's thighs.

I knelt down behind that crouching body and put my hands on her, sliding them around her to hold her small, stiff-nippled breasts. She gave a muffled sound of pleasure and widened her legs for me, though she didn't raise her head.

It would have been nice to have her undivided attention, but I was not in a mood to quibble. Pressing forward, I found her sweetly moist vagina and slowly, easily joined our bodies. A small stifled gasp from Edna, and we were soon rocking pleasurably to the sound of Betty's moans.

Those moans rose in intensity and volume as Edna's mouth did its work (abetted to what extent by our rhythmic motions I can't really say). Then they rose to a shriek and died away. By then I was quite absorbed in the pleasure of what I was doing, and was only vaguely aware that Betty, after a minute, had pulled away from Edna and crept around behind us—until I felt something on my back. Touching me. Stroking . . . kissing . . .

I leaped up as though Betty's hands and mouth had been branding irons, turning to confront her, and hearing a groan of protest from the abandoned Edna.

"No!" I bleated. "Damn it, Betty, you said you wouldn't . . ." I faded out, feeling stupid, with my erection waving in the breeze.

Betty reached for it. I pulled back.

"I just want to touch it," Betty said. "Oh, please, Steven. I just want to . . ." She reached again, this time with her mouth.

A wise (if somewhat sexist) man once said that women have no sense of honor. There were times—such as right then—when I wished I didn't either. I had to keep the image of Miss Greenglass firmly in mind to keep from giving in to Betty. On the other hand, I was also honor-bound to complete my liaison with Edna if I were not to forfeit my wager.

"I just want to kiss it," Betty pouted. "Kissing doesn't count."

"It counts, it counts," I growled hoarsely. "Edna—can't we just tie her up or something?"

"I have a better idea," Edna said. "She can kiss me instead."

"But—" I started.

"Be quiet," Edna said. "You'd like that, wouldn't you, Betty? Wouldn't you enjoy that?"

"Well, it's not the same," Betty said. Then she grinned. "But hell, it's not bad either."

And in a moment Betty was lying on her back again, but this time the ingenious Edna was crouching over her face, lowering her crotch to the redhead's eager mouth. Edna gasped as she made contact; then, with Betty well engaged, she beckoned me toward her.

Standing astride Betty's supine body I was well positioned to enjoy the ministrations of Edna's fine, passionate and highly talented mouth. Not to mention tongue, lips and teeth.

Edna groaned around my flesh as Betty pleasured her, and as she climaxed, the moaning and twitching of that wonderful mouth brought me higher and higher, until I too was pushed over the brink, spurting with splendid intensity into Edna's sweetly gulping throat.

Ah, women! Women! Who needs honor anyway?

Chapter 6

FORTUNE, MY FATHER USED TO TELL ME, IS AC-quired by dint of hard work, diligence and as-siduity. And he was his own best example, having through those means acquired quite a sizeable for-tune indeed—which he then passed on to me, with no effort whatsoever on my part. From this I learned three precepts which have stood me in good stead throughout my life; choose your parents with care; never work hard when you don't have to; and beware of generalizations.

However, even inherited wealth is not completely without its responsibilities. Although I delegate to others most of the labor of maintaining and enlarging the family firm and its ever-increasing profits, and never except on dire occasions actually visit its depressingly businesslike offices, I am still its nominal head, and as such must spend a certain amount of time pretending to guide and oversee its activities—a responsibility which I manage to discharge from an office in my home, with the assistance of my highly efficient and highly desirable amanuensis, Miss Greenglass.

Aside from the tedium of actually having to apply oneself to business, this position has other drawbacks, one of them being that the success of the firm apparently gives me the aspect of a financial wizard, or at least some kind of expert on the business world. Consequently I am occasionally sought out by the media for a knowledgeable opinion, or even an interview, on the state of the economy or some such topic. Unless I am feeling particularly pontifical, I generally turn down these invitations, preferring to avoid anything connected with work whenever possible.

Thus, when Miss Greenglass informed me that one of the local television stations had called with a request for a brief interview the next day on one of those late-afternoon "news" shows, which consist of a soupçon of news surrounded by an ocean of trivia, both she and I expected that I would decline handily.

"What happened?" I asked. "Did an astrologer cancel out? Some diet book author have another engagement?"

"It seems they want to get your views on the latest economic downturn," Miss Greenglass reported. "It will only be a ten-minute segment, the booker said."

"Pass," I said. But then a thought hit me. "Wait a minute—which show did you say this was again?"

"It's called *More at Four*," Miss Greenglass said, indicating by her tone her not very high opinion of either the show or its title. I knew that tone well.

"*More at Four*," I mused. "Isn't that the one Fern Forrester is on—you know, the sexy redhead with the cute lisp?"

"I wouldn't know," Miss Greenglass said.

"I believe it is," I said. I glanced at my watch; it was three-fifty. "We can check it out in a few minutes. This

Fern lady is very attractive indeed. And as you know, I just happen to be in the market for an F lady right now."

Miss Greenglass raised an eyebrow. "Fern Forrester?" she said. "You don't think that that's her real name, do you, Mr. Walling?"

"Oh no," I groaned. "Here we go again. Look, I understand about nicknames not being proper names—I remember Betty all too well—but this is not a nickname, it's—perhaps—a stage name, or whatever. Surely that counts. If Marilyn Monroe were still with us, would I have to put her under N for Norma Jean? A little common sense here, please."

Miss Greenglass sighed. "I suppose it's a debatable point," she said. "I shall leave it to your own conscience, Mr. Walling."

"Good," I said, though I was not completely happy with that reply—as she had no doubt foreseen.

A few minutes later I found the remote that operated the television set in a corner of the office, and tuned it to the desired channel. "Ah yes," I said as the program began. "That's the lady, all right."

Fern Forrester shared the anchor desk with one Larry Brewster, a fellow with a teased toupee and a perpetually sardonic expression. Fern's hair was reddish blond—at least this season—and she had a marvelous set of cheekbones, a ripe mouth and what appeared to be a sleek, well-engineered body, although most of the time only the top half of it was visible behind the desk. Watching her did nice things for my hormones, and I saw no reason why, given her first name and my fortuitous means of access, she should not be the next step in my progress toward winning my wager with the even more delectable Miss Greenglass.

"You may tell *More at Four* that I will be happy to appear on their estimable program," I said to her. And with that I decided I had done enough work for one day.

The following afternoon I arrived at the television studio shortly before the program was to start. The producer quickly turned me over to Larry Brewster, who proceeded to ask me what questions he should ask me on the show. It was evident that his knowledge of the subject was about as abundant as his hair. When he had written down my suggestions, I mentioned casually that I would be pleased to meet his lovely co-anchor. He shrugged briefly, and pointed to a small vanity table to one side of the set, at which sat Fern Forrester herself.

"Behold the queen," he sneered.

Thanking him for his courtesy, I strolled over. Fern was applying last-minute touches to her face and hair, which already looked perfect to me.

"Miss Forrester," I said. "So nice to meet you. I'm Steven Walling." I explained why I was there, throwing in a compliment or two along the way. She didn't look at me; her eyes never left her own face in the mirror.

"Well, I'm glad Larry has to do you," was the first thing she said. "Usually I get all the dull stuff."

"Um—yes," I said, smiling, although she didn't notice. "But I'm not always that dull, you know. I can be quite charming, actually. I'd like to show you. Perhaps if you're not busy we could have a drink after the show."

"In your dreams, fella," she said flatly and, still without looking at me, got up and walked away. Her legs, I saw, were as luscious as the rest of her.

I turned to see Brewster, who had wandered over unnoticed. He was smiling his most sardonic smile, which made me want to knock his toupee off. "Sweet girl, isn't she?" he chuckled. "Want some advice?"

"From you?" I said. "I don't think so, thanks."

He shrugged again. "Tell you anyway," he said. "Try her after the show. Whole different story. Once she's in front of the camera she gets so hot she'll fuck a wino. The bitch."

I wondered if Brewster was speaking from experience, but I wasn't about to ask him. However, I decided to hang around until the program was over, just in case.

I watched the show on an offstage monitor as I waited for my segment. On camera, Fern seemed a different person—warm, open, charming and apparently unaware of the sexuality that came so strongly through the screen.

The producer came by to tell me that my segment would be next. "Quite a gal, isn't she?" he said when he saw me watching Fern.

"Indeed," I said. "Tell me, is Fern Forrester her real name?"

He laughed. "No way. She was born Frances Malzetech. And she's not the twenty-seven she claims to be either!"

I didn't care about her age. But I was glad she was a genuine "F," and that neither I nor Miss Greenglass would have to worry about my conscience.

My interview went smoothly, and no doubt just as boringly as Fern had anticipated. I watched the rest of the program. Near the end, while some giggly clown was doing the weather report, Fern came off the set for a moment to check herself in the mirror again. She saw me standing nearby.

"Still here?" she asked, looking at me closely for the first time. There was something different about her. Her eyes were glowing. Her skin was flushed under the makeup. She almost gave off sparks.

"I enjoyed watching you," I said. "You're very . . . professional."

"Well, thanks." She sat at the mirror and started poking at her hair.

"About that drink . . ." I began.

She looked at me again swiftly. "What do you want, fella?" she said. "You want to screw a TV star?"

"Well . . ."

"Sure you do. Everybody does. You wait right here. I'll be back."

I waited right there. I watched on the monitor as she and Larry did a little cutesy patter as they closed out the program. Before the credits had stopped rolling, she was beside me. "Come on," she said. "Follow me." And walked away before I could say a word.

I thought probably I should be offended at her attitude, and for a brief moment I thought of just walking out of there. A very brief moment. Watching the elegant carriage of her slender body and the shapely lines of her long legs, my groin throbbed. Of course I didn't like her much, but my groin didn't care about that. I followed her.

She took me to her dressing room, which was small and cluttered. There didn't seem to be much room for sexual activity. But it was bigger than the dressing room at Brooks Brothers, and I'd done all right in *there*. I noticed a lot of mirrors around. Aside from the dressing-table mirror, there was a full-length looking glass on one wall, and a smaller one hanging on the back of the door, plus a few others here and there. Fern closed the door and locked it. Then she turned to me, looking me up and down. "Okay," she said. "This is your lucky day. Take

your clothes off while I get rid of some of this makeup."
Just to show some independence. I didn't start stripping
right away. I leaned against the wall and looked around
while she sat at the table and started removing her TV
makeup. "When you brushed me off before," I said. "I
took you for the frigid type."

"Well, usually I am, dear," Fern said. "I don't want
you to think I'm a nympho or anything. But I do get hot
after a show. Damn hot. Ask anybody around here." She
smiled at me in the mirror, a twisted smile, but her eyes
were burning. I figured I had shown my independence
sufficiently, so I began to undress.

"You know why?" Fern asked, although she didn't
wait for me to reply. "Because when I'm on, I know that
men—hundreds, thousands of men—are watching me
and lusting for me. It's true, you know. Men tell me that.
And they write to me about it. Not just weirdos, either.
All sorts of men. They watch me on the air and they think
about fucking me. Sometimes they sit there and jerk off,
watching me. When I'm on camera and I think about that,
I get hot as hell. My nipples go all hard and I get wet between my legs. Then, afterwards, I have to have somebody. I just have to."

I took my pants off. "So you latch on to whoever's
around," I said.

"Don't be nasty, dear." She stood up and faced the full-
length mirror. "You're getting what all those men only
dream about. They strip me in their fantasies, imagining
how it would be to see me take my clothes off." She
raised a hand to her dress and began to open the buttons
down the front, then slipped the dress off her shoulders
and let it fall to the floor. Her figure in the bra and panties
was fuller than I expected, but the overall effect was still

one of slender elegance. My cock stood up to show its appreciation. But she wasn't looking at me. She was staring at her own reflection. Her hands brushed over her body, lightly caressing it. Then they reached back for her bra catch.

"They would give anything to see what my breasts are like," she murmured. And took off the bra.

They were terrific. Perfectly round, with hard brown nipples. She touched them. Her eyes never left her own body in the mirror. Neither did mine. I dropped my shorts.

Fern took off her panties. "They dream of seeing me naked," she said, a little breathlessly. "Look, I'm naked. This is my naked body." She moved closer to the mirror, until her nipples touched the glass, then pressed herself against it. A tiny gasp came from her throat. For a moment I thought she was going to kiss herself in the glass. But then she moved back a few steps. Still gazing at herself as if in a trance, she slid a hand down over the front of her body. Her legs moved apart slightly and her fingers went between them. "Look at me naked," she moaned, stroking herself. "Fern Forrester, naked."

I had the feeling she wasn't talking to me any more, but to the unseen hordes of lusting TV viewers. I wasn't even sure she knew I was still there. But the throbbing in my groin told me I was there all right. I moved forward and reached for her. At my touch, she gave a start. Then she pressed herself back against me.

"Fuck Fern," she said breathlessly. "Fuck the TV lady."

"That's the idea, all right," I said, rubbing my hardness against her smooth derriere.

"Wait," Fern said, pulling away. She reached for her

dressing-table chair and swung it around so it faced the full-length mirror. "This way," she breathed. "Sit down. Sit down here."

I sat. There was no bed or couch in the room, so the chair was probably as comfortable a place as any. I assumed she would straddle me face-to-face. Instead, she lowered herself into my lap with her back to me. Of course—that way she could still see herself in the mirror. All of herself.

She sat down on me slowly, her thighs spreading wide, and as she moved back against me she reached down between them, found my stiff penis and guided it into her descending pussy. We both gasped as it slipped into her. Her tight warmth slid down over me like a custom-fitted sheath.

Fern hissed with pleasure. "Ah," she said. "Ahhh. Oh. Ahhh."

"I agree," I said. And I did.

Fern spread her legs as far apart as they would go, which let me slide more deeply up inside her. It also gave her—and me, over her shoulder—a good view in the mirror of my cock stabbing into her vagina. In fact, the view of her whole body in that position was pretty spectacular.

Her hips began to squirm as she gazed at the reflection in front of her. I encouraged her by pumping myself up and down slightly, and she took the hint and began a slow movement, rising and falling rhythmically.

"Look," she breathed. "I'm fucking. I'm fucking you. Ohh . . . oh, look how beautiful . . ."

It was beautiful, with her sleek body in motion, her breasts quivering, her legs open to show the long stretch of her inner thighs. She watched herself as she fucked harder. I reached around her to put a hand over her breast and rubbed the hard nipple, bringing a moan from her. I slid my other hand down over her stomach to her moving pussy.

She inhaled sharply when I touched her little button, and then moaned again as I gently brushed my fingers across it. I continued to explore that sensitive area, while with my other hand I played with her breasts, squeezing and stroking them and twiddling the nipples. Fern's breathing became harsh and she began to move harder. My own breath was coming faster, and I moved with her as much as I could beneath her writhing body.

"Uhh . . ." Fern gasped. "Unnh . . . Aaahh . . ." Her movements got jerkier, and I knew she was on the way. I brought my head forward and licked at the skin of her shoulder, suppressing a desire to sink my teeth into it.

"God, I'm . . . I'm going to come . . ." she panted. "Oh, look . . . I'm coming . . . watch me come . . . ooh . . . watch Fern come . . . Aaahh . . . Unnnhh . . . Aahh . . . ! Look at me . . . aaahhh!"

I watched her, and she watched herself. Her hands clutched at my legs and her body spasmed once, twice, three times. Her mouth was open and gasping. Her eyes never looked away from the mirror.

She went limp then, slumping in my lap like a deflated plastic doll, with my hard cock still inside her. I had held off to give her her orgasm, and now it was my turn. But Fern didn't seem interested. I gave her a few moments to recover, but the occasional involuntary twitch of her pussy kept me on the edge. I moved my hips suggestively. No response. I fondled her nipple and licked the back of her neck, trying to raise some interest. Fern only made a noise that sounded like a sigh.

"I'm finished," she said.

"But I'm not." I moved up and down as strongly as I could beneath her.

Fern sighed again, more loudly this time, and wiggled her hips a bit. She had gotten what she wanted and didn't give a damn about anything else—but what was I supposed to do? Her squirming was bringing me to climax. At the last minute I tightened my hold on her and, with a supreme effort, lifted her body just enough to allow me to slip out of her. I held her against me as I began to spurt strongly, and the silver jets shot up into the air and fell onto her body, splashing across her breasts.

Fern slithered out of my slackening grip. "Nice going!" she yelled. "Now I'm a mess."

I got up. She didn't look half bad, actually. In fact I had to smile. "Relax," I told her. "Think of all the TV fans who fantasize about Fern Forrester with come all over her tits."

"Yeah, sure," she said under her breath as she turned to the mirror. But I guess I'd said the right thing. Her eyes softened as she gazed at herself with the slick white stuff dripping from her flesh. Slowly she raised a hand to one breast and began to rub it over her skin, while all those unseen men lusted and jerked themselves off in her mind.

I'd had enough. I got dressed as quickly as I could. By the time I was ready to leave Fern wasn't mad at me any more. She even kissed me good-bye and offered to give me her autograph, but I told her I hadn't brought my book with me.

Chapter 7

"GET THE HELL OUT OF HERE!" THE MAN shouted. As well he might have, considering that I had just opened the bedroom door to reveal him standing with his pants and shorts down around his ankles, while a lovely young blonde lady knelt in front of him, her head bobbing steadily as she pleasured him with her mouth.

"Oops," Grace said. "Wrong room."

Although I didn't know the man, I recognized the girl. "Sorry, Ginger," I said, and closed the door.

"You know her?" Grace asked.

"Just met her a while ago," I said. "Your husband introduced us."

"Russell does like to pamper his guests," Grace said. "I don't think he'd approve of his wife doing it, however."

"Then let's not tell him."

"What a good idea," Grace said.

* * *

I hadn't been to one of Russell's parties in years, though I was always invited. This time I was there for only one reason, which was that Russell had a wife who was considerably younger than he was, that she was an attractive, effervescent brunette with an extremely alluring figure—and that her name was Grace.

Grace and I had never had the pleasure of each other's intimate company, but I had the feeling that, given the opportunity, this unfortunate situation might well be rectified. And I intended to create such an opportunity that very evening.

Russell's parties were always the same. Only wealthy and successful men were invited, and with the occasional exception, men who have devoted their lives to the pursuit of wealth do not make the most stimulating company. (Since wealth managed to find *me* without any pursuit on my part, I of course do not fall into that category.) Fortunately there were also the women. Many of these men had, like Russell, divorced their first wives and married younger, more attractive ladies. Others brought their mistresses. And there were always a number of highly decorative and apparently unattached young women, hired by Russell to be friendly and amenable to one and all.

Upon my arrival Russell had greeted me warmly, escorted me to the bar and, while waiting for my drink to be served, introduced me to several men whom I already knew.

"Where's Grace?" I asked him.

"Oh, around somewhere," he said vaguely. "Probably fixing her makeup or something. You here alone? That's not like you, Steven." He grinned. "Or are you here to see what you can pick up?"

"Something like that," I said.

"Look around," Russell said. "Anybody I can introduce you to, just let me know."

"Actually I'm looking for a particular . . . ah . . . type," I said.

"Name it, we probably got it."

"I need a G girl," I said.

"A what?"

"A G girl. Someone whose name begins with the letter G."

Russell gaped at me. "You kidding? Why a G, for God's sake?"

"Personal reasons. You know any?"

Russell looked around the room. The fact that his wife's name began with a G never occurred to him, as I had expected. "G . . . G . . ." he muttered. "Let's see . . . nope . . . nope . . . Oh, hey! Yeah! I got one!"

"I know," I said.

"Over there by the bookcase. See the blonde in the green dress? Name's Ginger. Pretty nice, huh?"

I looked. She was indeed pretty nice. "Lovely," I said. "Who's she with?"

"Nobody. She's a party girl. She's available. Help yourself."

"No, thanks," I said. "I don't pay for it."

"You don't have to," Russell said. "It's already paid for. She's all yours. On the house. Hey, Ginger!" He waved to the girl, calling across the room. "Ginger! C'mon over here!"

Ginger, who had been talking with two men, excused herself and made her way toward us. Her body swayed alluringly in the brief but tasteful dress.

"Ginger, I want you to meet Steven Walling, an old friend of mine and a great guy."

"Hi," Ginger said brightly.

"Nice to meet you, Ginger."

"He likes you because your name begins with G," Russell said. "Well, have fun, you two." He wandered off.

"What did he mean?" Ginger asked, smiling at me.

"Uh . . . Russell tends to be somewhat impetuous," I said. "I apologize for dragging you away from your conversation, but actually I'm looking for someone else. Our hostess, in fact. Russell's wife. Have you seen her?"

"I wouldn't know her if I did," Ginger said. "Does her name begin with a G too?"

"It does indeed."

"I've seen a lot of fetishes," Ginger said. "But that's a first."

"Long story," I said.

"Well, won't I do?" Ginger said. "I bet I'm as friendly as she is. And I'm not even married."

"And you are an extremely attractive lady," I said truthfully. "If only you weren't . . ."

"If only I wasn't what? For hire?"

"I'm sorry," I said. "Nothing against you, I just—"

"Won't cost you a cent," Ginger said. "It's all taken care of."

"I know. It's the principle of it. I'm sorry."

Ginger shrugged. "Your loss," she said, and turned away.

I watched her go, regretfully. My pride was intact, but my hormones were not happy about it. But I had other plans for them. I went in search of Grace.

I soon found her circulating among the guests, a slim, dark-haired vision in a simple but sexy yellow gown. She smiled at me dazzlingly. "Steven! I didn't know you were here!"

"How are you, Grace?" I said, kissing her. "You look fantastic."

"Good to see you too, Steven. I thought you avoided Russell's parties like the plague."

"I couldn't stay away from you any longer," I said. "I've missed you, Grace." I looked into her eyes and felt again that mutual desire which we had never gotten around to exploring. "I've missed you a lot. Isn't there somewhere we could get away from this crowd and . . . talk awhile?"

"Talk?"

"Or . . . whatever."

"You're still a very naughty boy, Steven."

"And you're still a very enchanting girl," I said. "I think it's time for us, Grace. Don't you?"

Grace hesitated. But not for long.

"Follow me," she said. When we got upstairs, she waited for me to catch up to her and took my hand. She led me to a door and opened it.

And that's when we saw Ginger with the man who yelled at us to get out.

I told Grace about my brief conversation with Ginger while we found another room. This one was happily unoccupied, and once inside I forgot all about Ginger.

But Grace didn't. After our first kiss, which was lengthy, passionate and extremely exciting, she said, somewhat breathlessly, "I wonder if she likes her work."

"What?" I panted. "Who?"

"That girl. The prostitute. Ginger."

"Who knows?" I said, kissing her neck as my hands explored her body.

"Steven . . ."

"Yes?"

She put her mouth to my ear. "Want me to do what she was doing?"

I pictured Ginger as I had last seen her.

"The thought is not unpleasant," I said.

"Will you reciprocate?" Grace breathed.

"Of course. Try and stop me."

Grace kissed me again, then sank down to her knees. I felt her hands opening my fly, freeing my stiff cock. Then I felt her mouth.

That mouth was warm and tantalizing and highly talented. I was soon floating on a soft cloud of exquisite pleasure. Then Grace raised her head for a moment to say, "I've thought about being one too, sometimes," before putting her mouth back where it had been.

I was breathing heavily and my voice sounded thick. "One *what?*" I asked.

Her mouth came off me again. "A whore," she said. "A prostitute." And she put it back.

I wasn't thinking too clearly at that moment, but this surprised me. "Why would you want to do that?" I asked.

The head went up again. "For kicks," she said. She kissed my cock sweetly. "I'm bored." She licked at me. "Besides, I'm kind of a whore already. I married Russell for his money, you know."

"Not the same thing," I said.

Her mouth had swallowed me again. "Mmmm-hmmmm," she hummed around my flesh.

I closed my eyes, swaying slightly. "Well, you'd certainly make a fortune at it," I muttered, giving myself up to the sensation of what she was doing.

"Mmmunnn . . . nummmm . . . mmmummm?" she said.

"What?" I responded. Which was a mistake, for she released me so she could better articulate my question.

"Would you pay to have me?"

"I never pay for it," I said. "But if I did, you'd be—"

"Why not?"

"It's a principle of mine," I said, arching myself suggestively toward her hovering lips. "Can we talk about this later, Grace?"

She kissed my throbbing hardness again. Briefly.

"I wonder what it feels like," she said. "To be a whore. A real one, I mean."

"Talk to Ginger," I groaned. "Later."

Then I felt her tongue again, slow and tantalizing along the length of me. "Steven . . ."

I sensed what was coming, and I didn't like it. "Grace," I groaned. "Let's stop talking now, okay?" I reached down to pull her to her feet, but her body evaded me—though her head remained in the general region of my crotch.

"Steven, I want to be a whore. Just this once. I want you to pay me. Please?"

"Grace, I told you I don't do that. Now come on, let me—"

"What's the going rate?" Grace asked. "A hundred? How about a hundred dollars? Is that a fair price?"

"It's a bargain," I said. "But you're not selling, Grace,

and I'm not buying. We're here because we like each other and we want each other. Right?"

"Of course," she said. "But, Steven . . ." And she lowered her head and caressed me again with that arousing mouth. "I'd be worth it," she murmured. "I promise."

It took some effort, but I pulled myself away from her. "Grace stop this now, for God's sake. I'm not going to pay for it, so let's—"

"Then you're not getting it," Grace said. She stood up and smoothed down her dress.

"You're kidding!" I exclaimed.

"Nope," she said. "I mean it. No pay, no play, isn't that what they say?"

"Cut that out," I said. "Be sensible, Grace." I could still feel the moisture of her mouth on my cock, which hadn't lost its stiffness.

"*You* be sensible," she said. "Come on, Steven. What's a hundred dollars between friends?" She reached behind her to open the catch and pull down the zipper at the back of her dress. Then she slid the gown off her shoulders and let it fall around her waist. The bra was built into the dress, and her breasts were now bare. And very lovely.

"Look, Steven," she said. "Aren't I worth it?"

My throat was tight. "I told you, it's a bargain," I husked. "But—"

"Only a hundred dollars," Grace said, "and I'll be your whore. I'll do anything you want, Steven." And she opened something else and let the gown fall down around her feet. Then she pushed down her panties.

"Jesus," I said, and started to move toward her.

She backed up. "No," she said. "You stay right there,

Steven. Until I get paid. A hundred dollars. Just put it on the bed."

"Grace . . ." I said. "Damn it, I'm not—I don't—"

"No?" Grace said. "That's too bad, Steven. I do want you. But . . ." She shrugged, which did interesting things to her breasts. "I guess I'll have to find somebody else to pay me." And she bent down for her panties and started to put them back on.

I groaned again. Not only was I dying to have that luscious body, but the thought of Grace getting away from me after we had finally gotten to this point was maddening.

And then something else occurred to me. The rules of my wager with Miss Greenglass limited me to just one woman per letter. Though I had not yet consummated my liaison with Grace, we had already had sexual contact, of a sort. It was true that the terms of the wager were not too specific in this area but, rationalize though I might, their spirit was clear. I had come close to bending them a couple of times, but having essentially kept faith with Miss Greenglass thus far, I meant to go on doing so. At this point it appeared that as far as G was concerned, it had to be Grace or nobody.

I sighed and gave up. "All right, Grace," I said, pulling out my wallet. "You win. I'll pay." I took out a hundred and put it on the bed. "I want you to know," I said, "that this is the first time in my life I have had to buy a woman! And by all that's holy, it'll be the last!"

Grace came forward slowly, then picked up the money and held it to her breast, a peculiar smile on her face. "Oh, yes," she breathed. "What a lovely feeling. I think I'll do this more often. Do you think Ginger could get me into the business?"

"Russell would love that," I said.

"Russell would never know," Grace replied. "I could be one of those wives who are call girls during the day. Wouldn't that be fun!"

"Before you do that . . ." I said.

Grace's smile widened. "Of course," she said. She dropped the money on the floor, then lay down on the bed and reached up for me. I joined her, and then kissed her for a while, quite thoroughly, during which time she and I managed to get my clothes off.

"Now," she said, "what would you like your whore to do first?"

"First, stop calling yourself a whore," I said. "I don't like it."

"Whatever you say, darling," Grace said. "You're paying, after all."

I sighed. "Well," I said, "I'd like to do some more of what you were doing before. Then I'd like to do it to you for a while, as I promised. Then . . ."

I stopped, because she was already doing it.

It was quite a while before Grace was ready to go back to the party, and I was worried that Russell would be suspicious; but she assured me he wouldn't even have noticed her absence. She also told me she was going to look into some of the better call girl services, and asked me if I would be one of her regular customers. I managed to avoid making a commitment on that score.

After a decent interval I rejoined the party myself, and since there was nothing more to stay for, I sought out Russell to say my good-byes.

"You missed a good thing there, buddy," Russell told me. "I hear that Ginger girl is just terrific! I'm thinking of trying her out myself. You should too. Forget that not-paying stuff. It's bullshit. Break down and make an exception. The exception proves the rule, you know? Isn't that what they say?"

"Yes," I said. "That's what they say, all right."

Chapter 8

"**H**ALLELUJAH!" EXCLAIMED THE REVEREND Jarret Jourdemayne. "And welcome to the Temple of Light, brother. Any friend of Sister Heather is welcome at any time. Day or night, brother. Day or night!"

"Ah . . . thanks," I said, refraining with difficulty from telling him that I was not his brother, and had not the slightest wish to be. I already had one brother, and that was enough. More than enough. I was there only because I wanted to see the man who had snatched Heather away from me, just as I had been on the verge of making her the next step in my alphabetical progression toward the winning of my wager with the tantalizing Miss Greenglass, and thus toward the possession of that very fine lady herself.

Heather, though only in her late thirties, was a widow—a very attractive widow whose husband had left her considerable wealth. I didn't care about her money, except as it had enabled me to meet her in the way of business, and thus to pay court to her until the time was ripe—

that is, until I had progressed to H. Heather, though not a cold woman, was somewhat skittish and required careful preparation. So I had nurtured her as I had made my way through Edna, Fern and Grace, and with impeccable timing had brought her just to the point of surrender.

And then she got religion.

In a fever of excitement she told me she'd been born again. She'd met the Reverend Jarret Jourdemayne, founder and chief preacher of the Temple of Light, and had been swept away by his charisma, his passionate religious faith, and his clear but penetrating blue eyes. She said they pierced her soul and let out the Spirit inside her. She was already preparing to become a member of the Temple. Faith, spirit and purity, in the person of the Reverend Jourdemayne, would be her guides from now on.

Thus I had good reason to resent the Reverend Jarret, aside from the fact that I strongly suspected he was less interested in Heather's soul than in her bank account — maybe even her body. I suggested this possibility.

"Oh, Steven, how could you!" Heather expostulated. "Why, the Reverend is a man of God!"

"Remember Jimmy Swaggart?" I said. "Remember Jim Bakker? This guy is out to swindle you, if not worse. Take my word."

"Oh, how can you say that? You don't even know him."

"Okay," I said. "I'll meet him and find out what kind of phony he is. When's the next sermon?"

"You'll come to a prayer meeting at the Temple?" Heather gushed. "Wonderful, Steven! You might even be born again yourself!"

"I doubt it," I said. "My mother tells me I was born quite adequately on the first occasion."

Which is how I came to be called brother by the Reverend Jarret Jourdemayne. I sat through the prayer meeting with some difficulty, mostly by concentrating on the two young women whom the Reverend had told me were his "acolytes." He introduced them as Sister Blessed Soul Martha and Sister Holy Virgin Mary, and they were knockouts. Even though they both wore loose, flowing robes of pure white, I could see that they were both built like brick—ah—temples. I strongly suspected they did more for the good reverend then lead the singing and pass the collection plates.

My plan was to find a way to expose the Reverend, not necessarily to the world, but at least to Heather, so she would forget about saving her soul (which, I was sure, was in no danger whatever) and think about pleasuring her body. And mine.

Of course it might have been simpler just to find another H lady, but I had put so much effort into Heather. Besides, I cared enough about her not to want to see her get taken advantage of. If my suspicion about his sexual designs was correct, I could just wait until he made a pass at her; but I didn't know how long that might take—or whether Heather might not even be flattered rather than indignant.

I wondered if it would be possible to catch him fooling around with Sister Blessed Soul Martha and/or Sister Holy Virgin Mary . . .

After the service, while Heather and a crowd of others, mostly female, clustered around the Reverend, I managed to get those two beauteous young ladies aside. "Very impressive service," I said. Very lucrative too, judging from the full collection plates. "Tell me, how did you ladies happen to get . . . ah . . . involved with the good Reverend anyway?"

It turned out they were sisters—real sisters—whose parents had been followers of Jourdemayne, and who had considered themselves blessed when he had suggested that their two young daughters become acolytes and devote themselves to helping him bring the word of God to mankind. Martha was nineteen; Mary was twenty. Martha had brown hair; Mary's was auburn. Martha was sexy as hell; Mary was sexier. And I had the distinct feeling that neither of them was as sweet or as innocent as their scrubbed faces and white robes suggested.

"It must be rewarding to be doing such important work," I said. "You and the Reverend must be . . . very close."

Mary smiled. "As close as you can get," she said. "The Reverend is a wonderful man."

"And very vigorous," Mary said.

"For his age," Martha said.

"You look vigorous too," Mary said.

"And younger," Martha said.

"But not too young," Mary said.

"Just about right," Martha said.

"Ah . . . thank you," I said feebly, and made a mental note to look these girls up again (one of them, anyway) when I got to M.

However, while I was now certain that the Reverend was doing more than praying with the M&M girls (as I began to think of them), I still had to find a way to prove it to Heather. Then I remembered Ginger. Faithful readers of this saga will recall that Ginger was a "party girl" whom I had recently met at the home of my friend Russell, and whose tempting but commercialized charms I had declined in favor of the less public (though still, as it turned out, costly) attractions of Russell's wife Grace. Ginger, I was sure, would not be averse to participating in a little plot I had in mind—for the proper remuneration, of course.

As soon as I had taken Heather home, I called Russell and asked him for Ginger's number.

Russell chuckled. "Taking my advice, eh? She's a hot one all right."

"How's Grace?" I asked wickedly.

"Wonderful. Seems very perky lately, for some reason."

When I called Ginger, she too thought at first that I had changed my mind about becoming one of her clients. But when I had explained my true purpose, not only was she perfectly willing to help me with my scheme, she even improved on it. It turned out that a former roommate had installed a pane of two-way glass in the connecting door between the two bedrooms in her apartment, so clients who were into voyeurism could watch activities in the next room without being seen. It was perfect. Ginger thought seducing the Reverend might be fun—as long as we could agree on the financial terms to her satisfaction. Which we did.

My next step was to pay another call on the Reverend Jourdemayne. I found him at his temple. I explained to him that I knew a young lady who was spiritually unhappy and who I believed could benefit from his ministry.

"Hallelujah, brother!" the Reverend intoned. "Another soul to be brought to the light. Praise God!"

"Yes indeed," I said. "The thing is, Reverend, this poor girl is very shy, very withdrawn. She's afraid to seek the very light which, as you say, would be her salvation. But perhaps the light could be brought to her. I was wondering if you might possibly visit her, so she could experience the power of your . . . faith."

As the Reverend looked somewhat dubious about this suggestion, I went on. "She's an orphan, you see, and though her parents left her a substantial fortune, she doesn't —"

That did it. "Why certainly, brother!" the Reverend boomed. "No exertion is too great for the chance to rescue a lost soul from the wilderness. Just point me the way, brother!"

But the best laid schemes of mice and men are often undone by women. Though I didn't want to go into detail with Heather about what I was planning, in order to get her to accompany me to Ginger's apartment I explained, putting it as delicately as possible, that I wanted to show her some aspects of the Reverend's character of which she was presently unaware. She flatly refused.

"I don't know why you are trying to discredit Reverend Jourdemayne in my eyes, Steven. A fine godly man like that! If it's some kind of petty jealousy, it seems unworthy of you. I can assure you I have the uttermost faith in the Reverend's probity and character, and nothing will shake it. No, I have no intention of going anywhere for such a purpose. Really, I'm surprised at you, Steven! I thought you were a man of character also. Perhaps I was wrong."

So much for that. But I had already paid Ginger her money, and I doubted that she would be very amenable to the idea of giving it back. So at the appointed time I showed up at her apartment, without Heather—but with a camcorder. Which Ginger at first objected to, until we did a certain amount of renegotiation. Compared to what this scheme was costing me, Grace had been a bargain.

Ginger had no trouble at all. She told the Reverend that she was a miserable sinner, and then she proceeded to demonstrate. Fully.

The Reverend did his best to drive her sins away. He called upon God, and upon Jesus Christ. In fact he did that quite a bit while Ginger was practicing some of her most accomplished sins on him. He inadvertently baptized her at one point; and it may have had some effect, for Ginger began to speak to him in tongues, as it were, until his rod and his staff were ready to comfort her. The Reverend was quite vigorous in his attempts to drive out the devil inside her. He must have succeeded in his task, for he ended by shouting his joy to the heavens . . .

I called Heather. "I have a tape," I said, "that I'd like you to look at. I think you'll find it very interesting indeed."

"Is this about Reverend Jourdemayne again?" she asked suspiciously. "Steven, I've already told you, I have no—"

"Just look at it," I pleaded. "Heather, the man is not what you think. This tape will prove it. It shows him—"

"I don't care!" Heather wailed. "I don't want to know! Oh, Steven, why couldn't you just let things alone? I thought you were—oh God. I don't want to see you any more, Steven. Not ever. Good-bye!"

"But—" I said, but I was talking to a dial tone.

Now I was angry. I had probably lost my chance with Heather for good, there was no other H lady in sight at the moment, and I had spent all that money for nothing. But I still had the tape, and one thing I *could* do was to put the

Reverend Jarret out of the preacher business. I headed for the temple.

But by the time I got there I had cooled down a bit. "I could use this tape to pull down this whole operation," I told the Reverend. "But what the hell, like the song says, we're all dodging our way through the world. So I'm going to hold on to it, but I just want one thing. Leave Heather alone. Forget about her money and anything else you're interested in, or the tape goes to *Hard Copy*. Okay?"

"Whatever you say, brother," the Reverend said. "The Lord works in mysterious ways. He giveth and He taketh away. Hallelujah, brother."

"I'm not your brother," I said.

As I was leaving the temple I met Sister Blessed Soul Martha coming up the front steps. She was wearing a skirt and blouse instead of the white robes in which I had first seen her, but her figure looked more heavenly than ever.

"Hi," she said, smiling angelically. "Coming to see me, by any chance?"

"Well, no, actually I came to see the Reverend," I said. "But it's nice to see you again. Where's Mary?"

"Home," Martha said, looking me up and down. "Did you want to see her? She'd love to have a visit from you."

"Well, I—"

"Or . . . I could go with you, and we could all have fun. The Reverend always enjoys that."

"I'll bet," I said. "But I'm . . . uh . . . not as young as I used to be. And I'm kind of tied up right now, but if I could look you up in a week or two, then . . ."

She frowned. "I thought you liked us."

"Oh, I do," I said hastily. "But . . . well, you see, I

have this unusual situation going. It's hard to explain, but you're an M, and I'm—"

"An M?" she repeated quizzically. "What's an M?"

"I mean your name begins with M," I said. "And—"

"No it doesn't," she said.

"It doesn't?"

"It begins with B. Blessed Soul Martha."

"Yes, but I mean your real name," I said. "You see—"

"That is my real name."

"It is?"

"Sure. Our parents were really religious, you know? And they christened us with these damn holy names so—"

"You mean—" I was flabbergasted. "Then your sister—she's really—"

"Holy Virgin Mary," Martha said. "Sure. It's on our birth certificates and everything."

"Well, hallelujah!" I said.

I said that again—or something like it—when, after a long and pleasurable dalliance, Sister Holy Virgin Mary's supple and voluptuous young body finally brought me to glory. I was truly grateful to her parents for their commendable piety in choosing names, but I was even more grateful to their daughter for not taking that choice too seriously.

She had indeed been happy to see me, and though we both regretted the circumstances that kept her sister from joining us, Mary proved to be so inexhaustibly eager, inventive and athletic that she made up for it. Perhaps the skills she displayed were the result of her study under the Reverend Jourdemayne but, having seen him in action, I doubted it. More likely it was just natural talent. A gift from God, as it were. Certainly by the time we were finished I felt more like praying than I had in years.

The Lord—as I remarked to Miss Greenglass some time later when recounting the events exactly as they occurred, and with a careful attention to detail that, I hoped, wasn't lost on my lovely assistant—does indeed work in mysterious ways. Miss Greenglass replied dryly that she thought the Lord had better things to do with His time than assisting me in winning our wager, but I said I was not so sure. And with a look heavenward, considered, not without some pleasure, the remaining eighteen letters of the alphabet.

Chapter 9

IT HAD NOW BEEN NEARLY SIX WEEKS SINCE I HAD made my fateful wager with Miss Greenglass, and while I was still technically ahead of schedule (with nearly a third of the alphabet behind me and a total of six months in which to complete it), I was not really happy with my progress. Having started out with a bang (so to speak), knocking off the first three letters in nearly as many days, in spite of complications, I had expected things to continue at that merry pace. Alas, they had not. I was still confident that I would accomplish what I had set out to do and win the favors, or at least the body, of the tantalizing Miss Greenglass; but I was admittedly a bit concerned about the Q's, X's and Z's that lay ahead of me, and I felt I should pick up the tempo.

In addition, the fact that my amorous activities were restricted to those women instrumental to the wager—and even those, only once—was galling. To a man accustomed to refreshing himself with female embraces on a daily basis at least, eight erotic encounters in six weeks (well, nine if you count Betty, who had been one of the complications) was not only highly depressing, it seemed to darken the universe and drain the essential forces of life from both body and spirit.

In other words, I was horny as hell.

A related problem, as I have mentioned before, was the many women of past acquaintance who naturally were somewhat piqued at my inexplicable neglect of them. I had to devise some complicated explanations in order to keep the doors open against the time when my wager would be completed; and alas, I was not always successful.

One such acquaintance was Phyllis, the passionate lady with the traveling husband and with whom, as it happens, I had been engaged in amorous dalliance on the very morning of the day on which Miss Greenglass and I first contracted our interesting wager. She had called me the last time her husband had gone away, and I had had to plead a fictional business trip of my own to put her off. But now, as I was strolling out of the Four Seasons after a pleasant lunch and trying to remember what had become of Inez, a Portuguese lady I once knew who had claimed to be a countess, I heard someone calling my name, and I saw Phyllis rushing up to me.

"Steven!" she cried. "I'm so glad I ran into you. I was going to call you. Something terrible has happened!"

I was not particularly alarmed. Phyllis is given to drama, and it is rare that twenty minutes of her life go by in which some crisis, catastrophe or ecstatic epiphany is not expressed. It's probably part of what makes her such a pleasurable bed partner.

"Tell me about it," I said, smiling at her. She was worth smiling at. Phyllis was an extremely pretty woman in her early thirties, with curly blond hair and a figure that stirred memories, which in turn stirred certain parts of my anatomy. I tried to concentrate on her face.

"Michael is going away again tomorrow!" Phyllis said tragically.

"What's so terrible about that?" I said, while at the same time trying to think of another excuse to avoid her. "He goes away all the time."

"But I'm afraid we won't be able to get together!" Phyllis wailed. "This cousin of mine from Colorado is coming to stay with me, and I'm going to have to entertain her. I don't know how I can get away long enough for . . . oh dear."

"Oh well," I said, trying not to sound relieved. "There'll be other times. Later on, you know . . ."

Phyllis came closer and took my arm. "What I was thinking, Steven . . . What I was wondering . . ."

Uh-oh.

"See, she's never been to New York, she wants to see the sights. I'm going to have to take her around and all. And if you could help me, maybe we could get a chance to . . ."

"Ah, I'm really busy right now, Phyllis," I said. "Couple of big deals in the works . . . lots of business. You know how it is."

"Oh, Steven, I'm so disappointed! I was hoping we could both show Irene around, and then maybe . . ."

My ears, as they say, perked up.

"Irene?" I said. "Your cousin's name is Irene?"

"Of course!" Phyllis said, as though that fact should have been self-evident.

"And . . . uh . . . is she as beautiful as you?" I said.

"Oh, Steven!" She hit me playfully on the arm. "Actually she's probably more attractive than me," she said, obviously not believing it for a minute. "She's younger, you know. Not by much," she added hastily.

"Well," I said. "Well. On second thought, I could make a little time."

"Oh, Steven! Thank you!" Phyllis could hardly control her joy.

"We can show her the town," I said. "The Rainbow Room . . . Bobby Short at the Carlyle . . . lunch at Le Cirque . . ."

"Oh, no, Irene says she wants to see all the touristy things. You know, the Empire State Building and all that."

"Oh," I said. "You know, now that I think of it, these business deals . . ."

"Steven!"

"All right," I said. "I just hope Irene . . ."

"What?"

"Appreciates it," I said.

I couldn't see much family resemblance between Irene and Phyllis, but I had no complaint. Irene's hair was dark, she was slightly taller than Phyllis, and her figure, while less buxom, was every bit as shapely. In my anxiety to get on with my schedule, I had determined to seduce Phyllis's country cousin, if at all possible, regardless of what she looked like; but I was relieved to find that the task would be anything but an onerous one. The difficult part would be to find a way to pry her away from Phyllis in order to accomplish this goal, while at the same time trying to avoid Phyllis's efforts to get me alone for the same purpose.

Irene was all of twenty-eight, she had been divorced for a year, and she was dying to see all the things she had always heard about in the big city. The three of us caromed around the town like demented pinballs, seeing every sight ever listed in every tourist handbook ever published. We went to the top of the Empire State Building, for the sake of tradition. But then we had to do the same at the World Trade Center, as it is even higher. We gazed reverently at Grant's Tomb. We toured Greenwich Village, for God's sake! We took the Circle Line around Manhattan. We tramped around Central Park. Irene was enchanted. Phyllis was excited. (She had lived in New York all her life, but Phyllis got excited by dust motes.) I was bored to death, and my feet were sore.

I did manage to squeeze in lunch at Le Cirque, but only because Irene's choice, the Automat, was no longer in existence, much to her disappointment.

In fact there was something childlike about Irene's enthusiasm (though certainly not about her body) that made her even more desirable in my eyes. Not that she wasn't bright—in terms of pure intelligence she had it all over her cousin Phyllis—but she had an open kind of eagerness that I found refreshing. Our sightseeing forays were made bearable for me only by my stealthy but determined attempts to establish a rapport with Irene—attempts which were not entirely unsuccessful. In fact, I got the definite impression that her New York adventure would be even more enjoyable if it included a brief passionate affair with a sophisticated, cosmopolitan gentleman such as myself. Gazing at the city from the top of the Empire State Building, I put my arm casually around her waist, and noticed that she did not pull away. At Grant's Tomb we briefly held hands, like kids, while Phyllis wasn't looking. And at the Museum of Natural History, while her cousin made a brief trip to the ladies' room, I managed to kiss her behind a dinosaur.

Of course when Irene in turn answered the call of nature, I had to kiss Phyllis as well. Not that this was a difficult task, but it did nothing to advance the program. Phyllis was in despair, seeing no way to ditch her cousin long enough for us to dally. That was fine with me, except that it worked both ways.

However, tomorrow was another day.

"Tomorrow is another day," I said to Miss Greenglass when I got home. She was packing up to leave for the night.

"I have heard that somewhere before," Miss Greenglass said, and left.

That night I soaked my feet and tried to think of a plan. I fell asleep wondering again whatever happened to Inez.

The following day did little to help my feet, but it did have a more salubrious effect on the rest of me. As usual, it was a lady that brought me luck, and this time one that I had no difficulty at all getting into: the Statue of Liberty.

I must admit that I was one of those native New Yorkers who had never actually visited the famed monument. Had it not been for Irene, it was an experience I would have willingly forgone for the rest of my days. I like to think I am as patriotic as the next fellow, but my impression of such a visit consisted of a crowded boat ride followed by an unending succession of steps, leading to yet another view of the Manhattan skyline, which by then one was too exhausted to appreciate.

And, dear reader, I was right.

Irene, however, was inexhaustible. By the time we reached the crown of the statue and looked out the little windows at the admittedly impressive view, even Phyllis's ebullience had waned, and she was quite happy to join me in sitting down on a convenient bench. Irene continued to gaze, oohing and aahing and exclaiming how beautiful it all was, and wishing we could go even higher.

Now it used to be that one *could* go higher—the spiral steps continue all the way up inside the statue's right arm and into the bottom of the torch—but for some time now that area has been closed to the public for safety reasons. I had been quite thankful to discover this, having, as I thought, climbed quite enough steps for one day; but Irene's remark gave me a glimmer of hope which overcame my fatigue in an instant.

The steps leading up into the arm of the statue were closed off, but apparently they had been doing some kind of maintenance work there, for the barrier was a makeshift one consisting of several sawhorses. A guard was stationed in front of them to prevent anyone from straying from the approved precincts.

We were not alone there, of course. Other sightseers wandered about with their cameras and other tourist appurtenances, but it was a weekday morning and the crowd was not so large as to interfere with what I had in mind. I rose casually and approached the guard. He turned out to be a friendly fellow, and we had a bit of pleasant conversation, during which a little money may have changed hands. Then there was more conversation, and more money, until finally our confabulation arrived at a mutually satisfactory conclusion.

I went to fetch Irene, hoping Phyllis would be content to stay where she was for a while, and I was gratified to note that the lady was dozing on her bench.

"Come with me," I whispered into Irene's lovely ear. "I am going to take you up to Paradise."

Irene looked at me quizzically, but she let me lead her over to where the guard was standing. We had to wait for the proper moment, but when no one seemed to be looking, the guard quickly pulled one of the barriers aside far enough for us to slip through. Irene started to say something, but I put my finger to my lips. "Climb," I said.

We climbed.

The stairs were narrow, and circled in a tight spiral, but I was not tired anymore. Irene was ahead of me, and the view up her skirt would have inspired me to climb the Matterhorn with an elephant on my shoulders. At one point I couldn't refrain from reaching up and briefly stroking her round, rolling rump. She stopped and half turned on the stairs.

"Steven!" she said—but not unhappily.

I wanted to take her right there, but the stairs were too steep for that. "Go on," I said. "Hurry."

We went on. And at last we arrived, breathless, at the top. I, at any rate, was breathless; but I chose to attribute that to my excitement over Irene's charms rather than to any physical debility.

There was a rather narrow walkway surrounding the staircase, with a waist-high iron railing all around, in front of the small windows set into the torch. The view was even more spectacular than from the crown, but at that point I couldn't have cared less.

"Oh, Steven!" Irene gasped, gazing at the city and the harbor laid out beneath us. "Isn't it beautiful!"

"It certainly is," I said, but what I was gazing at was Irene. I stepped up behind her and put my arms around her, pulling her back against me. She didn't resist, but still stared out at the view. "It's just fabulous!" she breathed.

"Fabulous," I said. I kissed the back of her neck, and slid my hands up to cup her breasts.

"Oh," Irene said. And then she said "Oh!" again, as she felt the rising hardness of my passion against her backside. This finally diverted her attention from the window long enough for her to look back at me, turning slightly but not dislodging my hands. I craned my head to kiss her soft mouth. After a moment it opened, and our tongues found each other. When my fingers began searching out the buttons of her blouse, she broke the kiss.

"Oh, Steven, God . . ." she panted. "We can't . . . not here . . ."

"Why not?" I said, opening buttons. "No one will come."

"But—" She looked dubiously at the dirty stone floor. "But how—"

"Just watch the view," I said. "And lean over a little."

"Oh, God," Irene said, but she leaned forward over the railing, clutching it with her hands on both sides. I abandoned the buttons and reached down to pull her skirt up, hiking it high around her waist. I then bent and pulled her panties down over those very fine legs. Irene said "Oh, God" again, but she stepped out of them, and then anticipated me by planting her feet as far apart as she could without losing her balance.

I stepped up close behind her, hastily opening my trousers and dropping them and my shorts around my ankles. It wasn't particularly elegant, but neither of us cared at that moment. Irene drew in her breath sharply as I found her sweetly moist opening and guided myself slowly inside her.

It was slow and sweet all the way. My hands found their way beneath her blouse and bra to hold her stiff-nippled breasts, as her hips moved in soft, sensuous rhythm. The New York skyline had never looked so wonderful to me.

"Oh, it's beautiful," Irene gasped. "Beautiful, Steven!" And this time I didn't think she was referring to the view alone.

I would have liked to go on looking at that vista, under those circumstances, all day long, but there was Phyllis to consider, as well as the guard, who had made it quite clear to me that he could only be bought for a limited period. So when Irene's breathy moans turned to soft shrieks and her body began to twitch spasmodically, I let go and joined her in rapturous climax.

By the time we had descended the arm and slipped back through the barrier, the guard was glaring, and Phyllis was awake and looking around, puzzled. We made haste to join her, and I came up with a story about having wandered down to a lower level; but I'm not sure Phyllis bought it. She kept looking suspiciously at Irene's glowing face.

Once again, I got back to my office just as Miss Greenglass was preparing to go home. She had, as usual, no discernible reaction when I informed her that yet another step had been taken in my progress toward the possession of her estimable person. I sat down wearily in my chair, and before regaling her with the details, I glanced casually through the small pile of phone messages she had left on my desk.

One of them made me sit up straight.

"*She* called?" I asked, showing the slip to Miss Greenglass.

That imperturbable lady merely nodded. "Yes, she wants to talk to you about doing a book on the market. I told her you usually turn down those offers, but she wants to talk to you about it."

"I'll be damned!" I said.

"Quite," Miss Greenglass murmured.

"Come on," I said, "aren't you just a little impressed? Hell, even I'm impressed. I mean, this is probably the most famous woman in the world!"

Miss Greenglass continued clearing her desk.

"And," I said after a moment, "she has great timing, too."

"Timing?"

"Yes," I said, adopting her cool tone. "Her first name, you know."

That, at least, made Miss Greenglass stop what she was doing and turn to look at me.

"You're not serious, Mr. Walling?"

"Why not?" I said. "I can try, can't I?"

Chapter 10

JUDICIOUS CONSIDERATION, IN WHICH I MUST admit I am sometimes deficient when it comes to women, would probably have prevented so hasty a declaration as that which I made to Miss Greenglass regarding the lady whose phone message I had just perused. After all, the challenge I had thereby set myself was nothing if not daunting. As I had said, this was perhaps the most famous woman in the world; a woman who had moved in the highest circles, and who even now was still a subject of eager interest to press and public.

I had been carried away by the fact that she had contacted me—though of course I realized it was a business call, in connection with her present occupation—and by the seemingly felicitous timing, as I had just that day effected a lovely consummation with a lady named Irene atop the Statue of Liberty, as described in the last chapter.

But perhaps I should have been less precipitate. There were, to be sure, no shortage of ladies of the J persuasion; it may, indeed, be the most common female initial in the

English language. It sometimes seemed that half the women I knew were named Jennifer; and there were plenty of Joans, Janes and Julies all over the place. It was, thus, ironic that I should undertake such a challenge just at the point at which my ongoing, and already difficult, task should have been easiest. I consoled myself with the thought that if I should fail with the lady in question, I would have a plentitude of J's to fall back on. But of course, having made my declaration of intent, I was obliged to do my best not to fail.

Although the perspicacious reader (and I trust I have no other kind) may be able to make a shrewd guess as to the identity of the lady in question, he or she will understand that this particular case necessitates a certain amount of discretion on my part. It may be objected that, up to now, this narrative has not been distinguished by any noticeable reticence or gallantry. However, in this instance even I quail at the possible consequences should she, or her notoriously close-knit and publicity-conscious family, take offense at any unwanted revelations. Powerful and influential in themselves, they are also rumored to have certain connections which . . . But never mind. Suffice it to say that the lady shall remain unnamed.

I knew that if I were to have any chance at all of making her the next step in my progress toward Miss Greenglass, I would probably need more than my celebrated virility and charm. This was no Irene, intrigued with the idea of a titillating affair with a sophisticated stranger in the big city. I would have to find a way to get past both her natural coolness and reserve, and the wary guardedness that had built up through all the years of adulation and notoriety. A challenge indeed.

My first step was to do nothing—that is, not to re-

turn her phone call. It was a risk, but not a very big one;
I was pretty sure she would call again. And she did, the
next day. Actually it was her assistant who called.
Echoing the message Miss Greenglass had taken, she
said her boss was interested in discussing with me the
possibility of a book setting forth my viewpoint on the
current economic crisis. I asked her why, in that case,
her boss hadn't called me herself. She explained, somewhat tartly, that her boss was a very busy woman, but
that she would set up a luncheon appointment at which
the lady and myself could discuss the matter. I explained, just as tartly, that I was a busy man and that I
never accepted invitations through third parties. And I
hung up.

Two days went by, and I feared I had muffed my
chance. But then there was another call, and after the
usual preliminaries between her assistant and mine, I
picked up the phone to hear the familiar breathy voice of
the lady herself.

"Mr. Walling?"

"Hi," I said.

"How do you do," she said. "You're rather a hard man
to get hold of."

"Not really," I said. "But you know how it is. So many
phone calls . . ."

There was a pause. Obviously she was accustomed to
having her calls returned immediately—and with defer-
ence. My idea was to put her off guard by eschewing def-
erence and treating her like anybody else. Or maybe not
even quite as well. It was another gamble but, as you
know, I am a gambling man.

"Of course," she said. "Mr. Walling, as my assistant
told you, we are interested in having you utilize your ex-

pertise in the area of finance to produce a book for us. It could be quite beneficial to your reputation, and if it were to—"

"Well, thanks," I interrupted. "But you know, I've gotten these offers before, and somehow the terms never seem to make it worth the effort. I'm kind of a lazy bastard, you see, and I don't think I'm really . . ."

"My company is willing to offer suitable terms," the lady said, somewhat coolly. "I'm sure we could reach a satisfactory arrangement, Mr. Walling. Why don't we meet for lunch and discuss the possibilities?"

"Well, I suppose I could do that," I said, feigning reluctance.

"Good. Shall we say tomorrow? Mortimer's at one?"

"I'm afraid I'm busy tomorrow," I lied. "How about Thursday? No, that's out too. Friday?"

Another pause. "Fine," she said. "Friday. I'll see you there."

Miss Greenglass, who had of course heard my end of the conversation, was busy at her keyboard, impassive as ever. "She hates me," I said cheerfully. "Good start, don't you think?"

"I'm sure you know what you are doing, Mr. Walling," she said.

"Well, I'm not," I said. "But I've got to do something. She's so used to everybody falling all over themselves for her that this might knock her off her feet."

"Or else she might just knock you off yours," murmured Miss Greenglass.

"It's a risk," I admitted, "but she's worth it. And so are you."

Miss Greenglass's mouth gave a twitch, which might have been the possibility of the beginning of the thought of a smile. "I'm sure the lady would be extremely flattered," she said, "to realize that you see her as merely a stepping-stone to be used for the attainment of someone else."

"And to avoid tripling that someone else's salary," I said. "Don't forget that."

"I assure you I have not forgotten that," Miss Greenglass replied.

I grinned at her. "Anyway," I said, "ask not what the lady can do for me. Ask what I can do for the lady!"

The lady, of course, was no longer in the prime of her youth, but the years had done remarkably little to detract from her beauty. If they had taken away the freshness of springtime, they had compensated by adding a strength and character to her fine features which made her as striking as ever. And her body was still slender and firm-looking, attesting to much time and probably money spent in its upkeep. There was an aura of elegance about her that was almost palpable, and I admit I had to make an effort not to be hypnotized by it as I sat down.

"Thank you for coming, Mr. Walling," she said, after our initial greetings. "I do hope we will be able to work together. It's my feeling that a book giving your views on the current fiscal crisis would be an enormous asset to our company."

I shrugged. "Hey, I don't know how I got to be such a big expert. All I did was inherit a successful company and not run it into the ground."

She smiled. "You're far too modest," she said. "Your name is well known in financial circles, and with the proper promotion I believe such a book could be—"

"I don't think so," I said.

"I beg your pardon?"

"I said, I don't think I want to write a book. Look, I get this all the time. I'm not a writer, I'm a businessman, and even that kind of reluctantly. My idea is to do as little work as possible, not give myself more. So as I said on the phone, I'm not really interested."

"I see," she said. The waiter had brought drinks for us, and now she picked up her glass and took a sip. She was annoyed, but she didn't want to show it. "In that case, Mr. Walling, why, may I ask, did you agree to meet me?"

I shrugged. "Curiosity," I said. "I wanted to see what you were like up close."

Her lips tightened. "I see," she said again, putting the glass down very carefully. "Well then, I think we have nothing further to—"

"You can't blame me for that," I said. "It's natural. Famous lady like you, I wanted to see what all the fuss is about."

Her face was white. She was boiling, but she controlled it. "Now that you have seen," she said, almost whispering, "I will not trouble you further." And she started to get up.

I didn't move. "That's it?" I said. "You're not even going to try to talk me into it?"

She stared at me as if I were a bug. "Into what?"

"Writing a book, of course," I said. "Did you have something else in mind?"

She took a long breath. She had had a lot of practice controlling her emotions. "You," she said after a moment, "are a very exasperating person."

"I bet you are too, sometimes," I said. "Look," I went

on before she could start to leave again, "I didn't mean to insult you or anything. I just meant that I wanted to see the person, the woman behind all the hoopla."

"Indeed," she said shortly.

"Indeed *indeed*," I said. "I know there's a real woman inside there someplace. I mean, sure you may be the most famous woman in the world, but you put your panties on one leg at a time just like everybody else, right?"

Two little red spots appeared high on her cheeks. I thought she was going to leave for sure, but instead she took another sip of her drink. "Really," she said. "You . . ." She took a breath. "People don't talk to me that way!"

"I bet there's a lot of things people don't say to you," I said. "For instance, I'm sure everyone tells you you're beautiful, but do they tell you you're sexy too?"

The red spots got larger. "Mr. Walling, I think—"

"You are, you know," I said. "You have a terrific body." And I let my eyes fall to her bosom, small but shapely under the designer blouse, and rest there deliberately for a moment before returning to her face. She glared at me, but her eyes showed something more than anger.

It was now or never. I leaned closer to her over the table, speaking softly but intensely. "I'd love to see it," I said. "Your body. Naked, I mean. I'd love to touch it. Kiss it. I'd love to have it beneath me, I'd love to see you with—"

"Stop it!" She didn't shout, but she looked as if she wanted to. She was rigid and pale. "You can't—what do you—who do you think—you must be—"

"I must be what?" I asked. "Crazy? Why? Is it crazy to want to make love with you?"

She gasped and started to leave. I took hold of her wrist, not very tightly, but neither did she pull it away. "That's what I want to do, all right," I said. "Fuck you, put my cock inside you, make you moan, make you crazy. Make you come. Over and over. I'd love to watch the great lady coming. I bet that's really a sight to see!"

I let go of her then. She didn't move. She seemed paralyzed, hardly even breathing. I saw her swallow. It took a moment for her to speak.

"This meeting is over," she whispered emphatically.

I sat back. "What about lunch?" I said.

"Mr. Walling, you—" she began, but then stopped. She stood up. "Good-bye, Mr. Walling," she said.

I got up also. "Let me get you a taxi," I said.

"Thank you, I have my car."

"Oh," I said. "Then maybe you can give me a ride back to my office."

She looked at me. Her face now was completely blank, devoid of any expression that I could fathom. For a moment she hesitated. Then she gave a very small shrug and walked toward the door. I followed.

An impressive-looking limousine was at the curb and, as we emerged from the restaurant, a uniformed driver got out and opened the back door, touching his cap to her.

"We'll be dropping Mr. Walling at his office, Peter," she said to him. I told him the address and then followed her into the car. The interior was quite roomy, and she sat as far from me as possible. But the partition was up between the front and back seats, isolating us from the driver, and the windows of course were opaque from the outside. My time was running out, but I couldn't bring myself to give up yet.

I slid closer to her. She glared at me. The anger and haughtiness in that glare almost stopped me. But there was also that other thing in her eyes.

"What are you doing?" she demanded.

"Look," I said, "it's only about fifteen minutes to my office. Why don't you tell your driver to drive around in the park for a little while?"

Her anger turned to disbelief. "You are outrageous!" she breathed.

"How long has it been since you made it in the back of a car?" I asked, moving closer. "A long time, I bet. Have you ever?"

"If you touch me," the lady said breathlessly, "I will scream."

"No you won't," I said, though I wasn't so sure. But I didn't touch her. I took a deep breath and said, "Please, pull up your skirt."

She only stared. If she was going to make a fuss, this was the time. But she only stared.

"What?" she whispered finally.

"Pull up your skirt," I said. "I want to see your legs. I know you have nice legs. I've seen pictures."

"You—you—how would you—"

I thought of reminding her of those nude pictures that had been published in the tabloids years ago, but I decided that was not a good idea. "I can tell," I said. "Come on, I want to see all of them. I want to touch them. I want to be between them and feel them around me. Right here."

"I have . . . never . . . I . . ."

"About time, then," I said. "Pull it up."

"Oh!" she said.

I waited.

"I won't," she said. She said it very softly indeed.

I waited.

"No," she said. "Oh, dear God," she said. "Oh, I—" She looked at me. Then she looked away from me. Then she said, "God help me." And she pulled up her skirt.

Her legs were fine, covered with the sheerest of pantyhose. The front of the skirt was up to the top of her thighs, though she was sitting on the back of it. She still wasn't looking at me.

"I want to see them bare," I said. "Take the hose off."

She shook her head slightly. Then she closed her eyes. She reached up beneath the skirt to her waist and pulled the pantyhose down, hitching herself up off the seat to do so. She pulled them off and dropped them.

"Gorgeous," I said. And I reached out a hand and put it on her thigh. She jumped, but didn't protest or make a move to push it away.

"Why am I doing this?" she whispered again softly.

"Because," I said, as steadily as I could, "you are a beautiful and elegant lady who is also sexy and passionate, and who should be able to act like an animal when she feels like it."

"An animal. Yes. Oh, God . . ."

I moved my hand higher. She gasped, and stiffened slightly.

"Tell him to go around the park," I again suggested.

"I—I don't know if—"

I moved my hand all the way up.

She fumbled for the little phone that she used to communicate with the driver, and pushed the button. "Peter," she said, "drive around the park, please. For—for a while." She dropped the phone. "Oh, God . . ." she said again.

I pulled her panties down.

She clutched at me then. She held me by the arms and looked straight into my eyes. I felt that she was about to make some fervent declaration.

What she said was, "You must never . . . ever . . . say anything about this . . . to anyone!"

"Okay," I said.

She gazed at me a moment longer, then released me and slumped back in the seat, naked from the waist down, her panties around her ankles. It was an interesting sight.

I started to fumble at my trousers, but I couldn't just pull it out and go at her with my clothes on. Not with this lady. So I undressed myself as swiftly and gracefully as I could, given the circumstances. She watched me, breathing rapidly but not moving or speaking.

"Show me your breasts," I said.

Her eyes closed, then opened. Her hands moved. She unbuttoned her blouse, pulled it open and took it off. Then she reached around to unclasp her brassiere, and she took that off too. I gazed at the gently rounded, shapely bosoms, then bent to kiss them. The nipples, already firm, became still harder under my lips and tongue as I moved from one to the other. I heard her catch her breath, then moan softly, and then her hands came up to softly stroke my body.

I stroked hers too, and kissed it, and played with it, until with a small, breathless cry she slid down onto her back on the roomy car seat, one leg bent up against the rear of the car, the other dangling to the floor. I pulled myself up over her and tried to kiss her mouth, but she turned her head away.

"No," she whispered. "Just do it. Please. Like an animal. Do it."

Whatever the lady wanted. I found her and moved slowly, but firmly into her. She groaned, and her body surged against me, her arms coming up to clutch at me. For a moment I almost lost it, as I had a sudden realization of where I was and who I was doing this with; but then I stopped thinking about it and became lost in the pulsing body underneath me. One leg curled around me as I moved, slowly at first, then faster, and I heard and felt her panting breath at my ear, louder and louder. Then the panting broke into a soft, husky shriek, and I felt her tense beneath me, felt her spasm and slowly relax.

Now I could think about it all right, and the thought of it kept me going, drove me to make this something she would remember. She still wouldn't let me kiss her, and she didn't say a word, but we grappled there in the back of that car until she had cried out twice more in ecstasy. And, finally, I did too.

Only then, as we lay there recovering our breath, did she kiss me—not lengthily or passionately, but a real kiss nonetheless. And then she gently but firmly pushed me away. We sat up and began to dress in silence. She told Peter to drive to my office, and from then until we arrived there she said only two more things to me.

First she said, "We should not, I think, meet again, Mr. Walling."

"Whatever you say," I said. And we never have.

And just before she dropped me off she said again, "You must never, under any circumstances . . ."

"I won't," I said. "I promise you I won't."

And I never did. Except for Miss Greenglass, of course; but Miss Greenglass is the soul of discretion.

And now you.

Chapter II

KISS ME, MISS GREENGLASS," I WARBLED, throwing myself carelessly into my chair and putting my feet up on my desk. "Anoint me with oils, shower me with accolades, proclaim my glory to the four winds, and make me a cup of coffee. Not necessarily in that order."

Miss Greenglass, as I had expected, did none of these things. She barely glanced up from the papers on her desk.

"I take it," she said dryly, "that you were successful."

"Did you ever doubt it?" I inquired, though I myself certainly had. "The bigger they are, Miss Greenglass, the harder they fall. And the harder they are, the—well, something or other . . ."

"I will make you that coffee," Miss Greenglass said. "You appear to be a little giddy, Mr. Walling."

"I'm just in a good mood," I said. "And why not? I am one step closer to winning our wager. And not only that, but I already know just who the next step is going to be."

"Indeed," she murmured. "And who is that fortunate lady, if I may ask?"

"Ask away," I said. "You remember me telling you about the girl on the plane, when I was coming back from my brief liaison with Bonnie in Monte Carlo? The stewardess who I thought was named Catherine, with a C, but who, alas, turned out to be Katharine, with not only a K but with two A's, as in the redoubtable Miss Hepburn."

"Of course," Miss Greenglass said.

"I had to turn her down, poor thing," I said. "But now she is in luck, for her proper time has arrived."

"If I were she—" Miss Greenglass began.

"Ah, but you're not," I said. "But don't worry, Miss Greenglass. Your turn will come too."

"We'll see," Miss Greenglass said.

A couple of phone calls to the airline, a discreet application of charm and a couple of well-crafted falsehoods soon got me the information I wanted. Katharine, it seemed, was still flying the New York–Monte Carlo route, and was scheduled for a flight departing JFK that Thursday morning. I had Miss Greenglass book me a seat. First class, of course.

I was looking forward with eager anticipation to meeting Katharine again, and in fact had been doing so ever since our abortive encounter in that tiny airplane lavatory. My blood warmed when I recalled the ample shapeliness of her figure in her blue stewardess's uniform, and the frank, unrestrained ardor she had demonstrated before I had called a halt. I could still feel the sensation of that agile, passionate tongue thrusting halfway down my throat as we kissed. And the warm breath of her ardent mouth caressing my hard flesh as she had almost . . . damn . . . almost . . .

But now nothing stood in the way of our delayed consummation. Nothing, that is, except Katharine.

I thought she might not remember me at first, but as soon as she saw me at the plane entrance as we boarded, her body stiffened and her deep brown eyes became chips of dark ice. I saw immediately that this was going to be a bumpy flight.

"Hello, Katharine," I said, smiling as I handed her my boarding pass. "It's great to see you again."

"Good morning, sir," she said stiffly. "First aisle to the right. Have a pleasant flight."

I had no chance to talk to her then. I found my seat and waited until the plane had taken off and the first flutter of drink-serving and other initial activity was over. Katharine passed my seat several times, but didn't even look at me. Finally I unhooked my seat belt and went in search of her.

I had to bide my time until I could approach her while she was temporarily alone in the small stewardess's cabin. "Katharine," I began. "I wanted to—"

"You shouldn't be here," she said coldly. "Go back to your seat."

"I wanted to talk to you," I said. "About what—"

"I have nothing to say to you," Katharine said, and tried to move past me. I blocked her way.

"If you don't move, I'll call for help," she said flatly.

"Go ahead," I said. "Call everybody on the plane. I'll tell them that I'm flying to Monte Carlo and back just so I could get to see you."

"Yeah, right."

"It's true," I said. "I want to apologize for what happened last time. And to explain."

She snorted. "It ought to be a pretty good explanation,"

she said, and added—unnecessarily, I thought—"you son of a bitch."

Now came the crunch. I have asserted that I try to avoid lying to women whenever possible; but there are times when that principle must take a backseat to practicality. Since making my fatal wager with Miss Greenglass, I had several times been confronted with the decision as to whether a more or less straightforward explanation of that wager would further my cause, or hinder it, with a particular lady. With Abigail, for example, it had worked like a charm. But given Katharine's present attitude, my intuition was that it would not have a salubrious effect.

So I lied.

"The thing is," I said, sighing deeply, "at the time, I was very much involved with someone—someone I was trying to remain faithful to. Even then our relationship was in trouble, but I felt obligated to try to save it." I gazed soulfully into her eyes. "I admit I was tempted—I wanted you so badly—I mean, who wouldn't?—and I almost fell . . . but at the last minute, I—I just couldn't be false to her."

Katharine showed no expression. "But now you've broken up, I suppose," she said.

"Yes," I sighed. "It's over. And I've found myself thinking about you. I haven't been able to stop thinking about you."

At first she just looked at me, but then, slowly, she smiled. She looked at her watch. "I have a few minutes," she said softly. "Want to share a bathroom again?"

"I'd love to."

"Come on."

Of course, I should have known it was too easy. But

perhaps my last conquest had made me overconfident; and besides, Katharine's alluring body tended to disrupt the thinking process. I followed her up the aisle, and waited while she slipped into an unoccupied lavatory. When I was sure no one was looking, I slipped in after her.

As before, the tightness of the space virtually forced our bodies together; but Katharine helped too. In a moment she was plastered against me, smiling up at me, and the sweet, yielding pillows of her breasts were mashed against my chest, with her loins grinding against mine with a slow, incredibly erotic movement that had me hard and pulsing in seconds. I clasped her tightly and started to say something, but her eager lips were on mine, and then that wonderfully talented tongue was in my mouth and all was right with the world.

She continued to grind against me as we kissed, and then I felt her hand moving down between our bodies, sliding caressingly across the throbbing bulge in my trousers, then finding my zipper and pulling it down. Her fingers searched and found and stroked, and all the time her tongue was playing with mine, as if in anticipation of greater joys to come.

Finally we broke the kiss, gasping for air; and then Katharine began to slide down my body as she went slowly to her knees. "Remember this?" she said breathlessly, kneeling in front of me and stroking my hard flesh, then bending her head to kiss it lightly. I felt her warm breath. Yes, I remembered all right. I strained forward. Katharine gave a little laugh. It set off a faint warning bell in my brain, but my brain was not what was occupying my attention at that moment.

"Remember?" Katharine repeated. "We were just like

this. And I was just about to . . ." Her head moved again, her mouth opened . . . I gasped as I entered the portals of heaven . . .

And then I gasped again, in quite a different manner, as I felt her lips squeezing tightly around the base of my shaft.

She squeezed hard enough to make me hold very, very still. And I heard that tiny laugh again, this time slightly muffled.

"Uh . . . Katharine . . ." I said. Very carefully.

She held me that way for another moment, and then let go and drew her head away. I made a small sound of relief and hastened to cover up my rapidly shrinking tool.

"I ought to bite it off!" she said. "You lousy bastard!" She stood up, but now she kept her hands between our bodies, fending me off in the small space.

"Katharine—"

"Screw you!" She tried to slap my face, but I managed to block it, so she settled for hitting me in the chest. "You piece of shit! How does it feel? You like it?"

"But I—"

"You expect me to believe that bullshit story?" She swung at me again. "First you walk out on me and then you—"

"Look, Katharine, let me—"

"Fuck off!" Katharine said. She pushed me with surprising strength, then squirmed past me and got the door open before I could stop her.

"Wait—" I said, but she didn't. She was out the door, and without thinking of caution I went after her, calling her name, only to find a stout lady passenger who had been waiting for an empty lavatory staring at me in shock.

"It's all yours, madam," I said to her, and she gave me a wide berth as she headed for it.

Another stewardess who had been passing had also evidently observed our nearly simultaneous emergence, and was standing there laughing quietly. I gave her an embarrassed kind of shrug, and she came up to me, smiling. She was very pretty and very young and very blond.

"Having troubles with Katharine?" she asked, looking me over rather boldly. "She can be pretty temperamental sometimes."

"I've noticed," I said.

"Anything I can do to help?" she asked. She wasn't talking about fetching me a drink, either.

"What's your name?" I asked.

"Diana."

"Damn. That wouldn't be Diana with a K, would it?" She blinked. "No."

"Didn't think so. Sorry, Diana. Another time, okay?"

Diana shrugged. "Sure," she said. "Maybe tonight? I'll be at the casino. A bunch of us girls are going."

"Oh?" I said. "Katharine too?"

She made a face. "It has to be Katharine, huh?"

"I wish it didn't."

"Me too." She turned and walked away. She had a lovely behind. For the hundredth time I hoped Miss Greenglass could appreciate what I was giving up for her.

Since I hadn't expected to spend much time in Monte Carlo, I had packed very lightly, and had not bothered to include a tuxedo, which is my preferred attire for visiting the casino there. However, standards have declined so precipitously in these casual times that my unassuming business suit was, if anything, conspicuous by its formality among the tourists, sharpers and local hangers-on in that once-elegant establishment. I was not particularly interested in gambling that evening; my focus was on that one great gamble which was rapidly becoming the central obsession of my life, and particularly on Katharine, who was to be the next counter in the game. It might have made more sense to just go home and find another K lady; but I hated to think I had made this long flight for nothing. And I kept feeling her breasts against me, and her writhing hips, and her fabulous tongue . . .

I roamed the casino for an hour or so before they showed up. There were four of them—Diana, Katharine and two others whom I hadn't met. It was, of course, the first time I had seen Katharine out of uniform, and she looked incredibly sensuous in a simple but formfitting black dress that plunged nicely in front. They were standing at a craps table, chattering excitedly as one of the girls I didn't know rolled the dice. She lost. As I approached, Diana spotted me and waved, then said something to the others. Katharine did not bother to look up.

"Hi!" Diana greeted me. "Nice to see you again. Hey, girls, this is—what's your name, anyway?"

"Steven," I said.

"Steven," Diana said. "He's a friend of Katharine's."

"No," Katharine said flatly, "he's not."

"They had a little tiff," Diana said mischievously. "In the bathroom on the plane." The other two giggled. Katharine rolled her eyes and moved a little bit away. I went over and stood beside her.

"Look," I said in a low voice. "I'm really sorry, and there really was a good reason for what I did, but it's just too complicated to explain."

"You don't say." She was still watching the play at the

table. At least she didn't walk away, which I took to be a good sign.

"I do. And believe me, it killed me to leave you like that."

"You managed, though, didn't you?"

"I'm sorry," I said again. "What more can I say? And if you can't forgive me—well, I'll go away and I won't bother you anymore. If that's really what you want."

She said nothing. I knew I had turned the corner.

"On the other hand—" I brought my mouth close to her ear and lowered my voice. "The bathrooms here in the casino are much bigger than they are on the plane."

She moved her head away, but then she turned it enough to give me a quick glance, and what I saw in her eyes in that instant made my pulse quicken.

"They're less private, though," she murmured.

"We can deal with that," I said. "Or . . . we could just go to my hotel."

"No, thanks," she said. "I like it here."

"Well then," I said. "My bathroom or yours?"

We chose mine. The gentleman in attendance there did not seem at all surprised at my suggestion that he absent himself for a while (in return for a substantial gratuity, of course); I got the impression that he received such requests all the time, and probably sent his children to college thereby. He could not, however, undertake to stand guard outside the door to keep others from entering. I waited until the room was momentarily empty, and then sneaked Katharine in as surreptitiously as I could, leading her quickly to a stall and shutting us in.

Even the toilet stall was larger than the lavatory on the plane had been. But the door, in the universal manner of such things, was set about two feet above the floor, so that anyone who cared to peek underneath could see the legs of the person (or in this case persons) inside. And it was highly unlikely that the bathroom would remain un-inhabited for long.

In fact, we had only just melted into a passionate kiss when we heard the outer door open and a couple of guys come in. I quickly sat down on the toilet seat and pulled Katharine onto my lap. Fortunately the seat was a wide one, just wide enough to allow her to place her feet on ei-ther side of me as she crouched there. It was not the most comfortable position in the world, but it was suitable enough for our purposes, except for the fact that we had all these clothes in the way. Also we had to be quiet. Other men were coming in now, and from that point on the traffic was virtually continuous.

I slid my hand down between us to open my zipper, my fingers brushing Katharine's crotch and bringing a soft moan from her. With my other hand I pulled her face to mine in order to muffle the sound with a kiss.

I got my zipper open and my cock free, and pushed Katharine's dress up over her thighs; but her panties were hard to pull off in that position. I tried pushing them out of the way, but finally had to make a little tear with my thumbnail and pull them apart until I could maneuver myself through the gap—and then into that sweeter gap, which appeared gratifyingly eager to receive me.

Our lips parted with a simultaneous gasp, and then she was moving on me, and I was helping as best I could. Her hands were tugging my jacket off, and I managed to get her dress open enough to slide her bra up and feast for a few moments on her round, hard-nippled breasts.

Then we were holding each other as she pressed her-self to me, moving harder, and we kissed again to stifle our panting and moaning, though I don't know how successful we were. Especially when I felt her spasming around my flesh as she went over the top, just as I was wondering how long I could hold out myself. As it turned out, not another second. But if the sounds of our climax were indeed audible outside our stall, at least no one was heard to complain.

Very civilized country, Monaco.

We continued to kiss as our passion subsided, though Katharine's restless, probing tongue made me suspect that she had further fun and games in mind. Not that I had any objections. My only regret was that, in these circumstances, she would be unable to use that marvelous mouth on me as she had come so close to doing twice before.

But what the hell, you can't have everything.

Chapter 12

ISTEN, HENRY," I SAID, TRYING TO STAY CALM. "I've told you I don't want you hanging around here. And especially around my assistant. Haven't I?"

"Hey, what's the problem, Steve-O?" Henry asked. He calls me "Steve-O" though he knows I hate it. Maybe because he knows I hate it. "Can't I drop in to say hello to my big brother? And if he's got a pretty secretary hanging around . . . well, hey, it's every man for himself, right?"

"Wrong," I said. "Firstly, Miss Greenglass is not a secretary, she's an assistant. Secondly, you're not a man, you're a cockroach. And thirdly, you're not worthy to shine that woman's shoes. So if—"

"Oho. Do I detect a little jealousy there, Steve-O? You want to keep this chick all to yourself, huh? Is she that good?"

I took a deep breath. "Miss Greenglass and I are simply employer and employee," I said. "For now, anyway. And I won't have—"

"What? A good-looking female like that and you haven't porked her yet? Hard to believe, Steve."

Faithful readers of this saga may or may not remember my mentioning that I had a brother. Henry, unfortunately, was he. It is probably evident that we were not on the best of terms.

"Henry," I said, "I'll tell you again. I don't want you here. This is a business office. It's a family business, Henry, but you chose not to be a part of it. You preferred to take your part of the money and be a playboy or whatever. Fine. Go play. But do it away from here. And away from Miss Greenglass."

Henry shrugged. "I guess that means double-dating is out," he said.

"What?"

"Well, sorry, Steve-O, but the fact is I have a date with the gorgeous lady tomorrow night."

I stared at him. "I don't believe it," I said finally.

"Why not? Hey, the chick knows quality when she sees it."

"You . . . and she . . . are going out?"

"I knew you'd catch on eventually," Henry said.

"No," I said.

"Well, Steve-O, if you say no and she says yes, now who am I gonna believe?"

"Get the hell out of here," I said.

"Okay, bro. But I'll probably see you tomorrow afternoon when I come here to pick her up."

I stood up then, and when Henry saw the expression on my face he decided to make his departure. I have often said that I am a lover rather than a fighter, but in this case I was quite prepared to make an exception.

* * *

It seemed so unlikely that my cool, unapproachable Miss Greenglass would choose to date such a person as Henry—and not at all unlikely that Henry would make up such a story—that I would not allow myself to believe it without further proof. When Miss Greenglass came in the next day I waited for her to mention something about it, but she didn't, and finally my curiosity drove me to broach the subject myself.

"Miss Greenglass," I began, at what seemed an opportune moment. "After you left yesterday, my brother told me that—well, I know it's probably just one of his stories—but he said that you and he were . . . going out together. Tonight."

There was no change in Miss Greenglass's placid demeanor. "Yes, Mr. Walling. Your brother was kind enough to ask me to dinner."

I stared at her. "And you accepted?"

"Yes, I did."

"But—but why?"

She glanced at me with only the slightest raising of her lovely eyebrows. "I beg your pardon?"

"Why?" I repeated. "Why would you go out with—with Henry, of all people? I can't believe it!"

Miss Greenglass's cool voice became cooler than ever. "I believe my private life is my own affair, Mr. Walling."

"Well, of course it is," I said. "But—but Henry! He's so—I just wouldn't have thought he was the type of person you would be—that you would want to—"

"Not that it is any concern of yours, Mr. Walling," Miss Greenglass said, "but perhaps your brother has certain qualities which you do not appreciate."

"My brother is a jerk," I said. "And you're wrong, Miss Greenglass—it is my concern. Once I win our bet,

I'm going to be taking you to bed. And I don't want my idiot brother getting there before me. I'm sorry if that sounds crude, Miss Greenglass, but when it comes to Henry it's hard to be anything else."

I couldn't be sure whether the swift glint in her eyes signified anger or amusement. "I am simply going to dinner with your brother, Mr. Walling," she said. "No one has said anything about sexual activity." She paused. "Although I have not ruled it out," she added.

"What? But—"

"Our wager, as you know, does not put any restrictions on me, Mr. Walling—only on you. And if, as you so charmingly put it, taking me to bed is indeed your object, perhaps you should be more concerned with your own social life than with mine, don't you think?"

The woman was infuriating. "Don't worry about that," I said. "I'm already at L. Hell, I know lots of L-women. Laura, Louise, Lana, Linda, Lonnie, Leslie, Lorna . . ."

"Most of whom you have already slept with, I'm sure," Miss Greenglass murmured.

"So what? Remember, that's not a rule. I just said that I would try to enlist new ladies in order to make my job a little less easy. But if you're going to sink to going out with my brother . . ."

"I fail to see what that has to do with it," Miss Greenglass said.

"Nuts!" I explained.

Laura's phone had been disconnected. Louise was away on a business trip. Lana was in the hospital with a broken leg. Linda was on her honeymoon. Leslie never wanted to speak to me again (I wasn't sure why, but there must have been a good reason). Lonnie, I learned, had become a lesbian (it was a '90s thing, she told me). Lorna was eight months pregnant.

I gathered all this information in a series of calls I made while Miss Greenglass was out to lunch. It did not exactly improve my disposition. Not that there weren't still more L-ladies in my address book; but the real source of my disgruntlement was my brother's rendezvous with my assistant and, try though I might, it was hard to focus my mind on other things.

I was not in the office when Henry came to pick up Miss Greenglass that evening; it was a spectacle I was not anxious to witness. I did, however, happen to see them as they left together. This was because I just happened to be sitting in the back of a taxi a few doors down, watching my building while the meter ticked happily away. And I just happened to notice them get into another cab which Henry hailed.

"Follow that cab," I said to the driver.

"You're kidding," he said.

"I'm not kidding. Come on, they're pulling out."

"You a cop or something?" the driver said.

"No. Will you just—"

"Twenty-three years I been driving a cab, nobody ever said that to me before."

"Please," I said, trying to keep an eye on Henry's taxi before it got lost in the traffic. "I'll make it worth your while, all right?"

"It's like I'm in a damn time warp," the driver said, finally putting the cab in gear and pulling out. He shook his head. "Follow that cab. Jeez."

"Hurry, it's turning the corner up there. See it?"

"How do you hurry in this traffic?" the driver said.

You didn't. When we reached the corner and made the

turn, there were several taxis up ahead, and I couldn't be sure which one was theirs. "Try to get closer," I said.

"I'm not a helicopter, buddy," the driver said.

"I thought you guys were all foreigners nowadays," I said.

"Yeah, I'm a dying breed," the driver said. "Your old-time, wise-cracking cabbie from Brooklyn. Wanna make somethin' of it?"

"No," I said. "You're the kind a man's supposed to say 'Follow that cab' to, after all."

"Right," the driver said. "Now that you said it, I can retire. Hey, which of those cabs are we following, anyway?"

"I'm not sure any more. I think that one, the one that's turning left. Follow him."

He did, and we managed to keep the cab in sight for several blocks, until it stopped to disgorge its passengers. There were two, but it was too far away to be sure they were the right ones.

"Stop here," I told the cabbie. I pulled out some bills and gave them to him. "Thanks."

"No, no," he said. "You're supposed to say, 'Stay right here, Mack—and keep the meter running!'"

"Next time," I said.

The cab had let out the couple in front of a Chinese restaurant called Jade Empire, and I had seen them go in, so there was a good chance I had chosen the right cab to follow. I walked toward the restaurant. Actually, I wasn't too sure just what I was doing, following them. What did I expect to see? I knew it was foolish, not to say sneaky— but both my brain and my conscience were a bit numbed by the thought of Miss Greenglass and my imbecile brother . . .

A peek in the window showed me nothing of interest. What now? I didn't want to be spotted, but I had come this far. I opened the restaurant door to take a cautious look inside.

"Good evening, sir. You like table?"

The query came from a young woman of Asian extraction who approached me as I stepped halfway in. She was carrying a handful of menus and was evidently the hostess or maître d' (maîtresse d'?) or whatever.

"Ah . . . no. No, thank you. I was just . . ." I was looking around the restaurant as I spoke, and on the far side I spotted a couple just sitting down. It was almost certainly the people who had gotten out of the taxi, and it was just as certainly not Henry and Miss Greenglass.

"Damn," I said. "It was the wrong cab after all."

"Sir?" the lady said.

"Oh, sorry." I looked at her closely for the first time. She was rather tall, and looked even taller because of the way her hair was pinned up atop her head. She was very pretty, and very Asian-looking, with high cheekbones and sleepy, entrancing dark eyes. Her voice was low, and her clipped accent was charming and somehow sexy.

"You like table, sir?" she said again. "Dinner for one?"

"Oh. No, thank you." I was about to retreat, when I noticed something that stopped me in my tracks. She was wearing a traditional Chinese dress, high-collared and clinging to her slim but lissome figure. It was blue and looked like silk, and pinned to it just above her left breast was a small name tag. It read, "Li Mai."

"On second thought," I said . . .

Her traditional dress had the traditional slit up the side, and as I followed her to a table I was mostly following her long, lovely leg. Not that there was anything wrong with the rest of her body, slender though it was. I had asked for something secluded if possible, and she obligingly led me to a corner table that was, if not private, at least out of the crowd.

"Thank you," I said when she had seated me. "Ah . . . I don't suppose you could join me? At least for a quick drink?"

She gave me a swift appraising glance from those obsidian eyes, but her smile was no more than polite. "Oh, afraid not, sir. I'm working now."

"Maybe when you get a break," I suggested.

She shook her head. "It will be another hour, at least."

I smiled at her. "I'll eat slowly," I said.

She didn't smile back this time, she just gave me the eyes again. "The waiter be right with you," she said, and turned away.

I ordered a drink, and then dinner, and ate slowly. Whenever she passed my table in the course of her hostess duties, I smiled at her with all my manly charm. She didn't smile back.

But while I was on my second pot of tea, she was suddenly there across from me. "I already know the line," she said. She was smiling, but warily.

"Good for you," I said. "Which line?"

"You want to know if it's true about Asian women."

"Good grief," I said. "Do you actually get that?"

"Many times," Li Mai said.

"And does it work?"

"Not many times."

"That's a relief," I said. "Actually, what I'm curious about is your name. Li Mai. Lovely name."

"Thank you."

"But aren't Chinese names sometimes reversed? I mean, the first name is actually the last name, and vice versa? Or something like that?"

She smiled slightly. "That's old-fashioned," she said. "Now we in America, okay? Different country. My name is Li Mai Chang."

"I'm glad," I said. Much more than she knew. "So is it?"

"Is what?"

"True about Asian women?" Actually, of course, I knew it wasn't. I had known a few very memorable daughters of the Orient in my time.

"Ah." She flashed the eyes at me. "Now I'm supposed to say, 'Why you don't find out,' right?"

"That would be nice."

"Then we go in back," she said. "Lock ourselves in storage pantry . . ."

"Sounds good to me," I said.

"There is even a table to lie on."

"Better and better."

"Or maybe you like the floor. More room that way."

"You're just playing with me, aren't you?"

"How you guessed?" Li Mai said.

"Damn clever, we Occidentals," I said.

She went back to work, and I ordered another pot of tea. It was another hour before she came back to me.

"Better leave waiter big tip," she said.

"I'm hoping it will be money well spent."

"You going to say you don't take no for answer?"

"Sometimes I do, actually," I said. "But you haven't said no yet, have you?"

"You patient man." She paused, looking at me. "Li Mai likes patient men."

"And I like women with beautiful cheekbones and slit skirts. And the legs to go with them."

"In China girls more modest," she said.

"And here?"

"Different country," she said. Our eyes met. She didn't look away.

"You know," I said. "It happens I've been making a study of the storage pantries of various ethnic restaurants. I'd certainly like to see yours."

Those dark eyes glinted slightly.

"Go in back," she said then. "All the way, then right. Fifteen minutes."

"Make it ten. I've been here so long the waiter looks like he's ready to hit me."

She smiled faintly. "That's not the reason he's angry."

"No? Then what is?"

"He's my husband," Li Mai said.

There was indeed a table, though it wasn't very big. Li Mai was sitting on it. As I closed the door and slid the bolt, she lay down on her back, bringing one leg up so that the slit skirt fell open, revealing that leg to the top of the thigh. In a moment I was in front of her, running my hand along the length of it, then pushing the dress up to her waist. She raised her hips in invitation, and I responded to her signal by pulling her panties down and off.

"It's not true," I said. "What do you know."

"You sure?" she said, somewhat breathlessly. "Maybe you need to look a little more close."

I did so. I bent down over her to get a really good look.

"I'm pretty sure," I said. "But I'd better check it out." Which I did, first with my fingers, and then with my mouth.

This took a while.

As I was doing it, she squirmed around a bit, partly with passion and partly because she was reaching around to unzip her dress, then taking off her bra. Her breasts were small and perfect. I held on to them to steady myself as I went on with my investigation.

When I had researched the question to my satisfaction—and even more, I think I can say, to hers—I hastily pulled off most of my clothes and climbed up to join her. The table was small, but fortunately sturdy. Our bodies fit together with no trouble at all, and her fine, shapely legs came up to curl around me. For a long pleasant time I probed deeply into the mysteries of the East—although the words Li Mai cried hoarsely into my ear from time to time were definitely English. Old English.

As we were dressing, I asked her about her waiter husband. I was not particularly anxious to be confronted with a meat cleaver upon emergence.

"Don't worry," Li Mai said. "This America now. I own restaurant. He want to keep his job, he keep quiet."

"God bless America," I said.

The next morning, I reported this bit of progress to Miss Greenglass, who received it with her accustomed *sangfroid*. Of course I didn't explain how it was that I happened to discover that particular restaurant, and fortunately she didn't ask.

"So that was my evening," I finished. And then added, as casually as I could, "How was yours?"

"Very pleasant, thank you," said my imperturbable assistant.

"You and Henry . . . got along all right?"

"Yes," Miss Greenglass said.

"But you didn't . . . I mean . . . Nothing happened. Did it?"

"I don't know what you mean, Mr. Walling."

"Oh, come on. You know exactly what I mean."

"I tell you again, Mr. Walling, that my private life is no concern of yours. I hope you will remember it this time."

"And I tell you again, Miss Greenglass, that it damned well is. Especially where my brother is concerned."

"The subject is closed," Miss Greenglass said firmly.

"You can be damn sure Henry would tell me," I said. "In detail."

"Then I suggest you ask him," Miss Greenglass said.

Which wasn't a bad idea. But I waited until she was out of the office before calling him.

"The chick is a dyke," Henry said.

"Aha," I said. "That means she wouldn't go to bed with you, I take it."

"She's frigid. She hates men. Probably a guy in disguise."

"She just has good taste," I said.

"Don't worry," Henry said. "I'll get her next time."

"Next time?" I said faintly.

"Saturday," he said. "We're going out again. I'll take her to a show this time, so maybe she'll come through."

I hung up.

"You're seeing him again?" I said incredulously, when Miss Greenglass returned.

"That's right."

"I can't believe this! How could you possibly—"

"Incidentally, Mr. Walling," Miss Greenglass said, "as Saturday is not a working day, he will be picking me up at my house. Seven o'clock. Just in case you'd like to try to follow us again."

"Grr!" I explained.

Chapter 13

MAYBE IT WAS MY IDIOT BROTHER HENRY'S irritating attempts to seduce Miss Greenglass that put me in a nostalgic mood, since it was in high school that he first started trying to steal my women—never successfully, of course. (Well, almost never.) Or maybe not; the fact is that for some time now, in thinking ahead to the letters of the alphabet still remaining for the completion of my wager, my mind had conjured up one name when it came to the letter M: the name of my first real girlfriend, Marcia Bradbury.

We had both been seniors in high school, eighteen years old and ready for anything, when our youthful romance had kindled. It took a while for our petting and gropings to progress to the point of actual culmination. And then, when the point had actually been reached—or to be more exact, when it was just *within* reach, and was just about to be grasped—

Her parents had come home.

And somehow our romance had never recovered.

Such frustration was not a very pleasant experience. I have labored assiduously to avoid such an experience ever since.

I had not thought of Marcia for years before making my bet with Miss Greenglass, but once she had come to my mind, I couldn't get her out. It would be wonderful, I thought, if I could go back in time, as it were, and at long last consummate that rudely severed relationship. Of course Marcia would no longer be the nubile virgin she had been then, but she might still be a very attractive woman, if she hadn't let herself go. I wondered if I would be able to find her.

Meanwhile, I had other problems.

My Miss Greenglass had indeed gone out with Henry a second time, although this time I had made no attempt to follow them. As before, I could learn nothing from Miss Greenglass about their evening together; and this time, when I called Henry, he was almost equally reticent. His general moroseness, however, made me fairly certain that he had still not succeeded in maneuvering my lovely assistant anywhere near a bed.

Of course I hadn't believed for a moment that he would. But still, the relief I felt was so powerful that it surprised even me.

"I assume," I said to Miss Greenglass a bit later on, "that you're not going to see my brother again. Two dates with Henry should be more than enough for anyone."

"You shouldn't assume anything, Mr. Walling," the lady said coldly. "And I don't wish to discuss this subject any further, if you don't mind."

"I do mind. As I've said before, Miss Greenglass, when I win our wager it would make me extremely unhappy to know that my imbecilic brother had claimed my prize before I did."

"You are still very far from that goal, Mr. Walling," Miss Greenglass said. "And if you do not concentrate on something other than this obsession with your brother and me, that problem will most certainly never arise."

"Hello?" A female voice. It didn't sound familiar; but then, it had been a long time.

"Hello," I said. "I'm looking for Marcia Bradbury. Does she still live there, by any chance?"

"Who?"

"Marcia Bradbury. At least that used to be her name. I don't know, she may be married or—"

"Oh, Marcia. Yeah, I think she's here. Hold on a minute."

I held on. I had looked up the number of Marcia's parents' house, and found it still listed under her father's name. Though I doubted that she was still living there, I had thought I might be able to trace her.

"Hello," came a new voice. "This is Marcia."

My heart, astonishingly, skipped a beat. "Marcia? Marcia Bradbury?"

"Well, not anymore. Who is this?"

"This is Steven." I felt ridiculously nervous. "Steven Walling."

A pause.

"Steven Walling," I said again. "From high school?"

Another pause. "Ah," Marcia said then, but without conviction. "From high school."

"Yes," I said. "We were . . . involved. Sort of. Our senior year. You remember? We were—going together."

"Senior year. Hmmm. That was a long time ago."

"Yes, but not *that* long," I said. I couldn't believe she didn't remember. "We had . . . we almost . . ." I was stammering like a schoolboy. This was absurd. "Remember the night your parents came home and caught us on your sofa?" I said. "We were just about to . . ."

"Oh dear," Marcia said. "Right in my living room?"

"Yes, and they caught us half naked, and after that—"

"What a shame," Marcia said. "How naked was I?"

"You don't remember?" I said.

"Oh, of course I do, dear," Marcia said, but not very convincingly. "And we never got to do it after that?"

"No. We broke up. Your parents . . ."

"Well, they're dead now," Marcia said. "They can't stop us anymore."

I blinked, though there was no one to see me. "I guess not," I said. "I mean, I'm sorry."

"I still have the sofa," Marcia said. "Well, maybe not the same one. But that doesn't matter, does it? What you want is to relive that night, only this time with no interruptions. Isn't that right, dear?"

This was weird. But she was right, that's what I wanted. "Well, I—I thought maybe we could get together, and then—"

"Why don't you come over, dear? You know the address?"

"I remember," I said. "But do you, Marcia? Do you remember me?"

"Of course, dear," she said. "Your name is . . . ah . . . what was it again?"

"Steven. Steven Walling."

"Yes. What was I wearing that night, Steven? Do you recall?"

Actually, I did. "A wool sweater," I said. "A blue one,

with a little pin on it. And a dark skirt. And you had a blue ribbon in your hair. We had just come back from—"

"All right, Steven. When would you like to come?"

"Any time," I said. "How about right now? I could be there in half an hour."

"I'll be waiting," Marcia said.

Both Marcia and I had grown up in Brooklyn Heights, a rather affluent enclave just across the river from Manhattan. As I taxied there I was filled with both anticipation and puzzlement. I was looking forward to seeing Marcia again; and it would be wonderful if we could indeed consummate our youthful passion at last. But it had appeared that she really didn't remember me at all . . . and in that case, why had she invited me over? Why had she all but promised that we would . . .

I paid off the cab driver in front of the familiar brownstone, and as I mounted the steps and rang the bell, I couldn't help feeling a bit like the nervous youth I had been when I had first performed those actions. The door was opened by a young and very attractive, if somewhat overly made up, blonde.

"Hi," she said.

"Uh—hi," I replied. "I'm here to see Marcia Brad— that is, Marcia. I'm Steven Walling."

"Oh, Steven, right. Come on in."

She took me into the living room. "She'll be right with you," the blonde said, and she went off, calling, "Marcia! Steven's here!"

The room was not exactly as I remembered it, but the sofa—a different one—was in the same place, and I was already feeling the grip of nostalgia. And then Marcia came in, and I was lost.

She was older, of course. She was not the girl of my memory, radiant with youthful beauty. And yet she was. Her smile was the same, her eyes held a familiar warmth. Her figure, if less slender, was still curvaceous and perfectly molded. And . . . she was dressed just as she had been that night, just as I had described on the phone. The woolen sweater, the skirt . . . the ribbon in her dark hair . . .

"Marcia!"

"Hello, Steven." She smiled that smile, and came up to me. I leaned to kiss her hello, but our lips met, and clung. My head was swimming when we parted.

Marcia backed up and pirouetted for me. "Is this how you remember me, Steven?" she said. "Do I look all right?"

"God," I said. "You're beautiful. You look——" I took a breath to steady myself. "But Marcia—do *you* remember *me*? On the phone I thought——"

"Never mind," she said. "Here we are now. Come sit on the sofa. Just like that night. Just think about that night."

She led me to the sofa and we sat down. She was very close. Her hair was long and loose, just as it had been back then . . .

"What about that girl?" I said. "The blonde, is she——"

"Don't worry about her," Marcia said. "She won't bother us. Nobody will bother us. Except maybe my parents. They might come home any minute. Isn't that exciting, Steven?"

"Oh, God . . ." I said. Then I kissed her. I kissed her for a long time, and her kiss was innocent and yet searching, just as it had been then, and after a while my hands started to roam.

She broke the kiss, but didn't pull away. "Oh, Steven," she breathed. "You make me so excited. But we shouldn't . . ."

"I know," I said. My hands slid slowly onto her breasts and squeezed them gently. I remembered the first time I had done that. I remembered how it had made me feel . . . just as I was feeling now.

"Oh, Steven . . ." Marcia moaned. But she kissed me again, and her lips and tongue said yes. One hand left her breast and slid down over her body to her thigh, and then underneath her skirt. She gasped against my lips.

"No, maybe we shouldn't . . ." she murmured.

"Marcia, I love you," I panted. I had said that then, in the heat of my need, with one hand on her breast and the other up her skirt, and I said it now.

"Oh, I love you too," Marcia breathed. "Oh, Steven!" she whispered as my hand found her soft moistness through the silk of her panties. "Oh, you're making me so hot . . ."

"Marcia—" I grasped her panties and pulled them down.

"My parents might come home . . ." she protested faintly, but her body was moving against mine, and her hands were fumbling with my shirt buttons . . .

And soon my shirt was off, and her panties gone, and her sweater was pulled off over her head, and it was amazing how much easier it was now to unhook a bra than it had been then . . .

It had been at this point, as I was kissing her beautiful breasts and struggling to open my pants, that her parents had come home and found us, turning our love and passion into a horror of embarrassment and recrimination. But now there were no interruptions, no barriers; there was only Marcia, as I remembered her, moaning and ready; and my rigid, clamorous, long-frustrated desire.

Her body was so warm, so sweet, and as I entered her she gave a sharp cry and clutched at me tightly. And then I was inside her, moving with her, and I was at last doing it with Marcia, loving her, and she was writhing beneath me, holding me with arms and legs, gasping and panting and calling out my name, our lust slowly but inexorably building higher . . . and higher. And then she arched strongly underneath me, and gave an ecstatic groan as her body convulsed and shuddered. And a moment later I, too, exploded inside Marcia's loving and marvelous body.

We said little as we cleaned up and dressed ourselves. I was still a bit lost in a fog of nostalgia and fulfillment and youthful dreams of love.

"Did you enjoy it, Steven?" Marcia said after a while. "Was it good for you?"

"It was—it was wonderful!" I said. "Fantastic! God, Marcia—"

"Good," she said. "That will be three hundred, dear."

The fog dissipated swiftly. I stared at her. "What?" I asked blankly.

"Well, I assumed you knew the price when you called," Marcia said. "Didn't whoever told you about us tell you that?"

"Wait a minute." My head was spinning again, but not so pleasantly. It was all coming together, and I felt stupid and humiliated. And dirty. "Wait a minute. Marcia. You mean . . . you mean this is—this place is a . . . Jesus Christ . . . a whorehouse?"

"No, it is not!" Marcia snapped. "Don't be so crude, Steven. This is a house of fantasy. We cater to special needs, to men who have particular scenarios they like to enact, roles they like us to play. Like you did."

"Oh, God!" I groaned. "I don't believe it. All this was . . . Christ, Marcia, you mean you don't remember me at all?"

She shrugged. "I don't know. It was so long ago. There've been so many men. And then when I inherited this house, I started this nice little business. So many men, you forget . . ."

"But I was the first . . . almost, right?"

"By senior year?" She laughed. "Don't kid yourself, dear."

"Oh, Christ," I said. "I was a sucker even then."

Marcia shrugged. "All men are," she said. "That will be three hundred, dear."

What could I do? I paid.

I returned home depressed, disgusted and disillusioned. Not only had I, for the second time within months, been tricked into paying for sex, something I had vowed never to do; not only had my long-cherished memory of my first romance been ground to dust; but my self-image as a suave, sophisticated ladies' man had taken a beating from which, right now, it seemed doubtful that it would recover. Generally I drink only on social occasions, but that night I disposed of half a bottle of bourbon before I took myself off to bed.

And then I had the problem of informing Miss Greenglass of this latest stage in my progress. I didn't need to tell her anything at all beyond the fact of the accomplishment. I knew she trusted me not to lie to her, but I was highly tempted to simply omit any mention of the end of the evening. Somehow, though, Miss Greenglass seemed to elicit total honesty, and at last I found myself telling it all.

I had no idea whether she would be contemptuous, derisive or totally indifferent. But once again I was taken by surprise. She listened calmly, and after a brief pause she looked at me with that level glance of hers. "You have nothing to be ashamed of, Mr. Walling," she said.

What could I say to that?

Miss Greenglass resumed her work. "Thank you for being so honest with me, Mr. Walling," she said, and then after a moment she added, "In return, I think I should tell you that I have no plans to go out with your brother again."

"You don't?" I said, perking up. "Well, that's good news. I knew you'd come to your senses sooner or later."

Miss Greenglass had nothing more to say. But Henry did. He called me to complain that she wouldn't see him anymore. "I told you she has good taste," I said. "Though why she ever agreed to go out with you in the first place—"

"Ahh, the girl's a nut case," Henry said. "All she ever wanted to do was talk about you anyway."

"What?" I said.

"Yeah. Crazy as a bat. Kept asking questions about you, what you were like as a kid, stuff like that. Listen, I still think she's a dyke, but I think you can have her if you go after her."

"I intend to," I said, and hung up.

I was feeling a lot better now.

Chapter 14

NOW, AFTER MY DEPRESSING, AND EXPENSIVE, experience with Marcia, I was halfway through my designated task—halfway to the winning of my wager and the possession of the delectable Miss Greenglass. And I was still technically ahead of schedule, as only two months and some odd days had elapsed of the six months allotted for that task's completion. But I was not nearly as far ahead as I would have liked, and I was determined to press on with dispatch and vigor in order to eliminate any risk, however slight, of failure due to unforeseen complications. I was also anxious to free myself up once more for the uninhibited pursuit of any female who crossed my path, mindless of her monogram; and, of course, to hasten the time when I could at long last consummate my desire for my remote yet tantalizing assistant, who seemed to become more alluring with each passing day.

Accordingly, I already had my next target firmly fixed in my sights. Nancy Dahlgren was a redhead in her late twenties whom I had met at some charity function. She was the type of woman one frequently encountered at such affairs (which is the chief reason I occasionally attend them), a type succinctly referred to as "beautiful but bored." Wives of wealthy husbands in whom they are no longer interested, they play their parts in society's rituals and alleviate the tedium wherever, however and with whomever they can.

Nancy was definitely one of those, and I had no doubt I could provide her with the kind of diversion she would enjoy.

My suspicion that she had harbored similar thoughts was confirmed by the fact that she was not the least bit surprised when I called her. "What took you so long?" she asked.

"Timing is everything," I said. "And since the time seems to have come, why don't we get together tonight?"

"Why not?" Nancy said. "Come over to my place. You know where it is, don't you?"

I did. Her apartment, in an exclusive building on Sutton Place, had been featured in several design magazines.

"Bruce will be out, I take it," I said.

"Don't worry about Bruce. See you around nine."

So I didn't worry about Bruce. Until he answered the door.

"Ah . . . good evening," I said, trying to seem casual. "I was just . . ."

"I know," Bruce said. "You're here to fuck Nancy. Come in."

Nonplussed, I think, is the word generally applied to the way I felt at that moment. I couldn't think of anything to say. So I went in.

"She'll be out in a minute," Bruce said, leading the

way into the sumptuous living room. He was a man in his early fifties, a bit stocky but in generally good shape. "You want a drink?"

"Uh . . . no. Thanks anyway," I said uncomfortably.

Bruce smiled, but it was not really a happy smile. "Don't feel awkward," he said. "This happens all the time. Nancy Nympho, I call her."

"Look . . ." I'm not sure what I was about to say, but I didn't have to say it, for at that moment Nancy came in. She wore a green dress which set off her lovely red hair, and she looked ravishing.

She smiled at me. "Hello, Steven. Did Bruce offer you a drink?"

"Yes. Um . . . I wasn't exactly expecting to see Bruce, you know."

"Oh, Bruce is going to watch us," Nancy said.

"What?"

"He enjoys it," Nancy said. "No matter what he might say. Isn't that right, darling?"

"You're a bitch," Bruce said.

"Whoa," I said. "What's going on here?"

"Nancy Nympho likes to show off," Bruce said with some bitterness. "It's her way of thanking me for marrying her and making her rich."

"Don't mind him," Nancy said. "He's just going to have a few more drinks and watch. Aren't you, Brucie? And if he's a really good boy, we might even let him join in."

"Hold it," I said. "I'm not sure what this is about, but it's not what I came for. I think I'd better just leave."

"Come on, Steven, don't be such a spoilsport," Nancy said, moving toward me.

"If you leave, she'll just find someone else," Bruce said.

"Good night, Nancy," I said. "I'm sorry."

Nancy smiled at me. "Can I just say one thing before you go?"

"Of course."

"How about this?" Nancy said, and she moved into me and pressed herself against me, bringing her mouth to mine. Her lips parted and her tongue brushed my lips, then slid into my mouth, searching. Her arms went around me and her body molded itself to me from shoulders to knees. She made a soft moaning sound deep in her throat as her tongue played with mine, her mouth opening still wider, as if to devour my soul. As the kiss went on, she started to squirm against me. Her breasts rolled, mashed so tightly into my chest that I thought I could feel the hard nipples through our clothing, and her writhing hips rubbed her loins sensuously against my crotch, until I knew she could feel the rapid swelling there. The kiss went on for some time, and after the first few moments I was no longer a passive participant.

We were both panting slightly when we broke apart. "See?" Nancy said. "You don't really want to go, do you, Steven?"

I had to admit she'd made a persuasive argument. At that moment I don't know if I could have moved even if I'd wanted to.

"Let me convince you some more," Nancy said, and she went down to her knees in front of me. Her hand stroked softly over the aforementioned rise in my trousers, and then she was pulling down my zipper. In a moment she had released my obviously eager manhood.

"Are you watching, Brucie?" she asked.

"Bitch," Bruce said. He was sitting on the sofa, drink in hand, and he was watching all right. I had almost forgotten him, and this reminder might even then have brought me to my senses if it hadn't been for Nancy's mouth.

Kissing me.

Licking me.

And then inviting me in.

All the way in.

I closed my eyes, shutting out Bruce, shutting out everything but the feeling of that moving, loving mouth. Then I opened my eyes, because I sensed her doing something else.

She was taking off her clothes.

Without releasing me, without missing a beat or disrupting the steady rhythm she had established, she proceeded to unbutton her dress and slip it from her shoulders. She reached behind her back to unclasp her bra, but as she did so, she turned her head toward the sofa to make sure her husband was watching.

He was.

The bra came open, and she slid the straps down. Then, on her knees, she moved closer to me, close enough that she could press her breasts against my thighs as she continued to suck me.

I felt weak, and my head was spinning. Reluctant as I was to lose Nancy's mouth, even for a moment, I didn't want to stand up any more. I lowered myself slowly to the floor.

Nancy let me go only briefly, then crouched over me as I lay down, taking me between her lips again. But when I began to groan and clutch at her hair, she raised her head, smiling at me. She'd slid her dress completely off, and the only thing now covering her magnificent body was a brief pair of black panties. Then she started to undress me, enlivening the process by kissing or licking or rubbing herself against each bit of flesh she uncovered. In the meantime, I managed to pull off her panties. My hands explored whatever I could reach of her body, but I have to admit that I still felt a bit inhibited by Bruce's presence. When I was naked, Nancy pushed me gently down on my back on the deep-pile carpet.

"Just lie still, lover," she murmured. She briefly stroked my throbbing stiffness, then swung herself over me until she was crouching astride my body, her sweet, red-thatched crotch hovering just above that erect pole. She'd positioned herself so that she was directly facing the sofa where her husband sat.

"Are you having a good time, Brucie?" she asked sweetly.

"Screw you," Bruce said.

"No, darling, I'm going to screw *him*," Nancy said. "Watch me now." She reached between us to guide me where she wanted me, then proceeded to lower herself onto me, slowly but steadily. She hissed sharply as she took me into her warm, moist depths, and I may have made a sound or two myself. Then I was buried inside her, and her buttocks were pressed firmly against my thighs.

I raised my hands to clutch at her breasts. She stayed that way for a moment, then began to move, taking it slowly, her fine, shapely thighs flexing as she raised and lowered herself easily.

"See, Brucie?" she panted. "See how I'm fucking him?"

"Yes, I see you, you . . . nympho slut," Bruce said.

"Damn it, Bruce," I said hoarsely. "Go away."

"Oh, no," Nancy said. "Brucie wants to watch. He

thinks it gets him hot. Are you getting all hot, Brucie?"
She was moving harder now, and I was matching her
movements as well as I could in my supine position. I
moved my hands down to her thighs, which allowed me
to watch her full, round breasts bobbing with her movements. "You want to join us, Brucie?" Nancy asked.

"Go to hell," Bruce said.

"Forget him," I grated. "We're doing fine."

"He'll join in later," Nancy said. "After you come inside me, Brucie can lick my pussy clean. He likes that,
don't you, Brucie?"

"I'm leaving," Bruce said.

"No you're not," Nancy said.

"Watch me," Bruce said. And he got up.

"Tell you what, Bruce," Nancy said, never missing a
beat. "On your way out, why don't you send Arnold in
here?"

"You would," Bruce said. "Wouldn't you, you whore!"

"You know he's always ready," Nancy said.

"Jesus," I groaned. "Who is Arnold?"

"Our houseboy," Nancy said.

"Forget it," I said.

"Don't worry, Steven," Nancy said. She leaned down
to kiss me, her mouth soft and sexy on mine, her breasts
brushing my chest. "You won't get cheated," she whispered against my lips. "I promise." Her hips were moving in little circles now as she intensified her rhythmic
motions. Any reservations I had about being part of this
weird scene were drowned in the sweet, hot sexiness of
Nancy's body.

Bruce had indeed left, but in a moment he was back,
followed by a thin young man in some kind of servant's
livery. He did not seem in the least surprised to see two

naked people engaged in sexual congress; obviously it was a spectacle he was accustomed to in the course of his duties. Bruce silently resumed his seat on the sofa.

"I knew you couldn't stay away, Brucie," Nancy said.

"The more the merrier," Bruce said. "Right, Nancy Nympho?"

"Of course," Nancy said. "Come on, Arnold. Take it out, dear. I want to taste it."

Arnold opened his trousers and took it out. I tried to concentrate on Nancy. The continued stimulation of her moving body kept me in a state of intense arousal, while the annoying distractions she was creating prevented me from getting too close to the edge. It was about the strangest feeling I had ever experienced during an erotic encounter. Except perhaps for the time when—but I digress.

"Come here, Arnold," Nancy said. "No, come on this side so Bruce can have a good view. That's it." The young man moved to stand at her side, facing her, his cock growing stiffer by the moment. Nancy leaned back, not breaking our connection or stopping her movements, but supporting herself with her hands on the floor behind her, her breasts lifting and growing taut. She put her head back and opened her mouth.

Arnold put his cock in it.

Nancy said something around his flesh. It was muffled, but there was no doubt in my mind that she was exhorting her husband to watch her.

I closed my eyes again, and reached once more for Nancy's breasts, clasping the resilient mounds, playing with the rock-hard nipples. I heard Arnold's breathing become louder and faster, then turn into gasps and moans. I'd had a sample of what Nancy's mouth could do, and was not surprised to hear him swiftly approaching his climax. Soon he groaned loudly several times, and when I heard him move away, I opened my eyes just in time to see Nancy swallowing the last of his sperm, smiling over at her husband as she did so.

"Did you enjoy that, Brucie?" she inquired.

"Not as much as you did, I'm sure," Bruce rasped.

"Damn it, I've had enough of this," I gasped. And with a strong effort of both body and will, I heaved up, unseating Nancy onto the soft rug, then rolled her over and got on top of her, quickly rejoining our bodies. But now I was in control, and began to thrust strongly into her, driving both her and myself toward a long-delayed consummation. Nancy moaned happily and clasped me with arms and legs, moving with me and against me, and crying out to her husband that she was going to come. Soon she did, bucking and twisting beneath me, and a moment later I joined her.

After a brief pause for breath-catching, I rolled away from her, certain that I was finished for the night. But not Nancy.

"All right, Brucie," she said, her voice still somewhat breathless. "You can come and lick me out now."

I looked over at Bruce, and was startled to see that Arnold was kneeling in front of him, doing unto Bruce what Bruce's wife had done unto Arnold. Evidently Arnold's duties in this household were many and varied.

"Never get enough, do you, you slut," Bruce asked rhetorically. But he pulled himself away from Arnold, got up and walked over to his wife. As he lowered himself to the floor, I started to get up.

"Don't go away, Steven," Nancy said, reaching out for

me. Her hand landed on my thigh, and swiftly slid upward to find my crotch.

"I'm through, Nancy," I said. "Besides, I've got to—"

"No, no," she protested, turning over and raising herself enough to look at me as I lay on my back. Her fingers stroked. "We'll get you ready again, don't worry."

"I don't think so," I said. "But it's been—"

I stopped because Nancy had taken her hand away and was now stroking me with her hair. Her head was bent over my crotch and she was moving it slowly from side to side, letting the soft strands of her silky red hair brush back and forth across my loins. And in spite of myself, I felt my incorrigible maleness twitching to life again.

"See?" Nancy breathed. She was on her knees, and I felt her warm breath as her mouth came closer to my reviving phallus. Then her lips, and her tongue . . .

"*Now*, Bruce," she said. And then Bruce was lying on his back, with his face beneath Nancy's crotch, pulling her lower body down to him. She moaned around my hard flesh. I was also vaguely aware that Arnold was crouching over Bruce's body, but I couldn't see what he was doing, nor did I especially want to. Bruce's moans were muffled in Nancy's flesh, and hers were muffled by mine, and mine was not muffled at all, as Nancy's magical mouth, lips and tongue brought me swiftly to full readiness again, and then slowly to explosive bliss.

It took me longer to recover this time, and when I did, Arnold was nowhere in sight. But Bruce and Nancy were holding each other, clinging together and crooning like wounded pigeons.

"Oh, God, Nancy," Bruce was sobbing. "Sweet Nancy. Oh, God, I'm sorry."

"It's all right, Bruce," Nancy whispered. "It's all right, darling. I love you. I love you, Bruce."

It was all too strange for me. I got dressed as quickly as I could, then headed for the door.

"Good night, Steven," Nancy called after me. "Call me soon, won't you, dear?"

"I'll do that," I said. "Sure." And I left.

In truth, however, I had no intention at that point of calling her again, soon or ever, and in fact I made a mental note to throw her number away as soon as I got home. Which I did.

But after a while, looking back over the evening, I started to remember how Nancy's body had felt moving against mine. And I thought about her high, round breasts, the silken sensation of her hair brushing my crotch. And her mouth—that marvelous, voracious, talented mouth. And finally I fished the number out of the wastebasket and put it back in the Rolodex.

One shouldn't be too hasty about these things.

Chapter 15

ONE OF THE MANY IMPORTANT FUNCTIONS OF my admirable and delectable assistant, Miss Greenglass—one that she fulfilled with tireless assiduity in the face of much discouragement and resistance on my part—was to make sure that my natural disinclination for any kind of work did not materially threaten the success or well-being of the enterprise of which I was the head, and of which she was, it goes without saying, a most essential employee. Distasteful though I may find it (and as liberally as I may delegate most of the responsibility, not to say the labor, to others), it is still the fact that carrying on a business does require a certain amount of unavoidable application to its needs. I suspect that, left to my own unfortunate propensity to neglect these things, my reputation as a successful businessman—not to say my income—would suffer drastically. But Miss Greenglass, calmly but firmly, in her often annoying but undeniably effective way, managed most of the time to prod, goad and manipulate me into performing whatever duties may have been necessary.

It was in fulfillment of one of these duties that I found myself, a few days after my interesting adventure with Nancy, attending a business meeting at the corporate headquarters of Carswell & Haynsworth, a large financial institution with offices on the topmost floor of a new midtown skyscraper. The proceedings, dull though they were, had a satisfactory outcome, and when the meeting ended I left the conference room in company with Philip Haynsworth himself. Outside, he stopped at a desk and handed a folder to one of the clerks. "June," he said, "ask Opal to type this up."

My ears, as they say, perked up. Opal? An Opal was just what I needed right then—an Opal or an Olga or an Olympia or an Odessa or . . . But Opal would do fine.

I swiftly said my adieus and casually followed the clerk as she made her way down a hall to a desk situated just outside an office which I took to be Haynsworth's. She handed the folder to the woman sitting there. I couldn't hear what she said, but it was safe to assume that the lady behind the desk was Opal. She was in her early twenties, and her skin was the color of coffee with just a small spoonful of cream. She had the largest, darkest eyes I had seen in quite a while. Her hair was curly and short, and what I could see of her figure afforded no cause for complaint.

I ignored the quizzical glance of the clerk as she passed me on her way back, and proceeded on to Opal's desk. Close up she looked even more stunning.

"Ah—excuse me," I said, smiling at her. "I'm Steven Walling. I've just met with Mr. Haynsworth, and there's something in that report we thought I'd better check out. May I see it for a moment?"

She regarded me with an indifferent glance, hesitated

for a few seconds, then shrugged. "Sure." She handed me the folder.

"Thank you," I said, and pretended to glance through the papers. "Oh yes," I said wisely. "Yes, that's fine." I closed the folder and handed it back to her. "Thank you, Miss . . ."

"Adams," she said. "Opal Adams."

"Miss Adams," I said, "I'm sure you have been told this many times, but may I say that you are an extremely beautiful woman."

She must indeed have heard that a lot, for the compliment did not seem to impress her favorably. "Thank you," she said rather coldly, and turned to start up her word processor.

"You know, this meeting ended earlier than I thought," I said. "And as it happens, my lunch appointment cancelled on me. Would you like to have some lunch with me, Miss Adams?"

"No, thank you," Opal said.

"Anywhere you like," I said. "I'll try not to bore you, I promise."

"I'm sorry," she said. "I have plans. In fact, I'm leaving right now." Turning off the machine which she had just turned on, she got up and swept past me.

I wasn't giving up that easily. I went after her as she walked down the hall and through the office, and caught up with her at the elevator bank outside the office doors. She did not look happy to see me.

"In that case," I said, "how about dinner? I mean, since we're hitting it off so well and all."

"I'm busy," Opal said. The elevator arrived and the doors opened. Opal stepped inside, and I followed. It was not quite noon, and there was no one else in the car. Opal gazed at the floor indicator.

"Look," I said, "I'm really not an ax-murderer or anything. I'm a respectable businessman, and I'd just like to spend some time with you."

She turned to me. "Now why you want to do that?"

Her manner was suddenly different from the corporate coolness she had projected in the office. Her voice was harder, and there was something in those large, dark eyes that was at once fierce and exciting.

"Why? Because you're a lovely woman, and I happen to—"

"Because you want to fuck me," Opal said. Nothing like a woman who gets to the point.

"Well . . . naturally, that possibility had occurred to me," I said carefully. "But at the moment I was just thinking of taking a meal together. You know, talking, eating, getting to—"

"Hey," Opal said. "Listen—what's your name again?"

"Steven," I said. "Steven Walling."

"Well, Steve, tell me something. You notice any difference between us?"

"Certainly," I said. "You're a beautiful female, and I'm—well, an average-looking male. *Vive la différence*."

"And?" she asked.

"And what?"

"I'm black," she said. "And you're white. You happen to notice that?"

"Sure," I said. "So what?"

"So," she said, turning away to face front again, "I don't fuck honkies."

I tried to think whether I had ever actually been called a honkie before. I didn't think so. "Why not?" I said.

She snorted. "Figure it out."

"I don't know," I said. "Prejudice, maybe?"

"Shit," Opal said. "You a white boy, and you talking about prejudice?" She snorted again. She was the only woman I have ever known who could snort attractively. "What you want to do, change your luck by fucking a nigger gal?"

"No," I said. "My luck is fine, thank you, and I have known black women before. I assure you that skin color is irrelevant to me."

"Yeah, well it isn't to me," Opal said. "Forget it."

By now the elevator had reached the lobby and we were heading for the front door. "Look," I said. "Just have lunch with me, that's all. Or don't you eat with honkies either?"

"Not if I can help it," Opal said. "Besides, I'm meeting a friend."

"Dinner, then."

We were out on the street now. Opal stopped just outside the doors and turned to face me. "Dinner?" she said, sounding skeptical. "You want to take me to dinner?"

"I'd love to," I said.

"Anyplace I want?"

"Name it."

"Fanny's Cafe," she said.

I'd never heard of it. "Okay," I said. "Where is it?"

"Right near where I live," Opal said, watching me. "One Hundred Thirty-Seventh Street, near Lexington."

Right in the middle of Harlem. She was trying to scare me off. I shrugged. "Okay. Why not?"

She looked at me another minute. "You're not scared you'll get your white ass stomped?"

"I'm sure you'll protect me," I said.

"Hell, no," she said. "Pick me up at six—if you don't chicken out."

Fanny's Cafe was small and crowded, and the food was excellent. Mine was the only white face in the place, and my presence was not exactly unremarked. Opal seemed to be well known there, but that did not stop the stares—mostly, it seemed to me, hostile—or the mutterings among some of the patrons. It was not the most comfortable situation I had ever found myself in, but I did my best to be casual and to make conversation with Opal, which was not easy. It was pretty clear that she had brought me up here only to try to intimidate or embarrass me, and that our relationship was not going to progress much further.

We had nearly finished our meal when a tall, husky young man came into the place, looked around and walked directly to where we were sitting. He did not look happy.

"What's goin' on, Opal?" he said.

"Hi, Calvin," Opal said calmly.

Calvin jerked his head toward me without looking my way. "Who's this honkie?" he demanded.

"Name's Steve," Opal said. "Steve, Calvin."

Calvin was not about to shake hands. "What you doin' with him, girl?"

"What's it look like?" Opal said. "I'm eating, okay?"

"Shit," Calvin growled. "Since when you eat with whiteys?"

I thought I'd better do something to assert my masculinity here. "Look, Calvin," I said, "Opal and I are just—"

Calvin turned to me, pointing a finger in my face, and

what blazed from his eyes was pure hate. "You shut the fuck up, honkie, or I'll fuckin' pulverize your ass! What the hell you doin' up here anyway?"

"I brought him, you creephead," Opal said. "Now fuck off, okay?"

"What the fuck is wrong with you, woman?" Calvin said. "You thinkin' you gonna do somethin' with this piece of white shit? You better think again, you hear me?" He turned back to me. "You get the hell out of here right now, man, or I break your face!"

"Hey! Who the hell you think you are?" Opal said. "I said he's with me, okay? You got nothin' to say about it, Calvin. Now fuck off!"

"You ain't gonna fuck no white trash, Opal, you hear me? You ain't screwin' no downtown ofay piece of shit, and that's it! You got me?"

Opal got up, her face blazing, and I rose with her. "Hey, Calvin, get it straight, man. You don't tell me who I fuck and who I don't fuck, okay? Nobody fuckin' tells me who to fuck. I'll fuck whoever I goddamn want to, and what the hell you gonna do about it?"

"Goddamit!" Calvin yelled. "You tellin' me you gonna fuck him!?"

"Yeah!" Opal yelled back. "I am! So go screw yourself! Come on, Steve." And she took me by the hand and practically pulled me out of the restaurant.

"Wait!" I protested. "I have to pay the bill."

"Let Calvin pay the fuckin' bill," Opal said. "Come on, my place is right down the block."

"Is Calvin your boyfriend?" I asked as we walked.

"Hell, no! He's just a guy, thinks he owns me or something. Fuck him! Son of a bitch. Nobody tells me who to fuck!"

"Look," I said. "You probably shouldn't go to bed with me just because you're angry at Calvin. You might—"

She glared at me. "What, you backing out now?" she demanded. "Shit, you want to fuck me or not?"

"I do," I said. "I surely do. I just—"

"Then shut up," Opal said.

Her apartment was small and neat, but I didn't have a chance to inspect it too closely. As soon as we were inside, Opal closed the door, turned on the lights and said, "Take your damn clothes off."

Much as I wanted her, I was still not really comfortable with the idea of her doing this to get back at Calvin. "Opal," I said, "are you sure about this?"

"Hell," Opal said, starting to unbutton her blouse. "It looks like it, don't it?"

"I thought you didn't fuck honkies."

"You gonna be the first," she said. "Also the last."

"Really? You've never been with a white man before?"

Opal pulled off her blouse. "I don't need to, baby. You white guys been fucking us for four hundred years."

"That long, huh?" I said, looking at the taut breasts pushing against her black brassiere.

"That's just in this country," Opal said. "You gonna get undressed, or do white guys keep all their clothes on when they fuck?"

She unfastened her skirt as she spoke, then let it fall around her feet and stepped out of it. She wore sheer panty hose, through which I could see black panties. Her body was a wonder, curving from the high firm breasts gradually downward to a surprisingly small waist, then flaring out into boldly rounded hips that tapered into the shapeliest thighs I could remember seeing. And all that flesh one smooth, dark, delicious color, without shade or blemish.

Opal rolled the panty hose down over her hips, then moved to a nearby easy chair and sat down to pull them off. Still half dressed, I went to help her.

"There's a switch," Opal said. "A white boy waiting on a colored gal. How's it feel, after keeping us in slavery all that time?"

"Not me," I said.

"Yeah, you," Opal said to me. "A white man is a white man."

"And a good cigar is a smoke," I said. "Where's the bedroom?"

"Forget it, honkie. This room here is fine. Fucking you is one thing, but I ain't taking no white boys into my bed."

"Damn it, not all white men are the same," I said. I placed both hands on her legs now and ran them up over her calves to her wonderful thighs. I pulled those legs apart gently. She didn't resist.

"The hell they're not," she said. "They all hate niggers. Black men are bad enough—most of them hate women. But white men hate blacks and women too. Man, it's pure shit out there!"

"You hate pretty good yourself," I said. I stroked her inner thighs, and that incredibly soft, warm flesh made it hard to concentrate on conversation.

"Yeah, well where you think that came from?" she said. Her voice was a bit huskier. I slid my fingers under the panties. Opal caught her breath and moved forward in the chair. I explored her moist crotch for a while, then reached to pull the panties down. She lifted her hips to help me.

"I don't hate women," I said, and my own voice was not exactly steady. "You can take that to the bank, Opal. If there's one thing I love, it's women. All women. All colors, all types." I took hold of her legs and hoisted them over my shoulders as I knelt there, pulling her forward still more, so that she was sitting almost on the edge of the chair.

"Yeah, right," she breathed. "You love to fuck, that's all."

"Among other things," I said. The words were muffled because my mouth was pressed against the inside of her thigh. I began to kiss and lick my way upward. The taste of her skin made my head swim.

Opal was breathing faster. "Eat me, honkie. Eat my black cunt."

"Try and stop me," I said. And then my mouth was jammed against the moist opening between her legs, and I was tasting and licking and kissing and breathing in the sweet dark mystery of her. Opal drew a sharp breath, then pressed harder against me. My tongue probed deeply as my mouth moved on her flesh, exploring her depths before searching out and finding her clitoris. I could almost feel it pulsating as my tongue moved over it, stroking and circling and teasing.

"Oh, yeah, do it, honkie," Opal panted, twisting her pussy against me. "Eat me, lick that thing . . . Come on, whitey, suck that black pussy . . . harder . . ." Her body was squirming in the chair, her soft thighs clutching my head. I could hardly breathe, but the essence of her was all the oxygen I needed. I nibbled and sucked and licked, and she writhed harder, her buttocks rising off the chair, her legs twitching against my cheeks.

"Come on, you white bastard, don't stop, you honkie son of a bitch, you pale-ass motherfucker, Jesus yes . . . right there . . . yeah . . . oh shit yeah . . . Now, you white fuck . . . now . . . now, honkie . . . Now!"

Her words turned into a near-howl as all of her convulsed at once, body, legs and pussy spasming and twisting as she came. It was some minutes before her trembling thighs opened enough to release my head. But I didn't mind. I was quite happy where I was.

"Damn!" Opal said finally.

"See?" I said. "You have to admit there are some things a white man is good for."

"Yeah? That all you know how to use, your mouth?"

"Let's find out." I stripped off the rest of my clothes. I was hard and very horny. Opal inspected my erection with some interest.

"Not bad for a white boy," she said.

"Well, thanks. Lie down here and let me show you what I can do with it.

"Uh-uh," Opal said. "You sit down here." She sat me down in the chair, then climbed onto me and straddled my hips, guiding my stiffness inside of her. "Let a white man get on top of you, he'll kill you for sure."

"Cut that out," I said. "I never killed anybody." And then I gasped as she sank down on me. Her vagina was slick but tight, in spite of her recent orgasm.

"Right," Opal said, and she began to move. "What about Medgar Evers? And James Chaney? And—"

"I wasn't there," I said. She was still wearing her brassiere, and as her hips rose and fell rhythmically, I reached up to unfasten it, then pulled it off. Her breasts didn't sag at all. The nipples were hard and dark, and I leaned forward to take one in my mouth.

"And Fred Hampton," she said breathlessly. "And George Jackson, and—"

"I swear I didn't do it," I mumbled against her breast.

"And Martin," she said, panting now. "And Malcolm. And—"

"Damn it, I—Wait a minute!" I said. "Malcolm was killed by black men!"

"So what?" Opal gasped.

"Oh, right," I said. "I should have thought of that."

I think she came up with a few other people that I had killed, but by then I couldn't hear anything but the roaring in my ears, and she was moaning too loudly to make herself understood anyway. And in a few minutes we were both shouting and holding on to each other as the world came apart . . .

"Okay, white boy," Opal said. "Time to go."

"I take it staying overnight is out," I said. "Can I call a cab from here?"

"I better do it," Opal said. "They hear your white voice, forget it."

As I was putting my clothes on, I said, "Will I see you again, Opal—sometime?"

"Nope," she said.

"Why not?"

"I don't fuck honkies," Opal said.

"Oh," I said. "What was it we just did?"

"We did nothing," Opal said, and her voice was belligerent, and very final. "It never happened, and it's never gonna happen again. You understand me?"

"Not really," I said. "But what can I do?"

When the cab honked, I went downstairs. Outside the building a man came out of the shadows. It was Calvin.

"Son of a bitch!" he shouted. "Did you fuck her, you white-ass motherfucker?"

I did my best to appear unintimidated, which was quite a trick. "That's really none of your business, Calvin," I said.

For a moment I thought he was going to attack me. But he glanced over at the cab driver, who was watching, then turned back to me. "You fuckin' better stay away from here, honkie!" he snarled, his eyes blazing at me. "You come up here again, I'll fuckin' carve your guts out! You don't come up here no more, you got that, shit-head? You ain't never comin' up here no more!"

"No," I said. "It doesn't look like I am."

Chapter 16

"PLEASE UNDERSTAND," I SAID TO MISS GREEN-glass, "that there is no question of special dispensation here. We have agreed on several occasions that there is nothing in the rules of our wager that disqualifies any woman simply because I have had the pleasure of knowing her, however intimately, before that wager was made."

"Technically that is true, Mr. Walling," Miss Greenglass said. "But you did agree with me some time ago that the abundance of women with whom you have had erotic liaisons in the past did make the challenge a great deal easier than it might be otherwise; and you did state that you would attempt to limit yourself, for the duration of this wager, to those females, few as they may be, who do not fall into that category."

I ignored the little sarcasm. "What I said—as you know, Miss Greenglass—was that I would, out of pure goodness of heart, and despite the fact that the rules do not call for it, concentrate whenever practical on women whom I have not previously enjoyed. And so I have. All the stations of my progress, as it were, have been accomplished with new women since that discussion; and in fact, from the very start of our bet there has only been one lady—Belinda—who was a previous amour. And that, as you may recall, was under rather special circumstances."

Miss Greenglass said nothing. She had a way of saying nothing that spoke volumes.

"However," I continued, "I definitely also made clear that this was not an absolute commitment, and that there might be occasions on which it might not apply. I recall making specific reference to the case of one Xanthippe, whom I am still hoping to locate before I have to deal with X."

"If you get that far," Miss Greenglass murmured.

"Fear not," I said. "Now in this case there's Phyllis. I know you are aware, Miss Greenglass, that the delectable Mrs. Dilsey has been importuning me incessantly every time her husband goes on another of his little trips. We were in the habit of spending a lovely night together on every such occasion, and poor Phyllis has been extremely perplexed and, I fear, a bit wounded at the plethora of excuses I have had to employ to avoid her since our wager. Though she is not perhaps the brightest lady in the world, she is beginning to get suspicious, and—"

"Especially since you seduced her cousin Irene virtually under her nose at the Statue of Liberty," Miss Greenglass put in.

"That didn't help," I admitted. "And now that Phyllis's opportunity has at last arrived, and I am in a position to assuage her suspicion—as well as her body—while taking the next step in my progression toward *your* body, it seems only decent that I should give the lady a break, don't you think?"

Miss Greenglass favored me with one of those looks. "How unutterably kind of you," she murmured.

"And of course it would be a relief to get her off my back for a while," I said. "So I just want it understood that I am not bending any rules here: Phyllis is a perfectly legitimate P. Okay?"

"If you are so certain of that, Mr. Walling, why bother explaining it to me now? Can it be that you actually have some inner reservations about Mrs. Dilsey's eligibility in this situation?"

"Not at all," I said firmly. "Not a bit. I merely wanted to forestall any possible objection based on false premises, that's all. Just making everything clear."

"I see," Miss Greenglass said, turning back to her word processor. "Then I will leave the matter entirely to your conscience, Mr. Walling."

"My conscience has nothing to do with it," I said. "My conscience is fine, thank you. Just fine."

"If you say so, Mr. Walling," Miss Greenglass said, and began to type.

The woman, as I have said before, was maddening.

Phyllis had been the last woman to grace my formerly busy bed before I embarked on my current challenge. In fact, as readers who have followed this saga from the beginning may recall, she had been there on the very morning of the day on which my fateful wager with Miss Greenglass had been contracted. She was in her early thirties, a bounteously curved lady with short curly blond hair and a generally cheerful manner, bouncy, open and excitable, both in bed and out. I was looking forward almost as eagerly as she was to having her in that bed again—at least so I thought.

I had taken her to dinner and then back to my house, where we proceeded directly to the bedroom. Phyllis knew the way well.

"It's been such a long time, Steven," she sighed, moving into my arms.

"I know," I said. "But we have all night to make up for it." And I kissed her. It was a long, passionate kiss. Her body molded itself to mine, pressing hard as our tongues met and tangled. I felt the sweet familiar sensation of her buoyant breasts mashing into my chest, her stomach pulsating against mine, her loins pushing to get closer as she moaned around my tongue. My hands roved, finding the round buttocks and holding on to them as that body twisted against me. Nothing aroused me faster than Phyllis's eager responsiveness, and I knew I was ready to . . .

But wait a minute. It seemed I wasn't as aroused as I expected. Or at least not as ready. This was a bit puzzling, but not really worrisome. Not really. It was early stages yet. When we finally broke for air, I picked Phyllis up and laid her on the bed, and as we kissed again I began to unbutton her blouse. I knew the sight of that splendid body would have me hard and throbbing in no time.

Phyllis loosened my tie and pulled it off, and between kisses and caresses we undressed each other. As I took off her brassiere I feasted my eyes on the high, thrusting, mouth-watering breasts which I always found so exciting. They were no less fabulous than I remembered, and I bent to kiss one, taking as much as I could of it into my mouth and running my tongue over the hard, red nipple. Phyllis gasped and clutched at my head. "Oh yes, Steven," she moaned. "Oh God . . ."

Oh God, indeed. What was going on here? Phyllis was as gorgeous, as sexy and as eager as always—yet while my mind wanted her as much as ever, my body seemed sluggish and unwilling. And now a faint, unwelcome suspicion began to sneak into my thoughts. Could it be that something in my conscience—that conscience which Miss Greenglass had so unfairly referred to—was troubling me? Did I perhaps indeed have doubts that I was being entirely fair as regarded my wager with that lady?

No! Absolutely not. I was completely convinced, as I had explained to her, that I was entirely within my rights as far as Phyllis was concerned. There was no doubt whatsoever.

And yet . . . as I finished stripping her, and then myself, and fell to caressing and tasting and reveling in the writhing voluptuousness before me, I couldn't quite manage to get my body into full gear—or to get the judgmental specter of Miss Greenglass out of my thoughts.

Damn the woman!

I determinedly concentrated all my attention on Phyllis's soft, creamy flesh. She was moaning steadily now, and her hands and mouth had begun to explore my body as mine were exploring hers. Inevitably, she soon became aware of the fact that my arousal was not manifesting itself with its accustomed aggressiveness. She made a small sound of surprise, and then moved to bring her body tight against me, throwing a leg over my hip and writhing sensually as her mouth moved over my face and neck in an evident effort to stoke my tepid fires.

I made an effort too. I knew Phyllis herself wasn't the problem. I never got tired of her eager wantonness, and it had been too long since we had shared this bed together. Then it occurred to me that in fact no woman had been in this bed since Phyllis had last inhabited it. Come to think of it (as you can see, my mind was wandering even as I held Phyllis's squirming naked body in my arms, an unprecedented phenomenon that only Miss Greenglass could have brought about), it had been some time since I had actually been with a woman in *any* real bed. I began to think back. Opal had not let me near her bed; we had coupled in an easy chair. My session with Nancy (and company) had taken place on her living room floor. Before that there had been Marcia on the sofa . . . Li Mai on that hard little table . . . Katharine in the men's room . . . my J-lady in the back of her limo . . . Irene at the Statue of Liberty . . . ah yes, I had to go all the way back to Holy Virgin Mary for the last time I had done it in a bed . . .

Strange, I had almost forgotten about that lissome young lady with the angelic name and the devilish body. I thought of her now, remembering the tireless abandon with which she had shown me the tricks that she, along with her sister, had been accustomed to lavishing on that old mountebank the Reverend Jourdemayne. I recalled how her hips had twisted beneath me as though on ball bearings, how her clutching legs had held me in a vise, how she had screamed so loudly at each orgasm (and she was the most orgasmic female in all my experience) that I had feared the neighbors might call the police . . .

And as I thought of these things, the blood that had been pumping so sluggishly through my veins began to surge, and the passion that had eluded me began to assert itself in no uncertain terms. Phyllis felt it, and purred happily into my ear as she pressed herself against it.

"Oh, Steven . . ." she breathed, and her hand moved down to investigate what she quite naturally believed that she had brought about. I remembered young Mary's talented hands, and the way her fingers had . . . But this wasn't fair to Phyllis. I forced Holy Virgin Mary out of my mind. Now that my momentary lapse was behind me, I could get on with the distinct pleasure of enjoying my blond companion—in spite of Miss Greenglass, who I wouldn't think about either.

I was deliberately not thinking about Miss Greenglass as Phyllis caressed my hardness appreciatively, causing it to . . . well, it wasn't exactly growing, but . . . but it was sort of throbbing . . . though perhaps not as strongly as it had been . . . maybe it was even shrinking a little . . .

Phyllis must have been as perplexed as I was, but she wasn't giving up. She moved down along my body and brought her sweet loving mouth into play. There was no doubt she knew what to do with it too. Her lips were soft and warm, her tongue was knowing. And I loved what she was doing. That is, I loved it in my mind. Hell, I loved it in my soul. But my body . . .

This was ridiculous. I concentrated. I closed my eyes to concentrate further. And suddenly I was thinking of another mouth, another tongue. I was thinking of Katharine, the beautiful flight attendant, kneeling at my feet in that tiny airplane bathroom and taking me halfway to paradise with her impossibly long, agile tongue, before I had reluctantly been forced to put a stop to her ministrations. That recollection brought me back to life again, and as Phyllis moaned with pleasure and took my renewed stiffness deep into her mouth, my mind flashed to still another such encounter. The little Chilean tennis player, Dolorosa, whose compactly athletic body I had first sampled against the wall of the shower in the ladies' locker room, and who had then urged me onto my back and proceeded to arouse me again with her avid lips, and then to bring me to climax with the same single-minded dedication, talent and pure joy of accomplishment with which she was used to trouncing her opponents on the courts . . .

These delightful memories had a most positive effect indeed, so much so that I was now getting dangerously close to spilling my seed into Phyllis's warm, luscious mouth, as I had done with Dolorosa—and as I had never, alas, gotten around to doing with Katharine. But Phyllis, wiser in the ways of the flesh than she was in most other things, pulled away before that danger could become irreversible, and swung herself over me so that she was sitting astride my hips. She guided my hardness to the eager opening between her legs as she lowered herself slowly down around me. It was in this position, I recalled, that we had been disporting ourselves that last morning, when Miss Greenglass had called up from the office and—

Oh-oh. No. Wrong memory. If I wasn't careful . . . I closed my eyes again. And remembered lying in Belinda's bed in her mansion at Monte Carlo, where that beautiful lady, with the skirt of her gown hoisted around her waist, and her dinner guests waiting downstairs, had straddled me in this way, taking me deep inside her, and riding me with a hard, steady rhythm, intent on bringing us both to a swift, dizzying climax so that she could hurry back to her party . . . I caressed the smoothness of her bare legs, then reached up to grasp her breasts, and felt naked flesh, stiff thrusting nipples. But Belinda had still been half clothed . . .

Nancy, I thought. It had been only recently that that uninhibited, redheaded creature—Nancy Nympho, her husband had called her—had been with me in this manner in the middle of her living room, with that very husband looking on, and her houseboy waiting in the wings.

I held on to her breasts and listened to her panting and moaning and gasping as her body moved up and down, and I remembered how she had—

"Oh Steven . . ." Phyllis moaned. "Oh god, Steven yes . . . Oh, it's wonderful . . ."

I opened my eyes. It was Phyllis, all right. Her face was flushed and twisted with passion, her hair was disheveled, her gorgeous breasts were bouncing. She looked fantastically sexy, and she felt even better. She was one thoroughly exciting woman, and I was happy to be with her . . . in spite of Miss Greenglass's niggling reservations, which . . .

Damn.

"Yes, Steven, oh God yes . . . so good . . . oh, darling . . ."

I closed my eyes again. Who had said that? Oh yes. I remembered. Christine. The sweet, almost virginal eighteen-year-old blonde whose long-standing crush on me had been consummated in my office—on Miss Greenglass's desk, in fact. "Oh, darling, darling . . ." she had gasped, her hands rubbing my back and her pneumatic buttocks slapping rhythmically on the hard surface as she twisted beneath me. "Oh harder, Steven . . . yes, darling . . . now . . . oh God, I love it, Steven, yes . . ."

Fired by that recollection, I reared up and rolled Phyllis onto her back, breaking our contact only momentarily before coming down on top of her. This was how it had been with Christine, except that instead of the soft bed it had been the hard wooden surface of the desk underneath our pumping bodies . . .

Which now brought to mind a more recent encounter on another wooden surface—the lovely Chinese lady, Li Mai, on the little table in the storage room in the back of her restaurant. Li Mai's exclamations had tended to be more graphic than Christine's, the stark English obscenities sounding strangely arousing in her clipped accent. And her long legs twined around my waist, clutching at me, pulling me deeper inside her . . . her fine supple body arching and thrusting with a strength that belied her delicate slenderness . . .

Phyllis was whimpering now as I thrust steadily and strongly into her, pleasuring both her and myself while driven by these visions of her predecessors. Interestingly, her whimpers sounded just like those her cousin Irene had emitted as I had plunged into her from behind while gazing out at Manhattan from the very top of the Statue of Liberty. That view was less memorable for me than the view up Irene's dress as we climbed the steep spiral stairs. And the feel of her fine round buttocks twisting against me, and her fine round breasts under my hands. And those high-pitched mewling sounds that were now being replicated, as it seemed, in my ear . . .

The whimpers turned to groans, and then to hoarse, gasping shrieks as Phyllis shuddered into her first explosion of the evening. Her climactic cries were different from Irene's, however. They were more like . . . like Betty, the voluptuous vixen who had been a near-fatal mistake in terms of my wager, but with whom I had eaten the sexiest take-out meal I'd ever had . . . among other things . . .

That memory kept me hard and ready while Phyllis recovered from her orgasm, moaning and catching her breath. With Phyllis it never took very long, however, and in a few moments she was up on all fours, eager for me to take her from behind. I complied with dispatch, and by now the memories came easily. I thought of Betty's friend Edna, crouching before me with her buttocks in the air and her dark head clasped between Betty's thighs. I thought of Fern Forrester, the TV lady, rubbing my sperm into her body while envisioning her vast male audience watching her as she did so. And I thought of Abigail, in the little dressing room at Brooks Brothers, half appalled and half delighted at her own youthful passion as she attempted to stifle her cries against my mouth . . .

These images, and others, ran through my mind almost unbidden now, as I held on to Phyllis's twisting, rocking, bucking body; and this time, when she came again, I exploded along with her.

Breathless, we collapsed side by side on the bed. I knew, however, that there was still a long night ahead of us. But I wasn't worried. Fortunately there had been, as Miss Greenglass had said, an abundance of women in my past. I was sure my memories would see me through.

It was with a certain sense of déjà vu that I picked up the bedside telephone next morning to receive Miss Greenglass's accustomed call informing me of her arrival at the office downstairs.

"I'll be down in a while, Miss Greenglass," I told her. "I am somewhat engaged just now."

"With Mrs. Dilsey, I presume," Miss Greenglass said, rather coolly.

"Of course," I said. "Incidentally, Miss Greenglass, do you realize that on the day we first made our little . . . ah . . . agreement, I had—"

"Yes, I do recall, Mr. Walling," Miss Greenglass said, interrupting me with unaccustomed asperity. "I recall that very well. And I take it that this—this repeat performance, shall we say, has caused you no qualms of conscience whatsoever, as far as that agreement is concerned."

"Qualms?" I said innocently. "I've broken no rules, Miss Greenglass; I've violated no stipulations. Why in the world would I have qualms?"

There are some things even Miss Greenglass doesn't have to know.

Chapter 17

I F I HADN'T SPENT MY ENTIRE LIFE LEARNING TO keep idle emotion from rendering me as helpless in a man's world as . . . well, as most other women I know, I might have begun to panic by now. Even so, there is a certain far-off prickling sensation gnawing at my hard-won composure that is both annoying and, I will admit in confidence, intriguing to me. Despite myself, I look forward now to the moment when my employer appears at my elbow to retail the stories of his sexual conquests. There was a time when his breath on the back of my neck caused only a shiver of disdain. Increasingly these days it brings a frisson of pleasure which I can hide from him only with difficulty. And yet I am determined to hide it. As I am determined to win the wager into which I so foolishly entered.

Anne Greenglass (you would be saying to yourself if you knew me well enough to use my first name), how could a sensible young woman like you be so foolish as to involve yourself in a bet with a man like Steven Walling? Not that it matters now, the deed being done (and I pride myself on not dwelling in the past), but I did it for the oldest of reasons, the mercenary one. I knew my employer's propensities before I came to work for him, and only accepted the position because the salary offered was so generous. My eyes were also open to the fact that Mr. Walling was interested in more than my office skills, but I felt competent to keep our relationship entirely on a business basis. And so I did during the first six months of my employment.

Then came the wager. At that time I hadn't begun keeping the records of our conversations, which will be so valuable to me in describing this strange progress, so I am unable to give you a word-for-word account of how it came about. I fear, though, that I was quite as responsible as he. Appalling as I would like to say I found his bed-hopping, I admit to a certain fascination at how easy and pleasant he made it all sound. My life had not been especially easy or pleasant, and I suppose like many people, I find a fascination with the lives of those who have everything they could want. That must be it.

Not that Mr. Walling is an unattractive man. On the contrary. And though I hate to admit it, his charm is genuine. So too, I think, is his delight in the multitude of women he beds with such maniacal regularity. But that isn't what brought me low. No, the idea of such endless repetition of the pneumatic function of sex fills me only with indifference.

It was more curiosity, together with my affection for order, which led me to suggest that he might organize his adventures by attempting to consummate relations with a series of women whose Christian names began with the letters of the alphabet, proceeding without deviation from A to Z. If only the conversation had ended there I wouldn't be in my current predicament. But my employer has an unfortunate propensity for recasting all ideas in sporting terms. Before I knew it he had offered to triple my salary if he failed to accomplish the feat in six months time. Now, as I have mentioned, my paycheck is already ample, and without a calculator it is possible to state with some precision that three times ample is very good indeed. That is why I consented to the wager.

Only recently have I begun to seriously consider the consequences if I lose. If he succeeds in meeting the terms of the agreement, the forfeit is my person. That is, I will be his twenty-seventh conquest. At the time the bargain was struck it seemed to me that I had a great many advantages on my side. The task is, after all, a daunting one on the face of it, no matter how effective Mr. Walling's powers of persuasion. And again, one stipulation of the bet is that he neither repeat his performance with any of his partners once he has achieved consummation, nor have relations with any other women during the six-month term of the wager. This, I felt sure, would be gall for a man who keeps two appointment books—one for business and one for pleasure. I might add that, although I have frequently been called upon to remind him where he left his business calendar, he has never to my knowledge misplaced his personal book. Most importantly, he is a notoriously lazy man. It is not self-flattery that leads me to say that his business benefits a great deal from my attention to it. My assumption (since proven woefully wrong) was that the entire episode would soon slip from his mind and that in six months I would be able to remind him of the incident and require the trebling of my pay in a single breath.

Curiously, he seems remarkably single-minded in his

pursuit of this seemingly trivial accomplishment, and this puzzles me. Although the amount of money involved would mean a great deal to me, he has often lost greater sums through an unwillingness to return a phone call early enough in the day.

My apprehension was piqued from the beginning, as Steven advanced immediately and repeatedly. My native caution warned me to begin keeping records of his steps, and I will now rely on these, interjecting some explanation of my growing anxiety as required.

I don't feel old enough to find myself so often shaking my head at the fecklessness of youth these days, and yet I do. The seduction technique employed by Mr. Walling on this occasion was to take the young woman to lunch and explain to her the terms of the wager and how she could help his cause. Fascination at this bald approach seems to have won out over self-respect, and before her mother would have let her go in swimming after the meal, the two were misusing a dressing room at her place of employment. I will let his description of the events complete the tale:

"The dressing rooms at Brooks Brothers are larger than those in many other establishments, but still not what you might call capacious. Fortunately the doors lock from the inside, and though for two people to lie on the floor, let alone conduct any strenuous activity there, might be somewhat impractical, the rooms are furnished with narrow wooden benches on which one may place one's clothing. Abigail and I did not use ours for that purpose. We occupied the diminutive bench ourselves, I seated on the hard wood, with Abigail seated on me, with her back to me, bent slightly forward and clutching at my legs for support, with my arms around her, my hands covering her fine round breasts and my rampant cock deep inside her sweet, pulsing vagina.

"In this position we could both see ourselves in the full-length mirror opposite the bench, and I must say that the sight of Abigail's delectable body slowly rising and falling against me did nothing to diminish my ardor. Abigail enjoyed it too, and the first time she came I had to put my hand over her mouth to stifle her cry. By the second time she had turned around to face me and we were kissing passionately, so that the sound of her climax was muffled against my mouth. As was mine against hers."

I expect Steven wanted to embarrass me with the luxury of detail in his description. Could it have been intended to arouse me? The question persists in spite of my efforts to dismiss it. At any rate, Abigail not only lay down to be his first stepping-stone, she provided the second. Almost. Maybe it was my first stab of concern when he announced on the second day that he had already secured a second triumph that brought out my legalistic side. Let me explain.

My conscience still pricks me over the disqualification of the friend proposed by Abigail. But not very much. After all, a given name may have any number of nicknames. For that matter, a woman named Theresa may be known to her friends as Bathsheba because she dated a man named David in college. My regret isn't that I insisted on a rule which any child would acknowledge was implicit from the start, but that I betrayed anxiety at the fact that he had advanced so rapidly. And I gained very little thereby as, with equal alacrity, he dispatched of Belinda the social butterfly, whom he ran to earth in Monte Carlo.

I gather she required no more wooing than Abigail had. His arrival seems to have been enough to put them both in the proper mood, as evidenced in this transcript of his report.

" 'It's so good to see you, Steven,' she said. 'But I've just managed to slip away for a moment. Even a hostess must go to the bathroom . . . but I can't leave my guests for long.'

" 'Then let's not waste time,' I replied, and pulled down my zipper.

" 'You are so wicked!' Belinda murmured. 'But you're right.'

Lifting her dress, she reached beneath it to pull off her panties.

" 'This will have to do,' she said; then, 'Oh, Steven!' as I released my already stiff, but still growing, penis.' "

Ah, romance.

Steven Walling is a resourceful man. And, I must confess, in his own perverse way an honorable one. His tryst with Christine needs no more mention than the fact that it occurred. More notable was, as they say, the one who got away. Delirious, I dare say, with how easily he slipped in and out of Monte Carlo, not to mention his mayfly romance there, he very nearly consummated an affair on his return trip which any jury in the world would find disqualified him from our wager. That is, he found himself on the runway and taxiing, as it were, in an airplane lavatory with a flight attendant whose name turned out to be not Catherine but Katharine. Even I must admit to being impressed by his willpower in refusing the temptation of so willing a partner, and his honesty in confessing how close he came to failing. Perhaps he embellished the story a little, but I will repeat what I was told verbatim:

"Katharine began to slide down my body, lowering herself slowly, letting her breasts rub against me all the way down, until she was on her knees . . . Oh dear Lord, I thought. Maybe . . . if there was no actual intercourse, would that really count? I tried desperately to convince myself that it wouldn't. Her fingers opened my fly and found my erection and pulled it out, and her head bent to me, and . . .

" 'No!' And somehow I managed to turn away from her, putting my hands down to shield myself, using them to tuck myself back in and zip up."

Much to my amazement, perhaps even to his, this episode didn't entirely disqualify him in the eyes of Katharine, as I will soon describe. Although he quickly made up lost time with Christine, this was as close as he had come thus far to a failure. His momentary flash of nobility, the feeling that at least I was matched with a genteel adversary, may have brought some color to my cheek. Briefly, it even seemed to me that I was actually feeling a touch of desire myself, but I have convinced myself otherwise.

I share with my employer an aversion to most intense physical activities, and part of the reason is that they have a tendency to overexcite the emotions. It hardly seems to me just, then, on the part of Providence, to have placed him in the way of perhaps the most overexcited package of human hormones in the Western Hemisphere just at a time when her Christian name allowed him to take advantage of the fact. Yet that is what happened. He was actually in quest of a woman named Deborah when he was overcome by this human steamroller. The seduction was much more her doing than his, he only pausing long enough to discover the convenience of her initial. Apparently winning a match invariably drove her into a sexual frenzy which she would cheerfully mitigate with the help of the nearest man. In this case, Steven Walling was that man:

"We were both panting when we broke apart. 'Is so good when I win,' she breathed. 'I am not care, me. We do big fuck, yes? Now, yes?'

" 'It does look that way,' I said, and grabbed her again. I meant to pull her down to the tiled floor, but she backed up against the wall, out of the direct spray of the shower, taking me with her. With her arms tight around my neck, she raised her legs and wrapped them around me, as though trying to climb up my body. I clutched at her tight buttocks, helping her, lifting her up, until I was able to join our bodies, and she sank down over my stiffness with a shout of joy, those marvelous legs squeezing me harder than ever."

I must say, Steven leaned unnecessarily close and spoke in a very low voice while dispensing these details, and it is possible that I haven't gotten every word right. Just possible.

There are times when my opponent's moves forward, and my efforts, however modest, to thwart him, take on the aspect of a chess game. In that game it can be more valuable to place a psychological rather than an actual obstacle to advancement. I never stipulated that Mr. Walling's conquest of Betty, inadmissable as such, made her unacceptable as Elizabeth. I merely suggested that it was hardly sporting for a man who had been so favored by ladies in the past to rekindle former relationships as a means to achieving the goal he had set for himself. Such repetition would hardly add luster to his legend. Enforcement of this guideline was left to his own conscience, which in the event has proved sufficient. Conscience did not, however, prevent him from capitalizing on his friendship with Betty/Elizabeth, who turned out to be equally friendly with another woman of the E persuasion, Edna. In the event, Elizabeth received more than the vicarious success of having proposed her friend:

"Betty was now lying on her back on the floor, with Edna crouched above her, kissing her way slowly down Betty's body. Kissing and licking. From her breasts down over her stomach, and on down to that flaming red triangle. And on down. Betty was moaning. She bent her gorgeous legs to give herself leverage to lift her lower body toward Edna's searching mouth . . ."

At any rate, suffice it to say that Steven managed to keep the letter of the wager by . . . participating directly only with Edna. I have mentally replayed the scene a great many times to satisfy myself completely of that fact, and I find myself quite satisfied of the fact.

If he had impressed me favorably in more than one way during his headlong plunge through the female population, my chessmate's next step was a distinct step backward. It surprised me mildly that he accepted an appearance on a television talk show in the first place. I was more, rather than less, surprised, to discover that his reason had to do with the name of the host. Fern Forrester is an attractive woman, in a superficial way, but widely known, even to people like myself, who do nothing to actively pursue such knowledge, to be as shallow, self-involved and uninteresting a person as even the singularly shallow, self-involved and uninteresting business of television gossip has yet produced. Nonetheless, he proceeded with his usual efficiency and quickly achieved his purpose. Further, he reported the incident with no trace of the embarrassment I, for one, would have felt at the thought that the person I had been so intimate with in the afternoon wouldn't recognize my name if it came up at dinner. In fact, he described their coupling with an unusual degree of detail. I offer only a brief taste:

"Her hips began to squirm as she gazed at the reflection in front of her . . . 'Look,' she breathed. 'I'm fucking. I'm fucking you. Ohh . . . look how beautiful.'

"It was beautiful, with her sleek body in motion, her breasts quivering, her legs open to show the long stretch of her inner thighs. She watched herself as she fucked harder. I reached around her to put a hand over her breast and rubbed the hard nipple, bringing a moan from her. I slid my other hand down over stomach to her moving pussy. She inhaled sharply when I touched her little button, and then moaned again as I gently brushed my fingers across it."

I think that he dwelt on the particulars of this encounter in order to provoke in me feelings of jealousy. An absurd idea. If he wants to waste his energy on a woman who isn't even fully aware of who he is, in my opinion he should feel free to do so.

The persistence with which my employer was sticking to business continued to surprise me. Conceit and self-flattery suggested that he was genuinely interested in enjoying intimacy with me, but I refused to accept such famously unreliable counselors. Why then his ardent pursuit? This is, after all, a man who has enjoyed the favors of more women than the kings of England back to William the Conqueror, inclusive. For now I consider this to be an open question.

My sympathies were much more excited by my employer's next victim. When he brought me the story he concentrated on the virtue with which he had resisted the easy opportunity presented by one Ginger, a paid entertainer provided by his host at a party. He neglected to explore the propriety of opting instead for the virtue of his host's spouse. What most drew my attention—and indeed sympathy—was not the alacrity with which he exchanged Ginger for Grace, but Grace's affecting desire to change her life with Ginger's. I am certain that if she knew what I do, never mind how, about the sort of life that Ginger is leading, she would quickly forget that particular fantasy so common to the idle rich. I expect also that Steven, on reflection, felt more sympathy for her unhappiness, and less for his own misplaced pride in never having paid for satisfaction. As it was, neither pride nor sympathy seem to have prevented him from achieving his customary result:

" 'Why would you want to do that?' I asked.

"The head went up again. 'For kicks,' she said. She kissed my cock sweetly. 'I'm bored.' She licked at me. 'Besides, I'm kind of a whore already. I married Russell for his money, you know.'

" 'Not the same thing,' I said. Her mouth had swallowed me again . . . I closed my eyes, swaying slightly. 'Well, you'd certainly make a fortune at it,' I muttered to myself."

It is to his credit, I think, that he reported to me all the details of this particular exchange. He must have had some misgivings about it. If I wanted to press a point I could have suggested that he had forfeited the bet by purchasing her favors. It was and is my opinion, though, that he had pursued the best course that was available to him under the circumstances.

Having praised my employer's honesty so thoroughly, I nonetheless fell into doubt when he delivered the name of his next inamorata. He had, after all, been making predatory passes at a woman named Heather, and appeared ready to stoop. There followed several days when he barely appeared in the office, and when he did was gruff and uncommunicative. I surmised from this that Heather had become uncooperative, and my spirits rose. This was, after all, virtually the first time that his mad career seemed to have encountered the sort of obstacle which might prevent his completing the alphabet in the allotted time. Apparently his intended had gotten religion. Rather than changing targets, he mounted an elaborate cloak-and-dagger operation designed to discredit the Reverend Jourdemayne, the spiritual obstetrician who had presided when Heather was born again. Just when I was allowing myself to enjoy the hope that this masculine obstinacy might prove to be his Achilles heel he appeared at my elbow looking fresh and cheerful. The change in mood, he explained, had been brought about by a religious experience. He had spent the night in bed with a young woman who bore the unlikely name of Holy Virgin Mary. Despite my obvious interest, I received only sparse details of the encounter, videlicet:

"She had indeed been happy to see me, and though we both regretted the circumstances that kept her sister from joining us, Mary proved to be so inexhaustibly eager, inventive and athletic that she made up for it. Perhaps the skills she displayed were the result of her study under the Reverend Jourdemayne but, having seen him in action, I doubted it. More likely it was just natural talent."

This left Mr. Walling nearly a third of the way through the alphabet in just six weeks, and left me squirming in my seat with uncomfortable anticipation of what the future might hold.

Fate, heaven only knows why, has been a staunch ally of Steven Walling. I had concluded that my best hope of winning my wager was that complications unconnected to women and womanizing might slow him down. Perhaps not entirely unconnected. I was therefore optimistic when he began spending extensive time with his friend Phyllis, whose initial was for the moment safely out of range, but whose friendship he wished to maintain against the time when he had won, or God willing, lost the bet, and could resume his old habits. My fool's paradise was exploded when I discovered that there was a third in their party, Phyllis's visiting cousin Irene, whose appearance at that very moment placed her at the intersection of Steven Walling's crosshairs. Sure enough, it was not many days at all before he informed me that the young woman had succumbed, picturesquely enough while sightseeing at the Statue of Liberty:

"I stepped up close behind her, hastily opening my trousers and dropping them and my shorts around my ankles. It wasn't particularly elegant, but neither of us cared at that moment. Irene drew in her breath sharply as I found her sweetly moist opening and guided myself slowly inside her.

"It was slow and sweet all the way. My hands found

their way beneath her blouse and bra to hold her stiff-nippled breasts, as her hips moved in soft, sensuous rhythm. The New York skyline had never looked so wonderful to me."

If I have given any impression of myself as cold or dispassionate, it is a misimpression. I do, however, believe in keeping business and pleasure separate. It is therefore in the nature of a confession when I state that the above scene caused me, just for a moment, to think that losing my wager with my employer might not be an unmitigated disaster. The moment passed, however, without, I hope, showing on my face, and my resolve to win redoubled. I can't quite say that I proposed his next challenge, one which I confidently believed insurmountable and hoped would occupy him fruitlessly for some time. I did, though, repeat the name to him several times at a moment when he seemed receptive, emphasizing the initial. The bait was sufficient, and I stifled my triumph. Just as well that I did, as the sequel will show.

The consummation I am about to describe made me wonder whether anything could halt this rake's progress. In this day and age men of much more modest gifts than Steven Walling can and do obtain sexual gratification with ease. I didn't expect the availability of willing partners to be his undoing, but rather his natural disinclination toward effort along with the six month deadline. When, therefore, he announced his intention of seducing one of the world's most famous women, a woman who was in large part famous for her reticence, I was, to put it mildly, surprised. Surprised that he would voluntarily make his task so difficult and that he would waste precious time laying a siege which would surely be lengthy and just as surely futile. I compliment myself on having performed a miracle by retaining my composure when he crowed his success to me after their initial meeting. My hands remained steady as he delivered the details, but my heartbeat, I think, became as highly irregular as the event he described:

"'I want to see them bare,' I said. 'Take the hose off.'

"She shook her head slightly. Then she closed her eyes. She reached up beneath the skirt to her waist and pulled the pantyhose down, hitching herself up off the seat to do so. She pulled them off and dropped them.

"'Gorgeous,' I said. And I reached out a hand and put it on her thigh. She jumped, but didn't protest or make a move to push it away.

"'Why am I doing this?' she whispered, again softly."

Why indeed? For purposes of the wager, it is only important that she did, so I will draw a curtain across the scene.

Having completed the first decade of his unholy rosary, one might have expected Steven Walling to take a moment to reassess his progress. That is not his nature. He plunged ahead immediately, and with effect.

I wouldn't say, going by Mr. Walling's usual detailed description of the event, that Katharine had been waiting for him since their first encounter with bated breath. In fact, she was so little impressed by our hero's willingness to fly to Monte Carlo, in order to have her as his flight attendant and renew his assault on her somewhat questionable virtue, that she offered to end his career as a ladies' man by removing the appendage essential to his craft. As she had the aforementioned appendage between her lips at the time, the threat was taken seriously. This led to a rather ticklish several minutes, during which he had to use the full measure of the charms God gave him simply to escape with his virility intact. Never one to thank the lord for small favors, he decided not only to escape in one piece but go ahead and complete his conquest.

As always, in the end the Walling suasion and suavity prevailed, and he enticed her into the casino bathroom. When our wager is over, I must cross-examine him about his fascination with fornication in water closets:

"We were holding each other as she pressed herself to me, moving harder, and we kissed again to stifle our panting and moaning, though I don't know how successful we were. Especially when I felt her spasming around my flesh as she went over the top, just as I was wondering how long I could hold out myself. As it turned out, not another second. But if the sounds of our climax were indeed audible outside our stall, at least no one was heard to complain. Very civilized country, Monaco."

I dare say.

Having determined to prepare myself for the possibility of losing this bet, I realized that my knowledge of my employer was in many ways deficient. I turned to his brother Henry to supply the want. It was an unanticipated but welcome fact that my attention to Henry inspired Steven with jealousy. I did nothing to discourage this. Very well, perhaps I not only allowed the misconception but fostered it. The green-eyed monster led him not to the perfectly chaste dinner I shared with his brother (and which at least yielded me the information I had hoped to glean), but to a love-feast of his own with the owner of a Chinese restaurant:

"The table was small, but fortunately sturdy. Our bodies fit together with no trouble at all, and her fine, shapely legs came up to curl around me. For a long pleasant time I probed deeply into the mysteries of the East—although the words Li Mai cried from time to time were definitely English. Old English."

Pangs of sibling rivalry may not have slowed Steven down, but they appealed, I confess, to my vanity.

It amused me to learn that Steven Walling's sexual adventures began in failure. Not through any fault of his own, or any unwillingness from his partner, but in the way so many adolescent attempts fall through. Her parents caught them in the act and gave them unshirted hell. Some perverse impulse made him determine that this wrong needed to be set right. Perhaps he was still struggling with my strong suggestion that he ought by rights to be cavorting only with women he had not previously enjoyed. It was only after he succeeded even more easily than is his wont in reaching his goal that he discovered the reason Marcia was so willing. His high school sweetheart had become a prostitute:

" 'Marcia, I love you,' I panted. I had said that then, in the heat of my need, with one hand on her breast and the other up her skirt, and I said it now.

" 'Oh, I love you too,' Marcia breathed. 'Oh, Steven!' she whispered as my hand found her soft moistness through the silk of her panties. 'You make me so hot!' "

The pathos of this story, from beginning to end, made me feel closer to Steven Walling than I ever had before. Once more there was the momentary confusion over whether I was quite determined to win. Barely more than two months had elapsed as he passed the peak and began his downhill run through the second half of the alphabet.

*   *   *

The sexual ethics of the upper class are notoriously lax. It might have been interesting to add a rule at the beginning of our wager limiting my employer to women of this group, but I doubt it would have made his task any harder. Indeed, it is notable that whenever he has approached his more affluent lady friends he has encountered very slight resistance, even from the mysterious J lady. The philanthropical Nancy was no exception. The fact that she was married deterred her not at all. On the contrary, the fashion in which she was faithful required only that her husband be allowed to watch. And in the long run to participate . . . along with the houseboy:

"Arnold opened his trousers and took it out. I tried to concentrate on Nancy. The continued stimulation of her moving body kept me in a state of intense arousal, while the annoying distractions she was creating prevented me from getting too close to the edge. It was about the strangest feeling I had ever experienced during an erotic encounter."

Apparently Mr. Walling's experience, while very long, is not unusually wide.

If my employer is learning something from his wayward journey, and I hope he is, it is unlikely to be any new technique of seduction. He is a past master of that art. Perhaps he will discover that the game is not invariably worth the candle, in this case when it involves actual risk of physical harm. His eye having settled on a beauty of African extraction, he began to limber up his toils and cast them her way. The danger in this case came not with failure but with success. Convinced that his only interest in her had to do with her heritage, she nonetheless cooperated in his quest, not out of a sense of fun, but rather to spite another lover. The venom she poured on him before, during and after their coupling was nothing compared to what the old boyfriend offered if he caught them together again. I don't think he will:

"Her body was squirming in the chair, her soft thighs clutching my head. I could hardly breathe, but the essence of her was all the oxygen I needed. I nibbled and sucked and licked, and she writhed harder, her buttocks rising off the chair, her legs twitching against my cheeks.

" 'Come on, you white bastard, don't stop, you pale-ass motherfucker . . . oh shit yeah . . . Now . . . now . . . now.' "

Escaping with his life, to say nothing of another feather in a cap that was starting to resemble a war-bonnet, he caught a cab to more familiar precincts and delivered his report to me.

Phyllis Dilsey may almost be called the cause of this whole mess. I am not a jealous woman, as I think is clear by now, but I don't like to see Mr. Walling diverting time from business to less worthy objects. I may, therefore, have been easily provoked on the fateful morning that our wager was forged. It had been necessary that morning to pry him from his bed, and the aforementioned Mrs. Dilsey. That explains why I was so easily led into a gambling venture. Add to that that she had been hovering around ever since looking for a repeat performance, and you will understand my vexation when Steven revealed that he planned to grant her wish. There were long pauses in the conversation, as I had no intention of revealing just how angry I was at what I considered a betrayal of the spirit of our agreement. My silence brought him as close as he had come to a failure.

Not that I have that assurance from his own lips. On his behalf, as on mine, silence spoke volumes. For the only time in our long odyssey he gave me bare assurance that he had accomplished his goal. In my experience (and never you mind what that is) this can only mean one thing. He must have encountered some difficulties in the performance of his wonted acrobatics. I would say that it must have been hard for him, but that might lead to some confusion.

Although, having accomplished this retrospective, I find myself less apprehensive about the prospect of his victory, it is not in my nature to go down without a fight. If I can throw a cross in his path with no sacrifice of honor I will do so. If, however, it is my fate to lose the wager, I hope to encounter that fate with grace. It would be such an easy thing to sour his victory (should he achieve it—I still have hopes of winning) by letting it appear that it was what I wanted in the first place. But you, dear readers, won't be fooled, will you?

Chapter 18

QUITE EARLY ON IN MY PROGRESS TOWARD THE winning of my wager with Miss Greenglass, I had begun to make provisions—or at least to attempt to do so—against the time when I would be faced with those letters presenting the greatest challenge. I must admit that on the whole I had not had much success in this endeavor. Almost half my allotted six months had passed, and while I had less than half of the alphabet to go, that half was by far the more difficult. I had stored up one or two vague leads, and in my hour of need I recalled a newspaper clipping I had torn out and squirreled away. I dug it out and perused it again.

It was an advertisement from a small-circulation weekly paper specializing in left-wing politics and New Age arcana. It promoted the offerings of an establishment known as The Astral Plane, and it read as follows:

Visit the Astral Plane, servicing the Evolved and the Enlightened. Spiritual counselling. Channeling. Crystal arrangement. Body piercing. Meditation training. Witchcraft. By appointment only.

This was followed by an address, and then at the bottom of the ad was a very small photograph of a young woman, under which was the name: Quintana.

Whether this was a first or last name, or actually a name at all, was something I could only find out by investigation. Oddly, although the ad specified "by appointment only," there was no phone number. How one was to make an appointment was not clear. I decided to risk just showing up.

The address was deep in what was once called the Lower East Side. I paid the cab driver, stepped around a couple of recumbent individuals taking their afternoon naps on the sidewalk, and entered the Astral Plane.

I was struck by the strong smell of incense and the faint sound of tinkling bells from somewhere deep in the pervasive gloom. The lighting consisted of a few candles scattered about on counters, which didn't appear to serve any other purpose. I heard a faint rustling noise from somewhere, and then a young woman came through a curtain in the back wall.

Given the general dimness of the place, and the fuzziness of the photograph, I was not certain that this was the lady in the ad, but it seemed likely. She had the same long brown hair floating freely about her face. She wore a long, loose white garment and she was barefoot. As she came closer I could see that she wore no makeup whatever, but that fact seemed somehow to enhance, rather than detract from, the limpid beauty of her face. The loose covering hid most of her figure, but it couldn't quite conceal the high thrust of an obviously unfettered bosom.

"*Namas te*," the young lady said. "Welcome to the Astral Plane."

"Thank you. Are you Quintana?"

"Yes," she said. "I am Quintana." Her voice was very low and soft, almost ethereal. There was something about her that made me feel disconcertingly awkward and intrusive.

"Forgive my coming with no appointment," I said. "But there was no—"

"Oh, but I knew you were coming," she said. "I received your emanation. I have been expecting you."

"Is that right?" I said. The girl was lovely, but seemed also to be something of a kook. "Do you know my name too?"

She smiled softly. "Names are immaterial. It is your spirit I recognize."

"But names are important too," I said. "Yours, for instance. Quintana. It's very unusual. Is it your real name?"

She shrugged. "A name is merely a convenience. An artificial symbol of outward identity. It means nothing."

"It means something to me," I said. "Is it your first name?"

"Please," Quintana said. "You have come here because you are in need. I feel that. Let me help you. You are an earthy person with a spirit yearning to rise up into freedom. Have you tried chanting? Do you seek a spirit guide?"

"Not exactly," I said. "I just—"

"No," Quintana said. "No, your aura is more . . ." She began to circle around me, one hand raised up as though feeling my aura. "It is earthly, tangible . . . it cries out for a physical solution."

"I think you're right," I said.

"A soul calling for release . . . perhaps a piercing of the body, allowing the spirit to escape from its prison . . ."

A piercing of the body was what I had in mind all right. But hers, not mine. "Thanks just the same," I said.

"You came here seeking something," Quintana said. "Tell me what it was, that I may best help you."

"Actually I came to find out about your name," I said. "I know it's just an artificial symbol of outward identity, but—"

Quintana sighed, which did interesting things to her bosom. "You cannot solve your spiritual problems by avoidance," she said. "Come with me." I followed her. Behind the curtain was a smaller room, just as dim but cozier, with rugs and cushions scattered on the floor. "Please sit down," she said. "We will have some herbal tea and I will consult the Tarot." She motioned to a pile of cushions, and I sat down on them, not very comfortably. I wondered where the tea was coming from. Maybe it was an emanation.

Quintana gazed at me solemnly. "You have been looking at my breasts," she said. "Would you like to see them?"

I blinked. "I certainly would."

She opened the neck of her robe and slipped it off her shoulders, and she was naked to the waist. Her breasts were high and thrusting, set wide apart, with nipples the color of raspberries.

"You must transcend your absorption with the physical," Quintana said. "The body is only a shell, a temporary structure, doomed to wither and perish. It is the soul that is immortal. I see your spirit yearning to soar beyond the material world. We must work to free that spirit. Have you ever meditated?"

I was meditating over her breasts at that moment. "Look," I said, "you're right. I'm a very physical person.

Maybe the way to free my spirit is through physical means. If your temporary structure and mine got together, that might bring about a liberation of the spirit . . ."

Quintana was shaking her head. "You are merely expressing what you *think* you desire," she said. "Not what is deep in your soul. It is the tyranny of the left-brain construct that leads you to see me as an erotic object. It is an illusion which only hinders your enlightenment."

"Oh, really?" I said. "Then how come I have this erection? I guess my penis doesn't know it's a left-brain construct."

Quintana didn't seem fazed. "An erection is simply a manifestation of your earthbound fantasies. Your true essence yearns for transcendence—"

"No it doesn't," I said. "It yearns for you. It yearns to hold those lovely breasts of yours. It yearns to be inside you and feel your legs around my body and your hips moving under me. And before all that, it yearns to know your name. Your real name. If you really want to help me, that's the best way to start."

She shrugged. Her breasts bounced. My cock twitched. "My name is Quintana," she said. "Just that. It is what it is. It is not what I am."

"All right," I said. "Fine." If that was what she said her name was—I think that's what she was saying—that was good enough for me, and it would have to be good enough for Miss Greenglass too. "Now about this erection . . ."

"You can will it away," she said. "It is not real. Concentrate. Look deep inside yourself and you will discover that this fleshly desire is a mirage—"

I pulled down my zipper and let my stiff straining tool out into the open, figuring if she could show me her temporary shell, I could show her mine. "Does that look like a mirage?" I asked her. "An illusion? An artificial construct?"

For a moment I thought her eyes grew even larger. She didn't move or say anything immediately, and as we sat there I began to feel a bit silly. But after a while she took a breath. "Perhaps . . ." she said softly, and paused. "There is a method—practiced by certain yoga adepts— of reaching enlightenment through . . . a—an aesthetic form of . . . of sexual contact."

"Now we're talking," I said.

"You must understand," Quintana said. "This is a spiritual practice. It does not involve lust, or what you think of as earthly passion."

"Oh, of course," I said. "Certainly. I wouldn't have it any other way."

"Undress," she said, and she stood up and followed her own command. I did likewise, but my eyes were on her as she slid the robe the rest of the way off. She was naked, and she was magnificent. My erection grew even bigger.

Quintana pulled just one pillow out of the pile on the floor and sat me down on it, with my legs sort of half folded in front of me. Then she stepped close and lowered herself, facing me, till she was crouched above my lap. I reached to put my hands on her breasts, but she shook her head sharply. "No. Just be still. Think of nothing."

That was easy to say, but it was very hard to do. It was even more difficult to keep my hands at my sides when her soft warm fingers made contact with my eager stiffness, holding it steady as she positioned herself over it.

This may have been a purely spiritual thing for her, but something about that spirit had made her moist and ready.

I let out a hiss of pleasure as she gradually enveloped me in that soft tightness. "Hush," she said. "Empty your mind of lust. Contemplate the joining of souls." As she said this she was taking me deeper and deeper, until finally she was sitting on my thighs, and I was buried completely inside her marvelous body.

"Quintana . . ." I croaked. My breath was coming fast, my heart was racing and my hands were twitching to touch her somewhere, anywhere. In fact I couldn't help brushing her smooth shapely thighs with my fingers—

"No," she said again, lifting my hands away from her flesh. "You must be still."

I don't know how those Yogis did it. It was impossible for me just to sit there that way and do nothing, and yet neither my desire nor my erection seemed to be diminishing one bit. Quite the contrary. I had to do something. In what I hoped was a subtle way, I flexed my leg muscles, pushing my hips upward just slightly, feeling myself burrowing still deeper inside her. At the same time I felt what was evidently a reflexive contraction of her vagina around my long-suffering erection. Quintana's mouth opened, undoubtedly to admonish me again, but instead the breath caught in her throat with a tiny gasp. This was encouraging, and I rocked a little harder, though still slowly.

"You must be still," Qintana said, almost pleadingly. "You must not—"

"I can't help it," I said. "I feel the spirit, Quintana. I feel the god within. Do you feel it, Quintana?" And I rocked harder.

"Oh . . ." she said. "Oh, don't . . . oh . . ." Her dark eyes, which had been gazing off serenely into the middle distance as though contemplating infinity, were now wide

and slightly glazed-looking. Then suddenly she gave a
kind of sobbing moan, and she was moving too, moving
with me, her breasts quivering and her fine thighs flexing
as she followed my rhythm.

"Yes . . ." she panted, gasping with each stroke. "Oh,
yes . . . yes . . . do it!"

I put my hands on her then, on her smooth thighs and
her flanks and then her breasts. I kneaded them lovingly,
rubbing the nipples between my fingers, moving harder.
Her head fell back and her mouth opened wide and she
gave a great cry. "Oh, Jesus!" she shouted. And then her
arms were around me, clutching me, pulling at me,
pulling my body forward as she fell backward.

Somehow we managed to stay together as we toppled
over, and then she was on her back and I was on top of
her, still inside her, and Quintana raised her legs almost
straight up into the air and spread them apart as far as
they would go. "Fuck me!" she cried wildly. "Oh God,
fuck me as hard as you can!"

I did my best. So did she. Her legs rose and wrapped
themselves around me, squeezing me as tightly as any
pair of legs has ever done, and her twisting body arched
clear off the floor, convulsing over and over, while her
stream of words melted into an incomprehensible babble,
which soon rose to a shrill, keening shriek, and finally
died away . . .

"You bastard," Quintana said when she had recovered her
breath. "You have interfered with my inner journey and
hindered my spiritual progression. You've set back the
process of my becoming a fully evolved being."

"Have I done all that?" I said. "I'm sorry, but—"

"Do it again," Quintana said.

Chapter 19

RELEASE ME THIS INSTANT, YOU MONSTER!" the woman said. Since I wasn't even touching her—was in fact sitting halfway across the room from her—and since nothing was holding her or even keeping her from leaving if she wanted to, this demand seemed unwarranted. But by that time I was no longer surprised.

I sighed. "Rachel," I said, "nothing is keeping you here. You can go any time you want. You said you wanted to discuss your husband's securities, and—"

"Oh, I know!" Rachel said, in her most tragic tone. "I know you have my husband at your mercy, and that if I leave without succumbing to your monstrous demands you will break him like a child's toy. Don't you think I know that?"

"Come off it, Rachel," I said wearily. "I don't even know your husband. I don't handle his business. I don't know what this game is you're playing, but I thought we were meeting because you wanted advice about investments, that's all."

That wasn't *quite* true, of course. She had asked me

about her husband's investments, but I had invited her to my office because her name began with R. I'd met her at a dinner party and had been attracted by her tall, slender, provocative body and her dark-eyed, dark-haired handsomeness. I figured her for about twenty-seven. When I learned that her name was Rachel, of course, she looked even better.

I hadn't intended to seduce her in the office, but there was always the possibility of taking her upstairs to my bedroom, or at least of making a future assignation. Some time ago I had determined to keep any sexual activity related to my wager with Miss Greenglass outside the office—though I no longer quite knew why. In any case, Miss Greenglass happened to be on vacation—and without her, my office routine, such as it was, had ground to a virtual halt, despite the fact that she had arranged for a temporary assistant to take her place. (The temporary's name was Brenda, which took her out of the running for me—a fact of which I'm sure Miss Greenglass was aware when she chose her.)

When Rachel agreed to come to the office, I was pretty sure she knew what was in my mind and didn't object. But what I didn't know was that she was some kind of . . . well, let's say she had a highly active imagination.

It had started the minute she had entered the office, looking gorgeous in a tight blue pullover sweater and an even tighter pair of dark slacks. She was mouth-watering, and she knew it. I was ready to take her upstairs at the earliest opportunity; but I wasn't ready for what Rachel had in mind.

"All right, Steven," she said at once. "You've got me here. Now what do I have to do?"

I blinked. "What?" I asked, puzzled. "You don't have to do anything, Rachel. Come on in and sit down."

"You don't have to beat around the bush, Steven. I understand the situation quite clearly. I know that if I want to save my husband from ruin, I have to pay for it with my body. I've come to submit myself to your whims."

I stared at her. "Now wait a minute—"

"I know I'll be forced to degrade myself," Rachel said. "That's what you want, isn't it, Steven? To have me debase myself before you. To make me crawl and grovel at your feet. To use me for your animal lust . . ."

"Hold it!" I said loudly. Then I took a deep breath. "Look, Rachel. Either you're under a very large misapprehension here, or this is some kind of nutty mind game, but whatever it is, I'm not playing, all right? What about your husband? Does he know you're here?"

"No," Rachel said. "I've come to face my ordeal alone. A sacrificial offering."

"Oh, for God's sake," I said disgustedly. "Rachel, look—you're a very attractive lady, and I won't say I haven't had ideas about taking you to bed. But not this way. It's just not my style. Now why don't we just forget about this and go have a drink or something, okay?"

"I suppose the first thing you'll want me to do," Rachel said, "is take off my clothes."

The thought sent a little tingle through me, but I fought it down. "Please, Rachel. I don't want you to do anything. Why don't you just go home?"

"Very well, Steven," Rachel said. "I have no choice." And crossing her arms in front of her, she took hold of the hem of her sweater and pulled it up. All the way up, and over her head, and off. She dropped it to the floor. She wasn't wearing a bra.

Naturally I stared at her breasts. What else could I do? Her breasts, not large but quite full in proportion to her slender body, stood up beautifully, round and firm, and her nipples were hard. Obviously she was turned on by the little drama she was playing.

After letting me look for several long moments, Rachel brought her hands up to cover her breasts in a gesture of phony modesty. It was then that she demanded that I release her, and I replied as related above, hoping that she would go before it was too late.

With a little sigh, she let her arms fall away. "What's the use?" she said tragically. "I know you won't allow me any dignity. You enjoy shaming me like this."

I took another deep breath, struggling with myself. "Rachel," I growled. "You came here to do what I want, right? Okay, I'm giving you an order. You understand? An order."

"You have complete power over me," Rachel said. "I must obey your despicable commands."

"Good. I want you to pick up your sweater and put it on. And then get the hell out of here. Is that clear enough?"

"I thought so," Rachel said. "You have no pity. You force me to disrobe completely before you." She opened a button at the front of her slacks.

"Stop," I said desperately. "Damn it, stop. Please stop. For God's sake, stop."

Rachel pushed her slacks down.

This was very interesting to watch. The slacks were so tight she had to work them down over her lusciously curved hips, pulling first at one side, then the other, gaining about an inch with each tug. This made her breasts shake and quiver and bump each other in a fascinating manner. I felt my erection getting stronger and my resistance weaker. I thought about getting up and walking out. I thought about it. Fleetingly.

"Rachel," I said—my voice was not completely steady—"you're doing this of your own free will. You understand?"

The slacks fell. Rachel kicked off her shoes and stepped out of them and the slacks together. She wore only panties. Thin ones. Her legs were bare. I looked at them. Not fleetingly. I think I gulped.

"Oh God, Steven," Rachel said, sounding as though she was about to cry. "Will you leave me no last shred of modesty? Must I strip completely naked?"

"Free will," I said weakly.

"You beast," Rachel quavered, and took off her panties.

Somehow I summoned up a last tattered remnant of strength. "Look, Rachel," I said. "If you don't stop this right now I'm going to call up your husband and tell him what's going on."

"God, Steven," Rachel said. "Are you so depraved that you would take pleasure in gloating to my poor husband over the shameful position you have me in?"

"Oh Lord," I groaned. But before I could think of what to do, the office door opened and Brenda came in.

Rachel seemed barely surprised, but I nearly jumped out of my chair. "Brenda!" I gasped. I didn't know whether to be relieved or disappointed. "I thought you were gone for the day!"

"I thought I'd just finish up those . . ." Brenda started, but her voice trailed off and she stared at Rachel standing naked in the middle of the office.

"Look," I said, "It's not—I mean—it's okay. Ah—the lady was just leaving."

"I see," Rachel said. "It's not enough for you simply to humiliate me and force me to your will. You're going to make me perform these vile acts in front of a stranger."

"What's going on?" Brenda asked. It occurred to me that she was not quite as shocked as she might have been. Brenda was about twenty, a pretty brown-haired girl with a very nice figure which I had been studiously ignoring for the past week.

"It's hard to explain," I said.

"What now?" Rachel said. "I suppose you'll make me get down on my knees. And crawl."

"I better leave," Brenda said, but I noticed she was not moving.

"No," I said. "Yes. No. Oh, Christ."

"All right," Rachel said, whimpering now. "You don't have to hit me any more. I'll do anything you say." She got down on her knees.

"Jeez," Brenda said. "This chick is out of her tree."

Rachel went down on all fours and began to move across the floor toward me. "Making me crawl to you on my hands and knees like an animal," she said breathlessly. "Naked. In front of a witness. How horribly degrading."

"Rachel," I said huskily. "I'm telling you for the last time—" I broke off when she knelt upright and put her hands on my legs. She pushed them apart so she could move between them. "The hell with it," I said. "I'm not fighting it anymore. Do whatever you want."

Her hands slid up my legs. One felt my erection through my pants while the other found my zipper. "I'm forcing myself to do this," she breathed. "I know you'll tie me down and whip me if I don't. And maybe even if I do."

"No such luck," I said. She was pulling my zipper down. Brenda moved in to get a closer look.

"Brenda," I said unsteadily, "maybe you'd better go now."

"No way!" Brenda said.

I didn't feel able to argue the matter just then, because Rachel was pulling my erection out of my pants.

"How disgusting!" Rachel declaimed. "And you're going to force me to take that loathsome thing into my mouth? And—and . . . oh, please . . . please don't make me . . ."

"I'm not . . ." I began, but I knew it was no use. And the truth is that at that point I was hoping to hell she wouldn't stop.

"Oh . . ." she said in a hopeless tone. "Oh you vile, perverted monster!" And then she lowered her head and took me into her mouth.

"Oh my God," I said. And then, "Oh, Jesus." I might have thrown in Buddha and Mohammed. I was having a very ecumenical experience. Rachel's mouth and tongue could convert an atheist.

Rachel's mouth moved up and down slowly. I began to gasp. Then I began to twist in my chair, gripping the arms for dear life. I felt as though I might take off at any second and fly up to the ceiling. Rachel was putting everything she had into this, and I knew I wasn't going to stop myself from coming right down her miserable little throat.

She moved faster. The room began to spin around. I saw Brenda revolving with everything else, her eyes bright, her hands gently squeezing her own breasts as she watched.

Then I didn't see anything but comets and rockets and shooting stars. My head fell back and I arched my bottom clear off the chair, pushing myself hard into Rachel's devouring mouth. I made some loud noises which I will not attempt to reproduce, and then I was spurting hard, my hips jerking uncontrollably as I emptied myself into her gullet while her lips sucked and pulled at me and her tongue caressed me encouragingly with each spasm. She swallowed it all as it came, moaning with greedy satisfaction.

Slowly I came back to earth. I sat panting and blinking stupidly until I could remember who I was, and the spinning of the office had slowed down a bit. Rachel was looking up at me, her nipples harder than ever.

"Oh, how could you force me to do such a horrible, wicked thing?" she moaned. "And what in the world are you going to make me do next?"

"Next?" I said dully.

Rachel's eyes widened. "Oh, no . . ." she gasped. "You wouldn't . . . you can't want me to . . . to do *that!*"

My eyes closed. "Do what?" I croaked.

"Do . . . do perverted things with . . . with this woman," Rachel said.

My eyes opened.

"Hey!" Brenda said. "Great idea!"

"Now wait—" I said.

"Oh, you filth!" Rachel said, and tried to sob. "Is there no depth to which you won't sink to get your twisted kicks?"

"Shit," I said.

With a pathetic whimper Rachel turned away and began to move on her knees to where Brenda was standing by the side of the desk. Brenda—who I had thought was the picture of sweet innocence—didn't waste any time. She had her panties off and her skirt up around her waist before Rachel even got there. She leaned back against the desk and planted her feet wide apart. Rachel moved close to her and, with another dramatic sob, buried her face between Brenda's well-formed thighs.

Brenda hissed sharply and dug her hands into Rachel's hair, guiding her head where she wanted it. But Rachel didn't seem to need much guidance. Brenda began to squirm and moan, and I got the impression that Rachel's wonderful mouth was giving her nearly as much pleasure as it had given me.

Keeping one hand clutched in Rachel's hair, Brenda raised the other to the buttons of her blouse, undoing a few so she could slip her hand inside and fondle her breasts while the kneeling woman continued to work on her. I watched all this with a fair amount of objectivity at first, but after a bit I felt the old phallus perking up again. It was a pretty erotic sight, after all, the naked woman kneeling before the half-naked one, her face in the other's crotch, both moaning now, Brenda writhing and gasping, twisting her own breast.

By the time Brenda cried out her climax, her violently jerking body bent forward over Rachel's still-working head, I was in full erection again. Feeling a little foolish, I stuffed it back inside my trousers and zipped it up. Which didn't seem to discourage it.

"Ohh . . ." Brenda panted, slumping against the desk as she released Rachel. "Oh, that was lovely," she said, "Lie down, honey—I'll do you now, okay?"

"Oh, no," Rachel said bitterly. "Steven doesn't want me to get any pleasure. Only shame and humiliation,

that's what he wants to see. Now he's going to tie me
down on his desk and . . . and . . ."

"Forget it," I said.

Rachel rose. Her face was wet, which made her look
even sexier. She bent over the desk, her upper body resting on the desktop, her sweet round behind sticking up
and out. It was a big desk, and she spread her arms across
it toward the far corners, flattening her breasts against its
surface, stretching herself as if she were indeed tied in
that position.

"Now I'm helpless," Rachel said. "You'll be able to
whip me until I scream. There's nothing I can do about
it."

Brenda was pulling her panties back on. She stifled a
giggle.

"And then," Rachel went on, "I suppose you'll take
me from behind like this, while I struggle frantically."

I wasn't interested in the tying and whipping, but that
sexy outstretched body and those curvy, jutting ass-
cheeks were tempting. Her widespread thighs were
smooth and shapely, and between them I could just catch
a glimpse of her beckoning vagina. My body wanted to
push itself up against that firm, round behind and slide
my cock between her legs and up into the sweet tight
warmth of her. My brain, on the other hand, told me to
just get the hell out of there.

Guess who won?

Chapter 20

S HE WAS NINETEEN YEARS OLD, AN INNOCENT-looking young lady with dark eyes, brown hair that was long and wavy and a scrumptious, almost voluptuous figure. She was sitting on the edge of her bed with her legs stretched wide apart and her heels resting on the floor. She had pulled her long skirt all the way up over her hips and was holding it around her waist. She was a tall girl, and her long shapely legs were as stunning as any I had ever seen. And she wasn't wearing panties.

"Is this what you want?" she asked.

It wasn't exactly what one might have expected from the leading symbol and poster child, as it were, of an organization called Stamp Out Smut—S.O.S., for short—and the daughter of its founder and executive director, the formidable Mrs. J. W. Dunbarton. On the other hand, I can't say that I was entirely surprised.

S.O.S. was the organization under whose auspices I was at the Dunbarton apartment that evening. There were about a dozen of us; we had been invited to imbibe cocktails, snack on canapés and, it was hoped, contribute with charitable generosity to the cause of guarding the endangered morals of our fellow creatures.

Now regular readers of this saga may suspect that this was not a cause for which I had much sympathy; and those shrewd individuals would be correct. My presence at this gathering was not occasioned by any desire on my part to join the swelling ranks of those who would impose their particular ideas of morality upon society at large. No, my motivation for attending this event had nothing at all to do with puritanism. Oh, no. Quite the contrary.

Mrs. J. W. Dunbarton had long been a well-known leader in the wars against pornography. Over the years she had enlisted her entire family in this crusade. Her husband, however, had been fortunate enough to die off several years ago, and soon afterwards her son had run off to Oregon, where, it was said, he immediately opened a chapter of the Sexual Freedom League. (Mrs. Dunbarton no longer acknowledges him as her son.) Her daughter, however, had remained faithful, and the two of them now functioned as a team, often appearing on television talk shows. It was on television, in fact, that I had first gotten a good look at Mrs. Dunbarton's daughter. Her name, not so incidentally, was Sabrina.

"It's a start," I said now, in answer to her question. I moved to the bed and knelt down on the floor in front of her, putting my hands on those beautiful soft thighs and spreading them still further. Then I put my lips to the silky inner surface of one of them and slip my mouth over it, my tongue trailing along the tender flesh. I heard Sabrina draw her breath sharply. I turned to the other leg and repeated the action, moving slowly toward her crotch. I lifted her legs then and put them over my shoulders. A whimper escaped her as I brought my mouth to her pussy, just grazing her labia and teasing very softly with my tongue. She moaned and leaned back on her hands, thrusting her crotch harder against my face. My hands roamed her legs as my tongue probed deeper, tasting the sweet female essence of her . . .

What had prompted me to attend this particular event had been no more than a vague feeling, based on a nebulous but niggling memory of the aforementioned television program. My attention had been focused on Sabrina whenever she was on-screen, and as her mother had spoken at length about the need to shield our young people from the filth currently pervading this great land of ours, and how the teaching of proper values is necessary to inculcate them with the traditional virtues, such as abstinence and chastity—pointing to her daughter as an example of such virtues, molded by a rigorous and pious upbringing—I thought I noticed, from time to time and very fleetingly, a swift flicker of the daughter's eyes, an expression so swift and almost subliminal as perhaps to be imaginary. For the most part she smiled and nodded as her mother spoke, and when it came her turn she more or less recapitulated what her mother had said, with great poise and forcefulness. There seemed to be no insincerity about her. And yet I could not get that feeling out of my mind . . .

"Sabrina?" a voice intoned from outside the door. It was Mrs. Dunbarton. I realized with a chill that the door was not locked. My first instinct was to pull away and assume some semblance of innocence, but Sabrina's hands suddenly clutched at my hair and kept me where I was.

"What is it, Mother?" she called. Her voice was a bit strained.

"What are you doing, dear?" Mrs. Dunbarton asked.

Her hands pulled me closer against her, and I responded by sliding my tongue up inside her. As long as I was there, I might as well keep busy.

Sabrina's body jerked and she gave a loud hiss. "I'm busy right now, Mother," she said unsteadily. "I'm—I'm discussing our work with Mr. Walling." I retracted my tongue and found her clitoris. "He's—oh!—he's very interested."

There was a brief pause. "All right, dear," Mrs. Dunbarton said finally. "But don't be too long."

"I'll be . . . I'll be there . . . in a few minutes, Mother," Sabrina panted, arching and twisting under the ministrations of my lips and tongue.

"Very well, then," her mother said, and I could faintly hear her footsteps moving down the hall, away from the sound of her daughter's soft shriek of completion.

"Jesus," I said, resting my head against a luscious thigh. "What if she had come in?"

"She wouldn't," Sabrina said. "She knows what's going on."

I was taken aback. "She knows?"

"Oh yes. She knows, all right."

When the notice of this fund-raiser had arrived some weeks before, I had not automatically consigned it to the wastebasket, as is my wont, but had deliberately held on to it, hoping that the timing might be such that when the indicated date arrived, the progress of my wager with

Miss Greenglass might just have brought me to the point at which I would be seeking an S. And that, fortunately, was exactly what happened.

I knew, of course, that I was deliberately setting myself a formidable challenge, the success of which was highly dubious, even given my notorious skill, charm and luck. But the vision of the luscious Sabrina (and, it must be admitted, my instinctive antipathy toward her mother) egged me on. Besides, it was not a huge risk; if I were to fail, there were Sallys and Susans and Sandras galore out there to fall back on . . .

"My turn," Sabrina said as I, with some bemusement, got to my feet. Without moving from her position on the bed she reached for my zipper and worked it down.

"Don't you have to . . ." I stuttered. "Your mother . . ."

"Don't worry about her," Sabrina said, pulling my very stiff member out into the open. "She'll be back."

"Ah . . . she will?"

"Mmmmm . . ." Sabrina purred affirmatively, gazing at my cock.

Earlier that afternoon, as Mrs. Dunbarton stood before us and again delivered herself of her burden of sanctity, emphasizing this time the urgent need for contributions from upright, caring citizens like us to carry on this important work, I again watched Sabrina closely. At first I saw nothing in her eyes but rapt attention and approval; but as her mother went on, those eyes began to lose focus, and then to stray around the room. After a moment she met my fixed gaze. I did not look away. Neither did she. For a long minute those dark brown eyes stared into mine, and while I could not definitely discern in them the ineffable expression I thought I had noted previously, there was one thing there that I was almost certain of: a kind of speculation.

When the presentation was over I joined the small crowd milling about our two hostesses, watching for the moment when the younger of them would be relatively disengaged. Seeing my opportunity, I approached her and introduced myself.

"I'm glad you could come, Mr. Walling," Sabrina said. "I don't think we've ever managed to inveigle you here before, have we?"

"I have been remiss," I admitted. "But I'm very interested in your work. In fact, I'd like to know more about it. Perhaps you and I could get together privately sometime to discuss it further."

"Of course," she said. "Our schedule is rather crowded, but I'm sure Mother and I could find the time to meet with you."

"Actually, I was thinking more along the lines of just you and me," I said.

"Oh, but Mother is much more knowledgeable on the subject, and besides, she is the head of the organization. You would get much more out of talking with her than with me."

Her voice was saying no, but her eyes, those inscrutable brown eyes, were saying something else. I just wasn't too sure what it was.

When someone else came over to talk to her, I excused myself and went in search of the lavatory. The apartment was large and spacious, and I wandered around a bit before finding what I wanted at the end of a long hall. When I emerged, I saw Sabrina standing in the doorway of a room halfway down the corridor.

She stood and waited as I walked toward her, and though I still wasn't sure what she was thinking, I was deliberately not subtle about letting my eyes run over her body as she stood there. She was wearing a white blouse with blue patterning on it and a long, tweed-like skirt which came nearly to her ankles. She showed no reaction to my scrutiny one way or the other.

"I was just getting something from my bedroom," she said as I came up to her.

I gestured at the room behind her. "Is this it?"

"Yes," she said. "Would you like to see it?"

"I certainly would."

She turned and entered the room. Following her in, I closed the door behind me, but she turned again, frowning.

"Why did you close the door?" she asked.

I shrugged. "For privacy?"

"Please open it."

"Okay." I did so. "But when a lady invites me into her bedroom, I usually assume—"

"You assume too much, Mr. Walling," Sabrina said sharply.

"Please call me Steven," I said. "Did you ask me in here just so I could admire the room? It's very nice, but . . ."

"I'm sure you're used to ladies' bedrooms," Sabrina said. "You do have something of a reputation, Mr. Walling."

"Steven," I said. "And I have seen a few bedrooms, yes. Does that excite you, Miss Dunbarton?"

She didn't suggest that I call her Sabrina, nor did she answer my question. "How many?" she said.

"I couldn't count them."

"Promiscuity," she said, sounding suddenly just like her mother, "is not only immoral and, in these days, dangerous, but it also indicates an immaturity and weakness of character."

"On the other hand, it's a lot of fun. Did you bring me in here for a lecture?"

"As you are obviously committed to the path of immorality and hedonism, Mr. Walling. I don't understand why you came here this evening."

"To see you," I said.

She just looked at me. The signals she was giving off were so confusing that I was . . . well, confused. But the only way I could see to play it was to press on.

"Are you really a virgin, Sabrina?" I asked.

A flicker in those bottomless brown eyes. "Isn't that a rather impertinent question, Mr. Walling?"

"Steven," I said. "Yes, it is. Are you?"

"What do you think?" she said.

"I doubt it."

"Oh?" There was no change in her expression. "And why is that?"

I shrugged. "Instinct. And the way you're playing with me now."

"But you know that my mother has brought me up to be—"

"I don't give a damn about your mother," I said. "And frankly, I don't think you do, either."

This brought a flush to her cheeks, and for a moment I thought she might slap me. But she just kept looking at me, and then she said, "Suppose I am a virgin. Would that make me less attractive to you? Or more?"

"Generally I prefer a bit of experience," I said. "But I

have nothing against virginity, provided the lady is ready to give it up."

"You are what they call a debaucher, Mr. Walling."

"And you, Miss Dunbarton, are what they call a cock-teaser."

This time she did slap me. Pretty hard too. I just stood there.

"Damn you," Sabrina said. "Close the door."

I closed the door, turning away from her for a second to do so. When I turned back to her I caught my breath, for she was sitting on her bed in the manner described above, her entire lower body open and exposed to my gaze, asking, "Is this what you want?" . . .

And she was sitting in the same position now, bent slightly forward as she suckled sweetly on my cock, which was fully engulfed by her sensuous lips. Meanwhile her hands worked at my belt, opening it and undoing my trousers and shorts till they fell to the floor. I cooperated by shedding the rest of my clothing, feeling slightly dizzy from the caresses of her mouth and tongue.

And then her mother's voice came again from outside the door.

"Sabrina?"

She took her mouth from me. "Yes, Mother?"

"Our guests are leaving."

"Please say good-bye for me, Mother."

"Sabrina, please . . ."

"I'm busy now," Sabrina said, putting her mouth back where it had been. I gasped, perhaps a bit too loudly.

"Sabrina . . ." The imperious voice was taking on a different quality now, the tone less commanding, almost pleading. "Sabrina, what are you doing?"

"You know what I'm doing, Mother." Her words were somewhat muffled around my cock this time, but then she drew her mouth away again to say, quite clearly now, "I'm sucking cock."

There was what seemed to me a deafening silence outside the door. Then: "I . . . I must . . . I have to say good-bye . . ." Mrs. Dunbarton said faintly.

"I'm sure you'll be back, Mother," Sabrina said.

"Jesus," I said. "What's going on here?"

"Don't mind Mother," Sabrina said. "She won't come in."

"But . . . look," I said, with some difficulty, as her mouth found me again. "I don't want to . . . I mean—"

"You want to fuck me, don't you? Isn't that why you're here?"

"Well . . . yes," I said.

"Then do it," Sabrina said, taking off her blouse. I hesitated, but when the bra came off I suddenly found myself bending over her, pushing her back on the bed as my mouth paid homage to her firm young breasts and her long, stiff red nipples. Our bodies collided and my hands found her long, smooth thighs and followed them up to the luscious curves of her backside. I drew my mouth from her bosom and looked into her glazing eyes. Then our lips met in a searching kiss as she wriggled into position beneath me. I found the soft, moist entrance and probed gently, then more urgently, sliding deeply into her as she moaned against my mouth . . .

"Sabrina?"

Jesus.

"Go away, Mother," Sabrina said loudly, pulling away from my tongue. "I'm fucking now."

"Oh, Sabrina . . . Oh, dear God . . ." Mrs. Dunbarton said. She sounded like she was about to cry.

I almost pulled away, but Sabrina's long legs wrapped around me, her ankles locked behind my back, keeping me where I was. I admit I didn't fight too hard.

Using her encircling legs as leverage, she began a slow but definite up-and-down movement of her hips, and with that stimulus I soon matched her endeavors. Our rhythm gradually got faster, and in a few moments the bedsprings began to squeak. Loudly. I remember thinking vaguely that Sabrina could easily have afforded a sturdier bed; but now I suspect she kept the noisy springs deliberately to torment her mother.

"Sabrina . . ." From outside, a wail of pleading and despair.

"Oh, God!" Sabrina cried—perhaps with more volume than would have been naturally engendered by what I felt was her quite genuine passion. "Oh yes, do it! Fuck me! Yes, fuck me hard!"

"Damn you, Sabrina!" her mother called out, anger now strengthening her voice. "Oh, damn you! Why must you do this to me?"

As little liking as I had for Mrs. Dunbarton, I was not particularly happy to be in the middle of this situation. But on the other hand, Sabrina's fine, supple body, her stiff-nippled breasts against my chest, her sensuous, clutching legs and squirming, eager pussy were more than enough to keep me there.

"Fuck you, Mother!" Sabrina shouted, moving harder, panting and gasping now. "Fuck you, you bitch! You wish it was you, don't you, Mother? Getting fucked silly with a big dick up your twat! Don't you, Mother?"

I was kind of panting myself, but I said, "Wait . . . wait a minute . . . you don't have to . . ."

"Fuck me in the ass!" Sabrina cried out, still moving. "Right up the ass! You hear that, Mother? I'm going to take his cock up my ass! You like that, Mother, you dried-up old cunt?"

This was too much. I stopped moving, but Sabrina didn't, and though in my mind I was getting turned off, my cock didn't want to know about that. Still, I tried to pull away, but Sabrina clung to me with her legs, and I succeeded only in rolling us over so that she was on top. I could have pushed her off by force, but I like to believe that I was too much of a gentleman to do that. So there wasn't much I could do but lie there and watch her bouncing breasts and her squirming body as she moved strongly up and down over my disgracefully dissolute but deliriously happy cock.

"Yes!" Sabrina screamed, her legs pistoning, her torso squirming wildly. "Yes! Yes! Oh, God, yes!!!"

Above her shrieks and the noise of the bedsprings— and the roaring in my ears—I could hear sounds from outside the door. They might have been sobs, or they might have been something else. I wasn't sure.

Sabrina climaxed with the shrillest, loudest scream of all, and she continued to shout out her defiant joy as her spasms of completion set me off, too. Ready to pop, I shot up helplessly into her twisting body.

She collapsed on top of me and we lay there recovering for a few moments. Finally she breathlessly said, "You didn't fuck me in the ass after all. Want to stick around and do it?"

Even in my depleted state, the prospect was definitely tempting; but I could still hear those strange, indistinct sounds outside the door. I decided I didn't really want to know what they were.

"Maybe another time," I said. "Without the audience."

"Oh, no," Sabrina said then, disengaging herself and getting up from the bed with surprising alacrity. "Believe me, it's not nearly as much fun without Mother."

It's always inspiring to witness family values at work.

Chapter 21

T HIS IS A RATHER . . . AH . . . DELICATE QUES-
tion," I said to Miss Greenglass. I was sitting at
my desk, drinking coffee and trying to ignore the
persistent throbbing in my head. "But I'm afraid it
is necessary, at this point, to bring it up. For purposes of clarity you understand." I cleared my throat.
"Exactly what, in your opinion, Miss Greenglass, consti-
tutes a sexual encounter?"

"That question seems not only delicate, but, coming
from you, rather peculiar, Mr. Walling," she replied with
the barest hint of amusement. "If you don't know the answer to that question, I can hardly conceive that there is
anyone in the world who does."

I sighed. "Flippancy does not become you, Miss
Greenglass," I said grumpily, though this statement is
doubly misleading. First of all, I can barely imagine Miss
Greenglass actually being flippant, and second, I cannot
at all imagine anything which would not become her. "I
am speaking, of course, of the terms of our wager," I
went on. "Having come this far, I do not wish to jeopar-

dize my eventual success through one of those technicalities which you are so adept at rooting up. And a, shall we say, circumstance has arisen that raises the question of what—technically speaking—may be considered a valid and mutually acceptable fulfillment of those terms."

"I appreciate your punctiliousness, Mr. Walling," she murmured. "But I think you have at least as clear a conception as I to what actually may define an encounter of that nature. Although we have differed on certain interpretations of the rules of our wager you have never been less than honorable in your conduct pertaining to it. I am certain I can leave this latest matter to your own judgment."

"Damn," I said bleakly. "I was afraid of that."

The perplexity I was feeling, not to mention my headache, was the result of an unfortunate rendezvous on the previous evening with a lady named Tamara Twindle, a supposedly rising young painter of whom you will probably not have heard, unless you are an aficionado of the most esoteric journals of contemporary art and a frequenter of the type of obscure gallery that specializes more in trendiness than quality. I had met this lady, in fact, in one of those very galleries, to which I had gone at the invitation of David Fenster, an artist-acquaintance of mine whose show was opening there. I attended this event neither from loyalty to my friend nor aesthetic curiosity, but rather because this acquaintance had lately acquired a lively blond girlfriend named Tina.

Of course, there was something of an ethical complication involved in taking a friend's woman, but with my usual strength of character I met that problem head-on. "I'm here to seduce your girlfriend," I said to Dave as we shook hands.

"Tina?" he said. "Be my guest."

So much for the ethical problem.

But when I was introduced to Miss Tamara Twindle, my thoughts swiftly betook themselves in a new direction. She was a tall, graceful lady in her mid-twenties with jet-black hair and a truly statuesque figure, shown off to perfection in a thin, low-cut dress. I turned on the charm full blast, and soon we were by ourselves in a corner, deep into what seemed to me a very promising conversation.

"Your work sounds fascinating," I said with as much sincerity and enthusiasm as I could muster. "I'd love to see it. Perhaps I could visit your studio sometime. I happen to know some very prominent art dealers," I added, figuring that if the aforesaid legendary charm didn't persuade her, the possibility of career advancement might.

Whichever it was, it worked. "I'd love to have you come up, Steven," she said, smiling alluringly at me. "Any time you like." Then she surprised me by taking a step back and looking me up and down. Then she surprised me again. "In fact," she said thoughtfully, "I think I would like to paint you, Steven. Would you consider posing for me?"

For a moment I just stared at her. Though I flatter myself that in face and form I am still far from unattractive, I can hardly claim to be the young Adonis type these days. Obviously this was some kind of come-on, which was fine with me, but I played it innocent. "I didn't think you worked from models," I said. "From what you described—"

"Oh, I don't usually," she said. "But occasionally I do like to use the human form as a starting point, as it were. And you have a certain ruggedly mature quality that I'm sure could translate into something quite strong on canvas."

"I see," I said. "Then you would want me to pose in the nude, I take it."

"Of course," Tamara said.

"Of course," I repeated. I couldn't really see myself posing, but I suspected there wouldn't be much actual painting going on once my clothes were off. "Sounds interesting," I said. "Why don't we do it right now?"

"That's a great idea."

Tamara had a studio loft not very far from the gallery, and once there I looked over some of her paintings, trying to make the appropriate noises of approval, while she set up a blank canvas on an easel. "Okay," she said finally, smiling at me. "Why don't you take off your clothes, and I'll change into my painting duds. And then we'll do it."

Certain that I knew what it was we were going to do, I followed this suggestion with alacrity. As I did so, Tamara moved to an alcove where some clothes were hanging. With casual ease she slipped the straps of her satiny, royal blue dress over her shoulders and let it drop to the floor. Beneath it she wore a brassiere and panties the same color as the dress but of even thinner material. Her body was truly magnificent, and I watched it avidly as she hung the dress up and took out an old, paint-stained jumpsuit. Naked now, and gazing at the high, proud thrust of those breasts, the sweeping curve of waist and hips, and the sculpted shapeliness of her legs, I felt myself growing stiff and hard.

With the jumpsuit in her hands, Tamara turned casually to look at me. Her eyes opened wide. "Oh, my!" she said. "Oh, Steven!"

Modestly, I said nothing.

"Oh, dear," Tamara said as the jumpsuit dropped from her hands. I waited confidently for her to approach me in yearning surrender. And then she laid it on me. "Oh, Steven, darling, you do know I'm gay, don't you?"

I stared at her.

"What?" came my brilliant retort.

"I'm gay," she repeated. "I'm a lesbian, Steven." She made a kind of apologetic gesture as I continued to stare. "Well, I thought you knew. I mean, it's no secret or anything. I'm sorry if you . . . Oh, dear. But you do understand, don't you?"

I couldn't believe it. "You mean you really just want to paint me?"

"Yes," Tamara said. "I still do. In fact, now more than ever. That . . . that *thing* you have there is truly classical. I'd really like to do something with it. Just in an artistic sense, you understand."

I understood, but I wasn't exactly happy about it. Even as she spoke, Tamara approached the easel and picked up a piece of charcoal, hastily beginning to sketch. But the classical thing to which she had referred was already beginning to diminish. She had forgotten the jumpsuit, and her scantily clad body was as enticing as ever, but the situation was different now. Despite her evident admiration of my physical attributes, I am not one of those benighted males who believes that all a lesbian needs to turn her around is a good dose of the male member. If she was gay, she was gay, and there wasn't much I could do about it.

Tamara was working feverishly. "Oh, Steven, it's shrinking!" she cried disappointedly. "Oh, no! Can't you keep it hard? Just for a few minutes? Please?"

"Ah, well, I'd like to oblige, Tamara, but I'm afraid it's not exactly—"

"Wait!" she pleaded. "Just let me get the essence of it, then I can . . ." But it wasn't waiting. Tamara groaned in frustration. "Wait," she said again. "Maybe this will help," and she took off her brassiere.

It helped. It helped a lot. Her breasts were slightly whiter than the rest of her body, firm and luscious and large-nippled, and my phallus instinctively came back to attention in tribute. Tamara immediately began sketching again, and the slight sway and jiggle of those breasts as she worked helped to keep me in the condition she wanted. But the knowledge that I was not going to get to play with them worked on me, too, and eventually . . .

"Just another minute," Tamara pleaded. "Oh, damn! Okay, here!" She put down the charcoal and took off her panties. Her breasts swayed as her body bent over, and an abundant tangle of pubic hair was revealed as she slid the garment over her hips and down the long columns of her legs. She stepped out of it to face me naked, and to consolidate the obvious success of this maneuver, she even turned completely around so that I could see all of that marvelous body. Then she quickly picked up the charcoal and went back to work.

This time my recalcitrant member stayed where it was until she was finished. Even after she was done I remained aroused, for in spite of myself my active imagination had begun to conjure up images of that naked body in various positions, and of various activities I would have liked to pursue with it.

"Okay," she said. "I've got the basics down. I can do the painting from this sketch. Of course, if you'd like to come again and pose for the actual painting, that would be—"

"I don't think I could stand it," I said. "Damn it, Tamara, put some clothes on or something. Unless you want to—"

"I don't do it with guys, darling," Tamara said. "Hmm, it's not going down this time, is it?" She moved toward me to give it a closer look. Still naked. "How come?"

"Because your body has got me crazy," I said. "Get dressed, for God's sake."

But she didn't. In fact, she stood there and stretched provocatively. "You like it, huh?" she purred. "Well, I'm sorry, Steven. I didn't mean to tease you."

"What do you think you're doing now?" I asked indignantly. "What the hell's going on here?"

She came closer, but when I instinctively reached out for her she danced back. "No, no," she said mischievously. "No touching, Steven." Standing just out of my reach, she struck a pose, hands on hips, legs wide apart, breasts thrust forward, her erect body swaying just a tiny, tantalizing bit. "But you can look all you like," she said. "And if you want to . . . you know . . . help yourself . . ."

I stared at her. "You're kidding," I said.

She shrugged, which made her breasts jiggle and my cock twitch. "I just don't want you to suffer, darling," she said. And she began to run her hands suggestively over her own body.

"Damn it, I *am* suffering," I said. "But I'm not a damn kid any more, Tamara, and I'm not about to—Oh, Christ." She had gone to her knees now, and was leaning back on her hands, her breasts straining upward, her legs wide enough for me to see right into her vagina. It was as if she was inviting me to try something, but I was pretty sure that if I did I would be met with a kick in the groin. This lady may have liked women, but she obviously got a kick out of teasing men. Now she lay down full length on the floor, twisting her body, caressing herself and rolling from side to side, her legs opening and closing salaciously. It was all I could do to stay where I was, and I have to say that I was tempted to do as she had suggested. But even I have my limits sometimes.

"Stop it, Tamara," I gritted. "You have a great body, but I'm not going to jerk off over you. Now if you'd like to at least give me a hand—"

"A hand?" She stopped wriggling and seemed to consider. At that point I would have settled for a hand—hers, that is. It wasn't what I wanted, but it would have been better than nothing. "No," she said finally. "I couldn't do that, Steven. You understand, darling, don't you?"

"To hell with you," I said. Not without some effort I turned away from her and began to get dressed. I stuffed myself into my pants and with some difficulty zipped myself up. By the time I finished dressing I had subsided enough (I hoped) not to be too conspicuous. Tamara called to me as I went out the door, but I didn't stop. I was angry and frustrated. I thought of calling Tina, but it was very late by now, and anyway it was the vision of Tamara's naked body that was churning around in my mind.

I settled for going to a bar and getting tanked.

Which accounted for my headache the next morning. My conversation with Miss Greenglass was the result of a forlorn notion that perhaps my evening with Tamara, unsatisfactory though it was, might actually be considered a sexual encounter. After all, we had both been naked. But the terms of our wager, however euphemistic their expression, had been understood by both of us to stipulate sexual contact, and there had been, unfortunately, no contact whatsoever. I could not truly convince myself that it met the necessary standards, and so when Miss Greenglass, before even hearing the circumstances, left it to my own conscience, I knew that hope was lost.

So later that day I called Tina.

David had been right. I didn't have to work very hard. "Hey, hi!" she said when I identified myself. "I've been hoping you'd call. Dave said you wanted to screw me."

"Uh . . . well . . . the thought did cross my mind . . ."

"Cool! Come on over! Dave's out right now."

"Um . . . cool," I said.

I can't in all honesty say that the memory of Tamara was completely absent from my thoughts during the pleasant hours I spent that afternoon in Tina's company and in her—and David's—bed, but Tina's own lissome, athletic and extremely talented body did a great deal to dispel it—most of the time. Her blond hair, it turned out, was dyed, but that did not detract from her appeal. She was smaller than Tamara, and thinner, but she was as curvy as a corkscrew, and she was certainly no tease; she was hot and inventive and utterly tireless. When she was underneath me she moved as though the bed was a trampoline, and when she was on top her twisting, bouncing body was a blur of motion. After my first climax—and her third—she brought me to life again with her incredibly knowledgeable mouth and tongue, and then begged me to, as she delicately put it, "ram that big cock up my pussy." Always willing to go to any lengths to oblige a lady, I complied. I was buried deep in Tina's tight, clutching cunt, one hand playing with her clitoris and the other clutching a quivering, hard-nippled breast while she, on knees and elbows, moaned and whimpered and squirmed and pleaded with me to do it harder. Right about that time, David walked in.

I stopped moving, which brought a groan from Tina, but David only grinned at me. "Hey," he said. "Quite a stud there, my man. Yesterday Tamara, and now Tina. Way to go."

I didn't really want to take credit where it wasn't deserved, but I felt this was hardly the time to disabuse him. "Uh, Dave? Could you give us a little privacy here? Just for a few—"

But Dave had other ideas. "Hey, don't mind me, man," he said, and then quite casually he unzipped his jeans, pushed them down—I noticed he wasn't wearing shorts—and sat down on the bed, positioning himself so that Tina could reach his crotch with her mouth. This she swiftly did, taking his cock with one gulp and at the same time squirming her backside as a signal to me to continue with what I had been doing. Which signal, with some amusement, I obeyed.

Four climaxes later—one each for David and me, two for Tina—in the peace of afterglow, I related the true tale of my adventure with Tamara the previous night. When I had finished, David burst out laughing.

"Very funny," I said bitterly.

"It is, man," Dave chortled. "You don't know. Listen, that chick is no dyke, that's just a routine she does. Turns her on or something. Tamara Tease, we call her. You should have stuck around, she'd have come across sooner or later."

I stared at him. "I don't believe it."

"Honest to God," Dave said. "Hey, don't worry. If she likes you, I bet you can still get in?"

But, of course, after Tina, Tamara was now out of bounds until my damn wager was over. My reaction to this might have been more pronounced had not Tina at that moment rolled over and started kissing my body again . . .

But when I got home, just for the hell of it, I called Tamara. "Oh, Steven darling!" she said. "So glad to hear from you! Why did you rush out so quickly last night? Darling, you didn't really think I was gay, did you? That was just kind of a way I have of testing a man's character, you know? And you passed marvelously, Steven. Why don't you come over tonight, darling, and we can really celebrate, okay?"

I took a long, deep breath. And when I said . . .

But never mind what I said. Some things just can't be printed, even in a book like this.

Chapter 22

"UNDER NO CIRCUMSTANCES WHATEVER WILL I accept this invitation," I said to Miss Greenglass. "It will be stuffed shirts and windy speeches and unmitigated dullness. Tell them thanks but no thanks."

"But it's a real honor, Mr. Walling," protested my lovely assistant. "To be asked to share your views with a Senate committee, and then to have lunch at the White House! Surely you can't turn that down."

"Surely I can," I said. "They have these conferences every year. They invite a dozen so-called business experts, everybody gabs a lot without saying anything, they put out an impressive-sounding press release and everybody goes back to business as usual. No thanks, I have better things to do with my time."

Miss Greenglass just looked at me. She can say more by being silent than anybody I know.

I looked down at the letter of invitation on my desk. "This senator is a sleaze anyway," I said. I looked more closely at the signature to see if I could tell whether it was genuine or photocopied. "I wouldn't—"

I stopped, because something had caught my eye. There beneath the signature, at the left-hand margin, neatly typed, were the senator's initials in capital letters, followed by a slash and, in lowercase, the letters "uj."

"Hmmm," I said. "Ah . . . Miss Greenglass. You are no doubt more familiar than I with the arcana of correspondence etiquette. Perhaps you can confirm for me that this means what I think it means."

I circled the symbol with a pencil and held the letter out to her. She came forward and took it, and as she glanced at what I had circled one eyebrow rose very slightly.

"As I'm sure you know, Mr. Walling, these initials constitute a record of who is responsible for this particular piece of correspondence. The capital letters stand for the initials of the person who dictated or originated the letter—in this case, obviously, the senator—while the lowercase initials are those of the person who typed or otherwise processed it."

"And as I'm sure you know, Miss Greenglass," I said, "I have recently arrived at a point in my progress toward winning our most exciting wager at which the initial U holds a certain interest for me. U is not the most common initial in the world, you know. In fact, I know no one personally who possesses it at this time. If, however, our dubious senator has in his employ a young lady who does boast that precious asset . . . well, it might even be worth attending this dull charade just for the chance of . . . getting to know her better, as it were."

Miss Greenglass returned to her desk. "I need hardly point out, Mr. Walling," she said dryly, "that you have no idea whether the lady is indeed young. Or whether the person who typed the letter is even a lady. To state only the most obvious of the many things you don't know about this person."

"That's quite true, Miss Greenglass," I said. "And so the logical thing to do, before committing myself to a day of tedium, is to find out, wouldn't you say? Why don't you call the senator's office for me and see if you can get this U.J. on the phone?"

Miss Greenglass gave me a look which I will not attempt to describe. Her lovely and placid features hardly changed a bit, and yet I knew without question that if I wanted to call the senator's office that day, I would have to do it myself.

Which I did, as soon as Miss Greenglass went out for lunch.

The person who answered the phone was a man, and I could only hope that this was not U.J. But then I realized that a senator probably had a quite extensive office staff. I was right, and I believe I must have spoken to every one of them, trying to explain who I wanted to talk to and why, before someone finally said, "Oh, I think you must want Ursula. Hold on please."

Ursula! "Yes," I said. "That's who I want, all right." But he was already putting me through, and the next voice I heard said, "Hello? This is Miss Jennings. Can I help you?"

She sounded young enough, as far as I could tell. At least she didn't sound old. "Ah," I said. "Miss Jennings. Miss Ursula Jennings, is that right?"

"Yes," she said. "Who is this?"

"This is Steven Walling, Miss Jennings." When this information elicited no discernible enthusiasm, I went on. "You—that is, the senator—wrote me a letter inviting me to the Senate Conference on Business and—"

"Oh, yes," she said. "Yes, Mr. Walling, I remember. If you are calling to accept, I'm afraid we will need your official—"

"Ah, no," I said. I liked her voice, but of course for all I knew she could have been fat as a house, or looked like Bela Lugosi, or been a confirmed lesbian. But I decided to take the chance. "That is, I do expect to attend, but I just want to clear up a few things first. For example, the invitation mentions that the conferees will be having lunch at the White House."

"Yes, sir?"

"And it says here, let me see . . . yes. It says 'Spouses welcome.'"

"Yes," she said, and then added, with a hint of amusement in her tone, "It used to say 'Wives welcome,' but that was considered sexist, assuming that the conferees would all be men, so—"

"Of course," I said. "We wouldn't want to be politically incorrect, would we? But you see, Miss Jennings, I don't have a spouse, or even a wife. So what I was hoping, Miss Jennings, was that you would do me the honor of accompanying me to that luncheon."

There was a long pause.

"I beg your pardon, Mr. Walling?" she said finally.

"Well, I'd hate to be the only one there without a date," I said.

"But—Mr. Walling—we don't know each other. We've never met."

"So it will be a blind date," I said. "I'm not too badlooking, Miss Jennings—may I call you Ursula? And I'm sure you—"

"I know what you look like, Mr. Walling. We have your picture in our files."

"Oh, I see." That knowledge made me a little uneasy, but that's our government. "Well, what do you think?"

"Mr. Walling, I—I don't understand. Why would you want to ask a total stranger to . . . to something like that? I don't . . ."

I wished I could just tell her the truth, but I have learned in the course of my life's adventures that truth, a most commendable virtue in the abstract, is in practice unreliable and can often screw everything up. So I lied a little. "I can't reveal my source," I said, "but I have it on good authority, Miss Jennings, that you are a highly attractive and personable young lady, and I would be grateful for your company. What do you say?"

Another pause. "I—I don't know what to say," Ursula said finally. "It's really most unusual. I don't know what the senator would—"

"Don't worry about the senator," I said. "As this invitation indicates, Miss Jennings—Ursula—I happen to be a most influential businessman, the head of a large and wealthy financial organization. I strongly suspect that nothing would give our senator greater pleasure than to cater to my every whim, unless it was knowing that you were doing that for him."

I thought I heard her suppress a giggle, though I wasn't sure. Still, I took it as an encouraging sign.

"Have you ever been to the White House, Ursula?" I asked.

"Well—only on a tour," Ursula said. "But not—not as a guest or anything. Or even as a guest's date."

I knew I had her now. At least for the date. But I was after more than a date, so I pressed my luck a little. "Then you haven't lived," I said lightly. "They tell me there's nothing like it. Eating in the state dining room, seeing the Oval Office, making love in the Lincoln Bedroom . . ."

Again there was silence, and I half-expected her to hang up. But she only said, "Well . . . I don't think we should plan on going that far, Mr. Walling."

"Call me Steven," I said.

The conference was every bit as dull as I had expected. The senators spouted platitudes, and the businessmen—myself included—gave them back bromides and clichés. Everybody smiled for the cameras and nobody gave a damn about anything that was said. Throughout the long morning I could only keep hoping that Ursula would be worth it.

Well, she was.

Not that she was a great beauty or anything. As a connoisseur, I would have rated her only average in the looks department, though she had a wonderful smile which lit up her whole face when she used it. Her figure was fine, but hardly spectacular. Her longish, light brown hair was neatly tied back, and though she wore no makeup that I was aware of, her bright fresh face did not suffer for lack of it.

She met me, as we had arranged, after the hearing, and we joined the group headed for the luncheon. After some initial reserve, she loosened up and we chatted easily as the official limousine bore us toward the White House. I liked her straightforward manner and her ready laugh, though I had the disquieting suspicion that this girl was nobody's pushover—not even mine.

The President greeted us all cordially, more platitudes were exchanged and we had an elegant if not especially tasty lunch. Afterward the President, along with a couple of his aides, accompanied us on a swift tour of the White House, including the Oval Office. I was hoping we would see the Lincoln Bedroom too, but we didn't. Even if we had, I had no idea how, in the circumstances, I could accomplish there what I had suggested to Ursula. But for some reason I now felt almost certain that if I had any chance with Ursula at all, it would only be in that very location. Maybe it was something in her voice when I had made that semifacetious suggestion. In any case, it seemed futile now, for our group was preparing to leave. And then I had a wild idea.

Who, after all, would be more sympathetic to the cause of seduction, the call of flesh to flesh, the ways of a man chasing a maid, than the current President of the United States of America?

So when it came my turn for a final handshake and a brief word with the President, I said swiftly, "Mr. President, I had hoped to have an opportunity to see the Lincoln Bedroom on my visit. You see, the lady I'm with would love to see it. And I would like to see . . . ah . . . more of the lady . . ."

The President, as I had suspected he would, understood immediately. He stared at me for a moment and then broke into the most genuine smile I had seen from him that day. In a moment he had beckoned to one of his aides and whispered in his ear. In another moment the aide was leading me and a somewhat bewildered Ursula away from the departing group and into an elevator.

We went down a corridor to a door which the aide opened for us. It was indeed the Lincoln Bedroom. A large portrait of the sixteenth President stared down from the wall, and the large four-poster bed was covered with a dark blue spread, Ursula gave out a soft gasp as we entered.

"I will be back for you in an hour, sir," the aide said, with no expression whatever in his voice. "One hour exactly." And he closed the door and left.

Ursula was staring around her. "Steven," she said, wide-eyed. "My God—how did you—"

"I always keep my promises," I said lightly. "Remember? I said we'd eat in the state dining room, see the Oval Office and—"

"I remember—what you said," Ursula interrupted. "But you're not serious—I mean . . ."

"Of course I am." I took a step toward her. She backed away.

"Hold on," Ursula said. "I mean, really, Steven . . . Even if we knew each other better—which we don't—I mean, this is the Lincoln Bedroom, for God's sake . . ."

"I don't think Lincoln will mind," I said, taking another step forward. "He's dead, you know."

Ursula stepped back. "They say his spirit still walks here sometimes," she said, almost whispering. "In this room . . ."

"Only at night," I said. "Ursula, we only have an hour."

"Steven, really, be sensible. We can't—" She stopped suddenly and stood still, as if listening to something. "Oh, my God!" she breathed after a moment. "Did you hear that?"

"Hear what?" I said.

"I thought I heard . . . a voice . . ."

"What voice? I didn't—" But I stopped, because she was listening again.

"Oh, my God," Ursula said again. "It can't be . . ." Her face was very strange.

"What is it?" I said, puzzled.

"He said . . . it said . . ." I could hardly hear her. She stopped, swallowed, then whispered, "He said it was all right."

My first thought was that she was crazy; my second was that she was making it up because she really wanted to do it. I never actually thought there was really any-thing—anybody—there. Well, yes, I admit I looked around pretty sharply, but that was just reflex . . . or something.

In any case, when I stepped toward her this time she didn't retreat, and when I took her in my arms to kiss her she by no means resisted. And then she was kissing me back, her arms around me, her mouth opening softly under mine . . .

And then she gave a sudden gasp and her body stiff-ened.

"What's the matter?" I said.

"Something touched me," Ursula whispered. "Oh. Oh . . ." The stiffness went out of her now, and her body melted against me. "Oh, yes . . ." And she kissed me again. Passionately.

I didn't know what was going on, but it was all right with me. Our tongues dueled, and the pressure of her body brought my cock to attention swiftly. My hands roamed her back before homing in on the tiny catch at the back of her dress, and then pulling down the zipper. She made a tiny whimpering sound against my mouth, but didn't try to stop me as I found the clasp of her brassiere and opened it.

But when I broke the kiss and stepped back to slide the

dress from her, she crossed her arms protectively over her chest. The look in her wide eyes was stranger than ever.

"He . . . it's as if he's watching," she breathed. And then she made a quarter-turn to face the picture on the wall. She drew in her breath sharply, and then, after a moment, her hands came down, and with them the top of her dress. The brassiere fell to the floor, and she was naked to the waist.

Her breasts were not large, but they were lovely, with prominent pink nipples which stiffened as I watched. With another small gasp she brought her hands to her breasts and began to caress herself, making those nipples even harder, still with her eyes on the picture.

This was getting kind of eerie; I felt almost like an intruder. I shook off the feeling. "Let me do that," I said, moving up behind her and reaching around her body. She allowed my hands to replace hers, and in fact pushed back against me, until I knew she could feel my erection pressing against her buttocks through our clothes. I kissed the side of her neck as I savored the touch of her sweet breast flesh and throbbing nipples. She moaned softly in response but still kept her eyes on the portrait.

After a moment I slid one hand off her breast and down over her smooth stomach, then under the waistband of the dress, which still clung around her hips. My fingers snuck inside her panties and moved slowly down . . . through a soft patch of pubic hair . . . down . . .

"Ohhhh!" Ursula gasped. "Ohh, my good God . . . ohh . . ." Her body stiffened, and then began to writhe gently against me as my fingers carefully advanced . . . searching, probing, stroking . . .

She had still been gazing at that picture, but now her head fell back and her eyes closed. Her breath was coming faster, and louder. For a few more minutes I continued to stroke her clitoris with one hand while caressing her breast with the other; then, without removing my hands, I started moving her toward the bed. She followed my lead as if in a daze, and though the journey was slow we eventually got there. I managed to maneuver her dress up and off before easing her down onto the bed, and then took a moment to swiftly divest myself of my own clothing, while admiring the delicious sight of Ursula in nothing but panties, stockings and garter belt. It was a delectable vision, and I was glad to see that she was old-fashioned enough not to wear panty hose on an occasion such as this. The number of ladies possessed of such good taste is, alas, rapidly diminishing in this modern world.

The sight was made even more arousing, if somewhat disconcerting, by the way in which her body was now squirming sensually as she lay on her back, her hands once again caressing her pink-tipped breasts. As I watched, her knees rose, her stockinged legs spread wide apart with her feet braced against the bed, and her hips began to move up and down, rhythmically, slowly at first but gradually picking up speed. It was as if someone was . . . but there was no one there. Not that I could see, anyway. Her heavy breathing turned to panting, her pants to moans, her moans to cries . . .

I couldn't stand it anymore. I moved to join her on the bed—and if I moved a little carefully, surely it was not because I expected to meet any impediments; perhaps I'm just not quite as young and springy as I used to be. But Ursula pulled away, and I had a sudden apprehension that perhaps I was not going to get lucky in the Lincoln Bedroom after all. But she only rolled onto her hands and knees, and crouched there—again facing that large portrait on the other side of the room.

"Oh, yes, do it . . ." she cried breathlessly. "Ohh, God, yes . . . do it now . . . now . . ."

Okay, so I wasn't sure who she was talking to—I was the only corporeal person there, as far as I could see. So I got up behind her, pulled down her panties and proceeded to do it. She moaned loudly as my straining cock found the entrance to her very moist vagina, and we both moaned still more loudly as it pushed its way in, gradually sounding the depths of her squirming tightness. My hands went beneath her to grasp her swaying breasts, and I held on to them until I was completely immersed in the warmth of her.

Then I began to sway back and forth, and she swayed with me, her moans deepening to abandoned grunting sounds which drove my passion still higher. Her shapely stockinged legs rubbing against my naked ones felt like an electrical current dancing on my flesh. I knew that she was still gazing at the portrait, but I didn't give a damn. I knew I was doing it with Ursula and she was doing it with me, and that I wished we could go on doing it until every damned President in history rose out of the grave and cheered us on.

But of course we couldn't. I thrust harder and harder into her squirming body, and her cries turned to groans of approaching climax, and I clasped her breasts and licked her back and gave her everything I had, and as she screamed and shuddered and bucked again and again, I let myself go too and we collapsed together.

We lay still, saying nothing until we had regained our breath, and then Ursula suddenly sat up and looked at me as if she were waking from a trance.

"Oh, my God," she said. Then she got up and began to dress. I noticed she kept her back to the picture.

I glanced at my watch. "We still have a little time," I said. "If you—"

Her face was slightly red, whether from exertion or embarrassment I was unable to tell. "I've never done anything like that before in my life," she said softly, turning so I could zip up the back of her dress.

I did so reluctantly, sitting on the edge of the bed. "Neither have I," I said and, for fear of misinterpretation, added, "Well, not in the Lincoln Bedroom anyway."

Ursula smiled at me, but it was a distant smile. I felt that we were still strangers, despite our recent intimacy. And then, to my utter astonishment, Ursula, now fully dressed, got down on her knees and, with no preliminaries, took my cock into her mouth. It hardened again quickly. I felt the stroking of a warm tongue and the moving touch of soft, caressing lips. These two inducements are always quick to capture my attention.

Her renewed enthusiasm was a surprise, but by no means an unwelcome one. I have increased the fortune I inherited by never neglecting a dividend, and I wasn't about to start at that moment. Finding a comfortable chair not far from my backside, I maneuvered us toward it as best I could without causing Ursula to break the exquisite suction she had set up. Having already accomplished my essential goal and advanced the wager, I could now give myself over to the pure luxury of my surroundings and the delightful treatment I was receiving from my new acquaintance. Reaching my goal, I gratefully sank my buttocks into the well-upholstered seat. The floor was deeply carpeted, so there was no fear that Ursula would be uncomfortable. Having so recently come, I settled in for a long, leisurely sucking.

It quickly proved, however, that Ursula's technique was very advanced. By twisting her lips on each descent she produced a wrenchingly pleasant sensation that caused my cock to jump each time she completed a stroke with my cock buried deep in her excellent mouth. Running my fingers through her hair, I concentrated on the twin goals of savoring her expertise and trying to make the experience last. A man can take just so much, and before I would have believed it possible I was on the point of coming again. When she lifted her eyes to mine, the sight of her hollowed cheeks and moist lips bent to the task of giving me pleasure, forced the crisis, and I let go once more, this time into her welcoming throat.

Delicately dabbing at the corner of her mouth with a handkerchief, she smiled at me more warmly now as she rose to her feet. "I didn't want you to think I was neglecting you," she said.

What a strange woman. But there was no time now to do anything but dress myself, which I had just finished doing when the aide came back to show us out.

As I followed Ursula out of the room, I glanced back for a final look at the Lincoln portrait. For just a quick moment I could have sworn . . . But no, it must have been a trick of the light.

When I arrived home and told Miss Greenglass about my latest bit of progress, I was gratified to find that even she was somewhat surprised. Of course she never doubted the veracity of my narratives, but in this case she could not suppress a certain curiosity about how I had managed to carry out my task in such an unusual and august location. I explained, rather smugly I must admit, that I had been aided and abetted in my cause by the President of the United States himself.

I didn't say which one.

Chapter 23

VARIOUS WISE MEN THROUGHOUT THE COURSE of history have made the profound observation that when a man is granted the fulfillment of his most delicious dream, the mischievous gods in charge of such things are wont to bestow the gift in such a way as to render it tasteless. Or at least to diminish its savor. I had at times looked upon this declaration as being somewhat overly cynical, and highly questionable. But that was before I encountered the Davenport twins.

Surely among the most delectable dreams or fantasies of every heterosexual male is the one involving twins—preferably beautiful, certainly sexy, undoubtedly voluptuous, absolutely uninhibited and very likely blond. Such were the Davenport sisters. And as far as I personally was concerned, that was only the beginning. Unbelievably, almost gloriously, as if they had been put on earth for my purposes alone, the names that their thoughtful parents had given to these gorgeous creatures were (are you ready for this?) Vinora and Winona—or, as they were more familiarly called by themselves and their friends, Vinnie and Winnie.

Admittedly, this delightful circumstance did not fall miraculously into my lap just at the ideal moment, which would have been after my highly satisfying if somewhat mystical afternoon with Ursula; that would have been carrying good fortune too far. I had become aware of the Davenports some time earlier, while attending an exhibition of foreign automobiles at the urging of an acquaintance of mine who wanted me to acquire his company. In addition to the cars, the exhibition also featured the usual generous sprinkling of scantily clad models whose purpose was to stand around the automobiles looking sexy—the idea being, I suppose, to make the buyers believe that such females came along with such vehicles, or at least would be magically attracted to their owners. The fact was that I was not in the least interested in buying an automobile company, and had attended only because my acquaintance had promised to introduce me to some of the models, in particular a spectacular pair of twin sisters whose names, he alleged, were Vinnie and Winnie. I could hardly credit this stroke of luck to anything but fate. I agreed to meet the young ladies and, incidentally, to listen to his sales pitch as part of the bargain.

As soon as I set eyes on this duo I had no further interest in automobiles, or even in the other models—almost none, anyway. They were indeed spectacular, two long-haired voluptuous blondes with figures that caused my eyes to light up and various other parts of my anatomy to come to attention. My company-president friend waved them over to us, and left me in their company. From what ensued I suspected he must have alerted them in advance to the fact that he wanted me to be . . . impressed.

"Hi," they said in unison. "We're Vinnie and Winnie!"

"So I understand," I said.

"She's Vinnie," one of them said.

"She's Winnie," the other one said.

"We're twins," Vinnie said.

"Identical," Winnie said.

"I can see that," I said.

"He's cute," Vinnie said.

"Nice eyes," Winnie said.

"Nice teeth," Vinnie said.

"Nice buns," Winnie said.

"How big do you think he is?" Vinnie said.

"At least seven inches," Winnie said.

"I bet more," Vinnie said.

"Eight?" Winnie said.

"Eight at least. Maybe nine," Vinnie said.

"Should we ask him?" Winnie said.

"He'd only lie," Vinnie said.

"Guys always do," Winnie said.

"We'll find out soon enough, I bet," Vinnie said.

"You think he likes us?" Winnie said.

"Guys always like us," Vinnie said.

"I believe that," I said.

"You better," Vinnie said.

"Because it's true," Winnie said.

"Because we're so sexy," Vinnie said.

"And gorgeous," Winnie said.

"And blond," Vinnie said.

"And we love fucking," Winnie said.

"And sucking," Vinnie said.

"And everything," Winnie said.

"Um . . . well, that's wonderful," I said. "That's just . . . um . . . wonderful."

At least it sure as hell seemed that way to me at the time.

But of course it wasn't that simple. At that point I had just gotten through my night with Phyllis and was now looking for a Q, so I had to find a way to put Vinnie and Winnie on hold for a while. Without managing to acquire an automotive company in the process.

And there was another problem.

"Uh . . . how does one tell you ladies apart?" I said.

"One doesn't," Vinnie said.

"One can't," Winnie said.

"There's no way," Vinnie said.

"We're identical," Winnie said.

"Like two peas," Vinnie said.

"Uh-uh . . ." I said. "And these things that you mentioned, that you like doing so much—do you do them . . . together, or do you sometimes—"

"Oh, we do everything together," Vinnie said.

"Everything," Winnie said.

"Always," Vinnie said.

"We're twins, you know," Winnie said.

"Yes, I know," I said.

"You want to take us to bed?" Vinnie said.

"Well of course he does," Winnie said.

"I know that, silly," Vinnie said. "I was just being polite."

"Of course," I said. "I'd love to. But I'm, uh . . . going out of town for a while, so it will have to be another time . . ."

"Anytime," Vinnie said.

"We'll be around," Winnie said.

"Just give us a call," Vinnie said.

Fine. Great. But there was that other problem. Most men thrust into such a situation, so to speak, would not have to worry about keeping track of who was who, but I obviously did if I wanted to keep faith with the terms of my wager. And, for reasons I did not completely understand, I did want to. There had been other occasions on which it would have been easy—and convenient—to fudge those terms just a little, without Miss Greenglass suspecting a thing. But thus far I had refrained from taking advantage of those situations, and I intended to go on refraining. Man of honor that I am, I admit I might have been tempted at times, had it not been for that unfathomable woman.

Though her opinion of my character was, let us say, less than admiring in many areas, she did have an inexplicable trust in my integrity and honesty, at least as far as our wager was concerned. And this was a trust that, wisely or foolishly, I chose not to violate, even if it meant losing that wager.

But I didn't intend to lose.

Nonetheless, I had a problem. Here were Vinnie and Winnie, who, as they made abundantly clear, did everything together. And, presumably, simultaneously. Obviously I could have both of them, and God knows I wanted both of them. But to be true to the wager, I would have to do Vinnie first. Vinnie first, Winnie second. But that wasn't all. Once I'd done Winnie, I could not then go back and do Vinnie again. Vinnie first, Winnie second, and stop. Now how was I supposed to manage that with two hot, sexy, gorgeous girls in my bed at the same time?

And furthermore, two hot sexy gorgeous girls who I couldn't even begin to tell apart?

"Just one thing, ladies," I said. "Uh . . . could we do it one at a time, perhaps?"

"One at a time?" Vinnie said.

"Separately?" Winnie said.

"Yes," I said. "Separately. Just for a change. Call it an experiment."

"Oh, we couldn't do that," Winnie said.

"We do everything together," Vinnie said.

"We're sisters, you know," Winnie said.

"Twins," Vinnie said.

"Identical," Winnie said.

"Yes," I said. "I get the picture."

Okay, fine. I did get the picture and it was wavering with the movement of double vision. I would just have to be careful.

Very, very careful.

By the time I had gotten through Quintana, Rachel, Sabrina, Tina and Ursula—all of whom I hope my faithful readers will remember as pleasantly as I do—my friend had sold his company to someone else, so I wasn't sure the twins would still be available. But I needn't have worried.

Two hours after I called them they were at my door, and ten minutes after that they were in my bedroom.

"We thought you'd never call," one of them said, unbuttoning her blouse. I had no idea now who was who.

"We thought you'd forgotten about us," the other said, kicking off her shoes.

"We didn't *really* think that, though," the first one said, pulling her blouse off.

"That's not very likely," the other one said, dropping her skirt.

"Because we're so sexy and all," the first one said, opening her bra.

"And gorgeous," the other one said, pushing her panties down.

"And we love to fuck," the first one said, starting on my clothes now that she was naked.

"And suck," the other one said.

And so on . . .

When we were all naked, the first thing I did was to walk slow circles around them, examining them very closely.

Very closely.

For one thing it was fun. But the main reason was to see if I could find something somewhere by which to tell them apart. A mole. A scar. A freckle. Anything.

Nothing.

High and firm of breast, taut and pink of nipple, smooth and flat of belly, round and tight of buttock, shapely and sweeping of thigh, curvy and flexible of calf . . . and not a mark, not a spot, not a blemish anywhere. On either of them.

On the one hand it was discouraging; but on the other hand, this examination made me so randy that I began wishing they were triplets.

"All right," I said finally. "Vinnie first."

"Why?" one of them said.

"Uh . . . I like to do things in order," I said. "Vinnie first, then Winnie. Okay?"

"Why don't we toss a coin?" one of them said.

"It's easier this way. Now who's Vinnie?"

"I am," one said.

"No, I am," the other one said.

And they both grinned at me.

"You can't both be Vinnie," I said, trying to hold on to my patience as well as my passion.

"Why not?" one said.

"We're twins, it's like we're one and the same person," the other said.

"We're both Vinnie."

"And we're both Winnie."

"No, you're not," I said, feeling silly. "Come on, girls. Who's who here?"

"But we both want to be first," one said.

"And neither of us wants to be second," the other said.

"Why not both at once?" the first one said.

Both at once. Why not indeed? Every man's dream. "No," I said. "Not both at once. No. It can't be done. No."

"But why not? It's such fun that way!" one of them said.

"Damn," I said. To say that I was strongly tempted to just jump in and take my chances would be an understatement. But then I recalled what had happened with Phyllis—and in that case I *hadn't* been breaking any rules. I didn't want a repeat of that.

I took a deep breath. I had to take a different kind of risk.

"Look, ladies," I said, trying to keep my voice steady. "I'm serious about this. I can't explain why, but it's important to me that we do this properly, okay? Now if we can't—if I don't know who is who here—then I'm going to have to call it off. Really. God knows I don't want to." Now *there* was an understatement. "But I will," I said.

"So please—I'm begging you—which one of you is Vinnie?"

Long pause.

"Okay," one of them said finally, sighing and pointing to the other. "She's Vinnie."

"Is that true?" I asked the designated Vinnie.

She nodded. "Yep. I'm Vinnie. She's Winnie."

I had to believe them. "Okay. Now I have to be able to tell you apart, so . . ."

I looked around and seized on my discarded necktie. Picking it up, I approached Winnie, who was closest, and used it like a ribbon to tie back her long flowing hair. "There," I said. "That's better. Now I can keep track of who's who."

"How does it look?" Winnie said.

"It looks dorky," Vinnie said.

"It does not," I said. "It looks fine."

"Where's the mirror?" Winnie said.

"In the bathroom," I said.

"I gotta go look," Winnie said.

"I'm going too," Vinnie said.

"Hold on," I said. "Vinnie, why don't we—"

"Be right back," Vinnie said.

And they left.

Well, they said they did everything together.

But in a minute Vinnie was back. At least I assumed it was Vinnie. Her hair flowed free and framed her lovely face. As she crossed the room toward me her hair and all the other parts of her moved and swiveled and bounced and jiggled. By the time she reached me my head was pounding. I grabbed her and we kissed, then fell across my bed with our mouths still fused. Her tongue probed deeply into my mouth, exploring every corner of it, while our bodies ground together. My hands moved swiftly over her, and then her legs opened for me.

Though I wanted to hold off taking her and spend more time doing all sorts of delicious things to her delicious body, her urgency—and mine—told me foreplay would have to come later. When it would be afterplay. Or whatever.

Crouching above her, between her raised and outstretched thighs, I reached down to find the soft warmth of her, moving forward, almost touching.

And then an indignant voice said, "Hey!"

I looked up. And there was—the other one. With her hair flowing free and framing her lovely face.

I leapt up off the bed as though shot from a catapult. And not a second too soon.

"Damn!" I shouted. "What the—You're not Vinnie!"

"Of course she's not," the other one said. "I'm Vinnie."

The girl on the bed smiled mischievously and shrugged. "What the hell," she said. "It was worth a try."

I was speechless. I had come that close—way too close—to taking the wrong girl! As it was, it was only by a technicality that I hadn't actually had sex with her. But that technicality was important. It counted.

I only hoped Miss Greenglass would agree with me.

"You cheat!" Vinnie said.

"Well, why should you have all the fun?" Winnie said.

"You can have your fun later," Vinnie said.

"You can just bet I will," Winnie said.

"Hold it!" I said. "The way I feel right now, nobody is going to have fun." And indeed this close call had diminished my passion. Visibly.

"Oh yes we will," Vinnie said. And she came over to me. Moving exactly as her sister had moved. Then she reached me and plastered herself against me from shoulders to knees, and moved some more.

Well, maybe we would.

We were on the bed. I was lying down, Vinnie was bending over me, completing the restoration of my passion by brushing her long hair over my crotch. I think I was moaning. Winnie was sitting next to us, observing.

Then Vinnie's mouth was devouring me, slipping and sliding and slurping. I was squirming and clutching at the sheets.

"She's good, isn't she?" Winnie said.

"She's . . . she's great!" I gasped.

"Mmmm-hmmm," Vinnie said.

"I'm better," Winnie said.

"Nnhh-nnhh," Vinnie said.

"You'll see," Winnie said.

"Jesus Christ," I said.

"She loves that," Winnie said. "Can't you tell?"

"Yesss, mmm, I can, and so do I," I said. My voice was muffled because my head was buried between Vinnie's thighs. I was reciprocating. I felt it was my duty. It tasted above and beyond the call of duty.

"You love that, don't you, Vinnie?" Winnie said.

"You know I do," Vinnie moaned.

"I love it too," Winnie said.

"Wait your turn," Vinnie said.

"Why wait?" Winnie said. She tapped me on the shoulder. "Can I do what Vinnie did while you're doing it to her?" Winnie said.

I raised my head briefly. I gathered my strength.

"Not now," I said. "Please. Not now. Okay?"

"Oh, damn," Winnie said.

"I agree," I said.

"Is it in?" Winnie said.

"Oh yeah, it's in," Vinnie said.

"Is it good?" Winnie said.

"Hell, yes!" Vinnie—Oh, no. Sorry. That was me.

"How does it feel?" Winnie said.

"Ohhhmigod . . ." Vinnie said.

"That good?" Winnie said.

"Ohh migod . . ." Vinnie said.

"I told you he'd be big," Winnie said.

"Sooo big . . ." Vinnie said.

"Good stamina too," Winnie said.

"Oh sweet mother Mary," Vinnie said.

"Are you gonna come?" Winnie said.

"Damn lordy fucking Jesus shit daddy," Vinnie said.

"Oh, she's gonna come all right," Winnie said.

"Yeeessssssss," Vinnie said. "Yesss. Nooowwwwwwww-www . . ."

Vinnie was experiencing what inspired the Star Spangled Banner. In technicolor. There were bombs bursting in air, rockets' red glare, the whole red, white and blue bit, and it was all happening between her legs. It was like firecrackers and the Fourth of July for her. For me too.

"That's the girl," Winnie said.

"Me too," I said.

"You're not a girl," Winnie said.

"You know what I mean," I said.

"It's about time," Winnie said. "It's my turn now."

*   *   *

I barely had the strength to roll Vinnie off me. I was pant-ing like a bellows.

"My turn," Winnie said again.

"I think . . . we'll have to . . . wait a while . . ." I gasped, lying helplessly on my back.

"Oh, don't worry," Winnie said. "I'll get you ready again."

"In no time," Vinnie said.

"Lickety-split," Winnie said.

"First I have to go to the bathroom," Winnie said.

"Me too," Vinnie said.

"Don't you run away," Winnie said.

"We'll be right back," Vinnie said.

"No!" I said, trying to get up. "No! Not again! Not to-gether! I'll never—"

But it was too late.

Chapter 24

WHEN THE TWINS CAME BACK FROM THE bathroom this time I knew I was in trouble. Four bouncing, bobbling breasts, four luscious shapely legs, two freely swinging blond manes, and two wicked, lubricious, determined smiles. And, of course, once again I had no idea who was who.

In spite of my recent activity with Vinnie, the renewed sight of those two splendid bodies revived my lust, as well as my apprehension. During their brief absence I had consoled myself with the consideration that I could, after all, go ahead and enjoy myself with whomever of the two presented herself as Winnie, without dire consequences. If it was the real Winnie, fine—I would be that far ahead (although I would have to avoid doing it with Vinnie again afterwards). If it turned out to be Vinnie, that could be considered simply a continuation of our initial encounter, after which I would be free either to do Winnie or some other W lady . . .

Besides, I figured that Winnie, having given way to

her sister earlier, would now be so eager for her turn that she wouldn't wish to play identity games at this point.

Wrong again.

"We both want to play now," one said.

"With you," the other said.

"Together," the first one said.

"No, no," I said, foolishly holding up a pillow as if for protection, as they advanced to the bed. "Not together. No!"

"We do everything together," one said.

"We're twins, you know," the other said.

"I know, I know," I said. "Which one is Winnie?"

"I am," one said.

"No, I am," the other said.

"We both are," the first one said.

"That sounds familiar," I said.

By this time they had reached the bed, and as they leapt for me I sprang up as though the sheets were on fire, while the thought flashed through my mind that somehow I had been brought to an incredibly low point. Here I was actually trying to avoid sex with two magnificent, naked and eager young females! What kind of spell did Miss Greenglass have over me anyway? Was winning that wager really worth this?

But what the hell, I had come this far . . .

"Look, ladies," I said, "much as I'd enjoy it, I can't do it with both of you. Not together." I realized I was now holding the pillow over my crotch, the condition of which betrayed the fact that I was ready to do it with somebody. I felt silly. Doggedly I pressed on. "I can do it with one of you," I said. "If it's Vinnie again, fine. But Winnie would be better for me, and it *is* her turn . . . So who's Winnie?"

"I am," one said.

"You are not," the other said.

"I am too," the first one said.

"Don't believe her," the other one said.

"Okay," I said. "Eenie meenie minie moe." I nodded at the one my finger had stopped at. "You," I said. I was taking a chance, but at least I wasn't breaking any rules. I could find out who she was later, I hoped.

The one I was pointing at grinned and jumped at me. The other one cried out in protest. "Hey! That's not fair! She's already had her turn!"

Aha.

Vinnie was sitting on the edge of the bed, watching.

"I can do that better," Vinnie said.

"No way," Winnie said.

"Ask him," Vinnie said.

"Didn't I do it better?" Vinnie said.

"Jesus," I said. "I don't know . . . I . . . I think it's a tie . . ."

"Watch this," Winnie said. I was on top of her, recruiting my strength with an interlude of slow, almost dreamy intercourse. It was my way of recovering from some of the wild contortions she'd been putting me through. Exciting and ecstatic as those activities had been, it was almost equally pleasurable to take her in this easy, rhythmic manner, while her fabulous body rose and fell gently in time with my strokes—writhing and twisting and undulating sweetly beneath me.

"Watch this," she said, but what she did then was not something to be seen, but to be felt. And I felt it—all along my overworked, happy penis. She was doing something with her vaginal muscles, controlling and contract-

ing them in such a way as to impart a squeezing sensation
that traveled with a rippling effect along the length of my
cock.

"Oh Christ," I said.

"Vinnie can't do that," Winnie said.

"I can so," Vinnie said.

"No you can't," Winnie said. Still doing it. "You know
you can't."

"I can. I've been practicing," Vinnie said.

"You still can't do it like I can," Winnie said.

"How do you know?" Vinnie said.

"Guys tell me," Winnie said.

"Guys lie," Vinnie said.

"Not about this," Winnie said.

"How about it?" Vinnie said to me. "Didn't I do it for
you?"

"Um . . . I don't remember," I said. A lie. If she had
done it, I'd have remembered.

"Ha!" Winnie said.

"I'll do it for you when you're done with her, then,"
Vinnie said.

I had to avoid that at all costs. "I won't have the
strength," I said. I speeded up my strokes to curtail this line
of conversation. With what Winnie was doing, I wasn't
going to hold out. I began to pump her harder and faster,
and Winnie was soon moaning and clutching me with
arms and legs, her body bucking satisfactorily.

"Oh good, she's close," Vinnie said. "Hurry up."

"Shut up, Vinnie," Winnie panted.

"She gets short-tempered when she's coming," Vinnie
said.

"Fuck you," Winnie said.

"That's how you can tell us apart," Vinnie said.

"Drop dead, silly bitch!" Winnie shouted. Her body was twisting wildly and arching so strongly she lifted me off the bed, her inner muscles still rippling more spasmodically now. "Ohhhh YEEESSSSSS . . ."

And she came just in time. I couldn't have waited a second longer.

"Now me," Vinnie said.

"I can't," I said. "I can't. No more. I'm exhausted."

"I bet I can fix that," Vinnie said.

"I bet we can fix it together," Winnie said.

"We like to do things together," Vinnie said.

"We're twins, you know," Winnie said.

"I know," I said. God, did I know. "But I can't. I'm sorry."

"What's wrong with him?" Vinnie said.

"Maybe he's gay," Winnie said.

"Gee," Vinnie said. "He seemed pretty straight up to now."

"Well, you can never really tell," Winnie said.

"That's true," Vinnie said.

"Some gay guys don't even know they're gay," Winnie said.

"Did you know you were gay, Steven?" Vinnie said.

"I'm not gay," I said.

"It's okay," Winnie said. "There's nothing wrong with being gay."

"I'm not—" I said, but then it occurred to me that this was a way to avoid further risk of messing up my bet. "Okay," I said. "You're right, I'm gay. Sorry, girls. It's been nice, but, well, you know how it is."

"That's okay," Vinnie said, patting me consolingly.

"Don't worry about it," Winnie said. She began to pat too. Patting me, stroking me, giving me little consoling kisses. Both of them. Pretty soon things were stirring again.

"Ohh look!" Vinnie said.

"I see," Winnie said.

"Wow," Vinnie said.

"Maybe he's not gay after all," Winnie said.

And the patting and the stroking and the kissing started to move downward.

"No!" I said. "I mean yes. I am. Gay. And I have to stop now. God damn it." And with a reluctance I cannot even begin to describe, I pulled away from them and slid out of the bed.

It may have been the most difficult thing I've ever done.

"Gee," Vinnie said. "He doesn't look gay."

"Not now, he doesn't," Winnie said.

"Believe me, ladies," I said, forcing myself to start putting my clothes on, "if I were ever to turn straight, you are the ladies I would do it with."

"We know that," Vinnie said.

"That goes without saying," Winnie said.

"Guys find us very sexy," Vinnie said.

"Straight guys, that is," Winnie said.

"I'll take your word for it," I said.

I had come to the point in my challenge that I'd been brooding about from the start.

I had to find an X.

Faithful readers of this chronicle may recall my mentioning that I had, long ago, known a young lady whose father, a classical scholar, had blessed her with the name of Xanthippe—although she preferred to pursue her career as an exotic dancer under the name of Tiffany. Who could blame her? After our brief but intense liaison I had lost track of the lady. I had blithely mentioned her to Miss Greenglass at the inception of our wager, and since that time I had been making sporadic, unsuccessful attempts to track her down. The time was growing uncomfortably short; I had just a little over a month left of the six months that I was allowed—and ladies with names beginning with X are not particularly plentiful.

Xanthippe's father, I recalled, had been a professor at Columbia University, but when I called the Classics Department I was informed that he had retired a few years ago. When I inquired of his present address, I was told they couldn't give out that information. And though I exerted all my charm, and even hinted at a bribe—two methods which are generally quite effective, especially the latter—nothing could change their mind.

I was desperate. So I called the cops. Actually one cop, Angela, an old friend of mine who might be willing to do me a favor. But there were strings. There were always strings.

"Been a long time, Steven," she said when I called her.

"I know," I said. "I've been kind of busy. Listen, Angela, I need a favor."

"Me too," she said. "A big hard one."

Memories stirred my blood, but I shut them out. "I just want to locate somebody," I said. "An ex-professor at Columbia. They won't give me his address, but if it's a police matter . . . Okay?"

"Easy enough," Angela said. "Why don't you come around and see me tonight and we'll talk about it. In bed."

Tit for tat, so to speak. I took a breath. "Angela, I can't," I said. "Not right now. I'll have to owe you one, okay?"

"Am I hearing right?" she said. "Is this Steven Walling, the stud of the stock market? The boffing businessman? The wolf of Wall Street? The Casanova of commerce? The fuckmaster of finance? The—"

"Cut it out," I interjected. Angela was sometimes too cute for her own good. Sexy as hell, though. "I'll make it up to you, I promise."

"Now," she said. "Make it up to me now. Right now."

"Right now? On the phone?"

"Right now. Right here. In the middle of the squad room."

"Angela," I said. "You're home. I called you at home."

"No," she said, and her voice was huskier. "Forget that. I'm in the middle of the squad room. At my desk. And all the guys are looking at me. I'm pulling up my skirt, Steven. I've got my legs up on my desk and I'm pulling my skirt all the way up over my panties and spreading my legs. All the cops are watching."

Angela, I forgot to mention, is a little kinky. It's a theory of mine that you have to be at least a little kinky to be a cop. "Okay," I said. "Fine." Whatever it took—as long as I didn't have to actually do it with her. Not that I wouldn't have liked to. In fact, thinking of Angela and envisioning her with her skirt up and those fine legs stretched out was having an effect on me. I adjusted myself in my chair.

"They're all watching me, Steven," Angela went on. "I can see their pants bulging as they watch me. I'm stroking my thighs, Steven. I'm touching my pussy through my panties, and they're all watching and going crazy. They want me, Steven."

"I believe it," I said. I believed she was doing what she said, too, although not in the squad room. I could hear her breathing getting heavier, less even. I recalled her sexy brown eyes, her quirky mouth, her short dark hair, and the way her taut round breasts pushed out against the starched blue of her uniform.

"Wait a minute," I said. "If you're in the squad room why aren't you in uniform? What's with this skirt business?"

"It has been a long time, hasn't it?" Angela said. "I'm not in uniform any more, Steven. I'm a detective now. Almost a year."

"Oh," I said. "Well, congratulations. But it's too bad, in a way. You used to look so sexy in your uniform."

"Don't you think I look sexy now?" Angela said huskily. "With my skirt pulled up to my waist and my panties showing? I'm wearing stockings and a garter belt too."

"I see," I said, and in my mind I did. I closed my eyes. Not a bad picture.

"All the guys think I'm sexy, all right," Angela said. "They're standing around with their tongues hanging out, watching me play with myself. Watching me spread my legs wide apart and slide my fingers beneath my panties to get at my pussy, Steven . . ."

"Uhhuh," I said, perhaps a bit hoarsely. I adjusted my position again; my trousers seemed to be getting a little tight. "Is that all they're doing? Standing and watching? Sounds like a pretty wimpy bunch of cops."

"They know they can't have me," Angela said. "There's a rule against police personnel becoming sexually involved with each other."

"Oh, right," I said. "And everybody knows the cops never break the rules, right?"

"Besides," she went on softly, "I only want you,

Steven. Come and take me. Take me right here with all these guys watching."

"Um," I said. I had called her from my office while Miss Greenglass was out to lunch. I glanced at my watch, seeing that there was still some time before she could be expected to return. I had a momentary twinge regarding the propriety of going along with this situation in terms of my wager. I shook it off. This couldn't really be considered sex, I told myself; after all, we weren't even really together, and I didn't intend to actually do anything anyway. But the inherent irrationality of the thing still made me hesitant. "Actually, I'm not much of an exhibitionist," I said. "Can't we go somewhere more private? Or even better, why don't we wait till we can really—"

"I see you, Steven," Angela murmured. "I see you standing here looking at me. Can you see me?"

Oh well, it was for a good cause. I closed my eyes again, thinking once more of the Angela I remembered, imagining her in that revealing position. "Yes," I said. "Yes, I can."

"What are you going to do?" Angela asked.

"What am I going to do. Well . . . ah . . . what do you want me to do?"

"You're sitting on my desk," Angela said.

"I am? I mean, yes, I am. Of course I am. On the desk."

"You've got your hands on my legs. You're sitting between my legs now."

"Really?" I said. "How did that happen?"

"Never mind. You're running your hands over my legs. Oh Steven . . . ohh God that's nice."

I kept my eyes closed. "Glad you like it," I said. "What am I doing next?"

"Steven . . ." There was a note of pleading in her voice. "Be serious, come on . . ."

I silently sighed. "Okay, I'm sliding my hands up to your crotch. Under the panties . . ."

"Yesss," Angela hissed. "Take them off."

"Well, I'm sitting between your legs," I reminded her. "I'll have to—"

"Oh for God's sake," Angela moaned. "Don't be so damned literal, Steven. Rip them off or something!"

"Fine. Consider them off. Now I can stroke your pussy. It's wet, Angela." It usually was, as I recalled.

"Yes. Ohh Steven, yes. Mmmmm, I feel your hands, Steven, you have such wonderful hands."

Her husky, moaning voice was getting to me now. The constriction in my pants was becoming more pronounced. I shifted position again, and then, hardly thinking about it, I pulled my zipper down—just to ease the tightness and let my cock breathe. That was all.

"I'm taking out my cock," I said.

"Lovely," Angela crooned. "Lovely cock. I always loved your cock. Stick it in me, Steven."

"Great idea," I said. My eyes were still closed, and I was breathing faster now. "I'll just slip off the desk so I can—"

"Can I suck it first?" Angela said. "Just a little bit? Put my mouth on it and lick it and suck it, before you stuff it into my pussy? Would you like that, Steven?"

"Damn," I said fervently. As I heard Angela gasping and whimpering, driving herself to climax with the thought of sucking my now-throbbing cock, my free hand involuntarily sought out my straining member and began very lightly to stroke it, while I mused on that fine sweet mouth and how it could feel when she . . .

Suddenly I heard the swooshing of air with movement. I opened my eyes with a start and nearly had a heart attack. There in the doorway—gazing at me with her usual inscrutable expression, but with her eyebrows arched higher than I had ever seen them, as much as a quarter of an inch, perhaps—stood Miss Greenglass.

I think I shouted. I know that in my frantic confusion I hung up the phone with one hand while swiftly trying unsuccessfully to stuff myself back in my pants with the other. I hate to think what shade of red my face was.

"I . . . I was . . . I mean . . ." I stammered. Miss Greenglass just stood there unmoving, and seemingly unmoved. "Look, I'm . . . it was just . . . you know . . . phone sex . . . sort of. Doesn't, um, count, really. I mean . . . how long . . . damn it to hell . . ."

"I think, Mr. Walling," Miss Greenglass said, "I think I shall take the afternoon off—if you don't mind." Her voice was even more controlled than usual—as though she was trying to repress something, mirth or anger, I wasn't sure. "I'm sure you won't need me, as you seem to have things . . . well in hand."

Before I could say anything more she went out again. As she walked away down the hall I thought I heard the faint sound of not-quite-stifled laughter. I looked down at my still-erect member. It looked up at me. Neither of us was happy.

Chapter 25

"X ENOPHON STUCK VERY STRICTLY TO THE facts," Professor Daltry was saying, between puffs on his cigar. "Whereas Thucydides had a tendency to embroider a bit here and there for the sake of drama, one has to be somewhat wary with Thucydides. Herodotus, on the other hand . . ."

For the sake of politeness I tried to look interested as the good professor rambled on. I had, after all, passed myself off as an alumnus of his department as plausible reason for seeking out his ex-colleague, Professor Anderpol—Xanthippe's father. He therefore assumed I would share his somewhat obsessive interest in the ancient Greek historians. He was wrong.

Professor Daltry had been head of the Classics Department at Columbia since Professor Anderpol had retired. I had come to see him as a last resort, hoping he could help me locate Xanthippe's father, and thus possibly find Xanthippe. My cop friend Angela was no longer speaking to me, after I had hung up on her when Miss Greenglass had interrupted our incipient phone fantasy.

(Miss Greenglass since then has not referred to that incident by word or deed, and I was too embarrassed to bring it up.) I had explained to Daltry that Professor Anderpol was an old teacher of mine who I was trying to find for sentimental reasons. Unfortunately, once I finally got him to focus on the subject, the professor informed me that Anderpol was on an extensive tour of Europe and Asia and had no fixed address.

"I see," I said, trying to conceal my disappointment. Then, clutching at straws, I asked, "Do you happen to know if his . . . ah . . . his wife and daughter went with him? His daughter Xanthippe?"

The professor looked surprised. "Why, I have no idea," he said. "Actually, I wasn't aware that Anderpol had a daughter."

"Oh yes," I said. "Oh, he did indeed. She was a—well, a kind of entertainer. Called herself Tiffany. For stage purposes, you know."

"Ah. Hmm. . . . Yes," Daltry said. "Understandable, I suppose. Too bad though. Fine old classical name, Xanthippe. You remember how Theopompus, in his Philippica, speaks of—"

I interrupted before he could get started on the classics yet again. "Very unusual though—isn't it?—for a woman to have such a name. One that starts with an X, I mean. You, ah . . . you don't happen to know of any others, do you?"

"What? Ah. Hmm. See what you mean. Yes. No. No, I don't believe I do, come to think of it."

I sighed. "I didn't think so," I said, and rose to go. "Well, thank you, profess—"

"Except for Miss Kanellopoulos, of course," the professor said.

I sat down again. "Miss Kanel—um—who?"

"Yes, Miss Kanellopoulos. Xenobia, you know."

"I don't know," I said. "Why don't you tell me? Who is this Miss Kanel—um—Xenobia?"

"Oh, she's an instructor here. In this very department. Oh yes. Teaches ancient Greek. Very good at it too, I understand. Not an easy subject, you know. Ancient Greek."

I wondered how ancient this Xenobia was herself, but I forbore from asking. "Ah . . . do you think I could meet her?" I said, trying to sound casual. "Just out of curiosity," I added hastily. "As I say, I have this interest in unusual names. And Xenobia sounds so . . . classical."

"Oh, indeed," Daltry said. "I believe it is Cratippus who makes reference to the female priests of—"

"Yes, I believe it is," I said. "Would this Xenobia be around now, do you think?"

"Um." The professor glanced at his watch, discovered he wasn't wearing one and looked up at the clock on the wall. "Well yes, I expect she would still be here. Perhaps you could find her in her classroom. Let me see—" He opened a drawer in his desk and consulted a chart. "Yes, three twenty-one. Right in this building."

"Wonderful," I said. "Thank you, professor. And give my regards to Thucydides."

On the one hand I was excited, as I made my way to the third floor, by the fact that I had discovered an actual X-lady—and one so conveniently located. On the other hand, I feared that this Ancient Greek instructress would be a doddering old frump with false teeth, thinning hair and a wen on her nose. But the pressure of time an the fact that X-ladies were so scarce as to be practically nonexistent determined me to do my best to add Xenobia to my list regardless of her age or appearance. As long as

I could manage to look at her without throwing up, I told myself, I could make love to any woman on earth. Or so I hoped.

My heart sank and my resolution wavered when I approached room three twenty-one and saw emerging from it a small, dumpy, snaggle-toothed woman of at least sixty-five. Oh well. While my dreams of ever bedding Miss Greenglass shattered into small pieces, I stopped the lady.

"Excuse me, ma'am," I said. "Are you Miss . . . uh . . . are you Xenobia?"

"No," she said. Suddenly I saw she was a beauty. "Xenobia's in there." Indicating the room she had just left, she waddled away.

I now took a deep breath. I knocked on the door and opened it.

The woman was sitting behind a desk at one end of the room. When she saw me enter she got up and walked around to stand in front of it. I looked at her with my mouth agape.

She was, I conjectured, about thirty-six or -seven. She had midnight-black hair, short but abundant, cut in a kind of circle that surrounded and set off the off beat beauty of her features. Her eyes were equally dark, and highly intense under heavy brows that would have seemed masculine on most women, but which suited her face perfectly. Her complexion was what is known as olive, and for the first time I understood and appreciated that description, for her flesh had the smoothness and translucence of that distinctly Mediterranean fruit. The erect and aristocratic posture she assumed as she stood on her own ground displayed the generous ripeness of her figure: breasts high and full, hips deliciously rounded, legs—at least the portion of them not hidden by her dark calf-length skirt—sculptured to perfection.

I tried to avoid staring too greedily and blatantly. "Excuse me," I said. "Are you Miss Kanel—um . . . Miss Xenobia Kanellop—"

"I am Ms. Kanellopoulos," Xenobia said. "Can I help you?"

"I think you can," I said, giving her my irresistible charming smile. "And I'd like to explain how."

Her expression was mildly curious.

I continued, "Would you like to have dinner with me?"

She hardly blinked. "No, thank you," she said. "What is it you want, Mr. . . . ?"

"Walling," I said. "Steven Walling. And what I want is—well . . ." What lie or half-lie I had on my tongue I cannot now recall. But whatever my story might have been, it was apparent from the way this woman looked at me with those dark all-seeing eyes, that it would be insufficient. Nothing but truth could pass muster under that gaze.

I took a breath and plunged. "What I want is to have sex with you," I said.

The heavy brows rose, but that was the only sign of surprise she gave.

"That's very flattering," she said, in a tone which revealed that it was anything but. "And why, may I ask, do you want to do that?"

"Because your first name begins with X," I said.

I wondered if the glint I saw in those deep dark eyes was one of amusement. Probably not.

"I see," Xenobia said. "Not a very common quality in a woman, I'm aware, but I hadn't realized that it was an erotic stimulus."

I had the sinking feeling that my mission was hopeless, but I couldn't give up yet; where was I going to find another X? Again I felt instinctively that the only thing that might work was total honesty—the more total the better. Since making my wager with Miss Greenglass I had not divulged the existence of said wager to any of the women who had been instrumental in my attempt to win it, except right at the beginning, with Abigail. Much as I believed—theoretically—in being straightforward with women, I had not thought that such a disclosure would do very much to further my cause. In this case, however, it seemed the only thing to do.

"The fact is," I said, "I have a bet. A wager. With . . . uh, with a colleague."

Xenobia simply looked at me, unmoving, but her eyes told me exactly what she believed—and what she didn't.

"With a woman who works for me, actually," I said hastily. "She's my assistant. Anyway—what I'm doing is, for this bet. I'm—well, I'm going through the alphabet. With women. Their first names, you see—A, B, C and . . . and so on." I was aware that I sounded awkward telling this tale, and almost absurd—in a way I had certainly not been with Abigail. But this Xenobia was unnerving in a way sweet innocent Abigail could never have been.

She gazed at me silently for another few moments. Then she threw back her head and laughed loudly. It was a good laugh but not very encouraging.

"And tell me, Mr. Walling," she said when she had subsided. "What are the stakes in this interesting wager of yours?"

I told her.

"I see," she said. "So that's why you want to have sex

with me. So that you can have sex with someone else. Very flattering indeed."

"That's not the only reason," I said. "I mean, that's the reason I looked you up, yes. But you must know that you are an extremely attractive woman, and any man would want you under any circumstances." As if to confirm this, I let my eyes travel slowly down over her splendid body, then back up to her eyes. I did this deliberately. My instincts told me that my only chance with this woman lay in being bold as well as forthright. Any sign of weakness and I would be blown away.

Xenobia looked coolly at me, unfazed by my frank survey of her body. "Have you had a good look?" she asked.

"Not really," I said. "I could look at you forever."

"I take it you approve of what you see," Xenobia said. She was, I fancied, a little less glacial now.

"Very much indeed," I said. "You have a marvelous body."

Her mouth twitched just a bit. "Thank you," she said. "But I think I should tell you, Mr. Walling, that I am a virgin."

I stared at her. "You're kidding."

"I am not."

"You're a virgin?!"

"That's right."

I couldn't believe it. But I couldn't believe she was lying, either. "Why?" I asked. "For God's sake why? It can't be for lack of suitors."

"Hardly," Xenobia said. "But I have yet to meet one who is worthy of the gift."

"Is that right?" I asked. "And you're telling me you have never had sex?"

"Oh, no," Xenobia said. "I didn't say that at all. The Greeks are an earthy people, Mr. Walling, and I am a very passionate woman."

"I don't understand," I said. "Are you a virgin or aren't you?"

"I am," she said. "Technically."

"Technically."

"Yes. My maidenhead is still intact. No one has had me that way."

"But there are other ways," I said. "Is that it?"

"Exactly," Xenobia said, still looking into my eyes. "I am Greek, you know."

I was—so to speak—a little taken aback. "I see," I said. "I think."

There was a small pause before Xenobia said. "Would you like to have me in the Greek way, Mr. Walling? If you could?"

"I'd like to have you any way I can get you," I said, truthfully.

"Then you may," Xenobia said. And with what seemed one continuous movement she turned around, pulled her long skirt up around her waist, bent sharply over the front of her desk, and pulled her panties down to reveal the most magnificent derriere I had ever seen.

I stepped toward her, taking in the delectable sweep of her legs and the mouth-watering curves of that splendid fundament. It was right there before me and all I had to do was take it.

But this was a little too cold, even for me.

"Not so fast," I said. I pulled her up and turned her around.

I stood very close to her, and looked into her eyes. She looked back, but this time I could tell it was an effort for her. She thought I was going to kiss her. So did I. But instead I raised my hands and placed them on her breasts.

"Ah," she said in a breathless voice.

We stood face to face, and I hefted her soft, resilient mounds. She drew in a slow, audible breath and even through her blouse and brassiere I felt the nipples harden. With her next breath her mouth opened slightly. Without releasing her tits I leaned forward to find that full, luscious mouth with my own.

She was passive for a moment, merely letting me kiss her—not resisting but not cooperating, either. But her lips were soft and warm, and when after a moment I slid my tongue between them, she gave a small gasp. Then her tongue came forward to meet mine, her mouth opening wider and fitting itself to mine.

We were still kissing when I slid my hands from her breasts to the buttons of her blouse. Her tongue did not stop its delicious investigation of my own, and she made a tiny whimpering sound in my mouth as I began to undo the buttons. Her hands urged my wrists to work faster. Once I had undone the blouse and it hung open, I caught a glimpse of her magnificent curved shoulders as I slipped it down over them. For the moment, it dangled from her waistband unattended. We had urgent matters to deal with.

Xenobia's skin was soft and exciting under my hands. Still kissing her, I deftly unhooked her bra. She pulled away from the kiss to look at me, her eyes wide and unfathomable, as I slid the flimsy cloth off her bosom. My own eyes dropped from that gaze to her breasts, and I caught my breath. The perfect smoothness of her flesh combined with that unique Mediterranean coloring seemed to impart a particularly erotic glow to the firm solidity of her bosom. Her nipples, of so deep a red they were almost purple, stood stiffly in the exact center of those lustrous melons. I dropped my head to one of them. My tongue sought and found the silkiness of the skin and I licked slow circles around the nipple before taking it into my mouth. I nibbled and tongued it and then drew it in deeper and devoured as much of her breast as I could. After a minute or two I released it and licked my way to the other breast. Meanwhile my hands slid over and around her body.

I heard her gasp close to my ear and then felt her fingers at the front of my trousers. She unbuckled my belt, unbuttoned the waist and pulled down my zipper. In a trice my trousers and shorts were down around my ankles and those fingers were playing on my very stiff phallus.

"Now," she whispered breathlessly. "Do it now." And she turned and bent over the desk again.

"Please," she said.

This was better.

I gazed again at that lovely out-thrust backside, and then I put my adoring hands on it and grasped and stroked it. This brought a soft, pleased gasp from Xenobia. Her ass felt as good as it looked. I slid one hand down between her legs, and some instinct made her press her thighs together, preventing me from reaching the center of all this femininity.

"No," I said. "Let me touch you."

She moved her legs apart slightly then, and my fingers found her vagina. I explored it gently, not too deeply but enough to coat my fingers with her sweet vaginal juices which I then brought up to her anus, spreading the moistness around and inside it for lubricant while she hissed and sighed in anticipation.

I spread her cheeks to expose her little asshole, then moved forward and placed the tip of my throbbing spear against it. At first it seemed it would never fit; but as I pressed forward gently and experimentally, and Xenobia pushed back into my prick, the puckered pink opening expanded somewhat. Soon I was able to slip the tip inside. She gave a soft gasp and pushed back harder on my cockhead. Now the head entered the sanctum, and I felt the walls of her anal passage tight and quivering around it.

"More," she said. "Oh God, more."

I gave her more. "Christ—Christ—Christ," she said.

She was squirming her buttocks from side to side as I pushed gradually deeper. Finally I felt secure enough to start a short back-and-forth stroking movement. She made hoarse whimpering sounds, and then she said, "Yes. Yes. Do it. Yes . . ."

I slid my hands between her upper body and the desk till I was holding her breasts. The nipples were hard and rigid against my palms. I hunched more deeply.

She moaned and sobbed and pushed back against me, working to take more of my staff into her anus. I gave her everything I had. Her body jerked and writhed and twisted, and the clutching of her tight passage around my tool was like nothing in all my experience. I heard myself grunting like a pig, and I had to concentrate hard to avoid losing myself entirely and ending it right there.

I didn't want it to end yet. I stopped moving and lowered my head to lick her slightly sweaty back.

It tasted salty; it tasted, in fact, like ripe olives. I licked my way to her neck and nibbled at it, and her body writhed and twisted beneath me.

"Do it," she moaned. "For God's sake do it. Aah . . ."

I tried to move slowly but she increased the pace. She pumped her buttocks back and forth against me and I was soon lost in her rhythm, in the sound of her moans and gasps and the sweetness of her flesh. Then her moans turned to sobs—sobs of joy—which soon became loud cries that culminated in a sudden raucous shout as her body convulsed repeatedly, then shuddered and went limp. The narrow passage that held my cock in its tight grip continued to twitch spasmodically, making it difficult for me to maintain self-control. I held on, however, and now that she was still I was able to moderate my rhythm again, pumping firmly but slowly back and forth in that clutching tightness, savoring the sensation of her firm but yielding buttocks against my loins, her stiff-nippled breasts quivering in my hands, her soft gasps and groans rising once more into urgent pleas as her desire came to life again.

Thus I was able to bring her to climax a second time before giving up the struggle myself, nearly collapsing on top of her as I shot burst after burst of pent-up passion hard and deep into that wonderful body.

Limp and spent as I was, I was still reluctant to withdraw myself from that snug harbor, or to take my hands from her heaving breasts. "Xenobia," I breathed close to her ear, "you don't really want to stay a virgin, do you? Just give me a few minutes and I can—"

I was interrupted by an elbow in my ribs. In the extremely unplayful circumstances, that took me aback. I straightened up.

"Wow, Xenobia," I expostulated. "What was that for?"

Xenobia stood up too, and quickly slipped into her blouse before turning to face me. Her eyes were ablaze with righteous indignation.

"Men!" she rasped. "Why are they never satisfied? Did I not tell you there is not a man on earth worthy of that gift?"

"What you said was that you had never met one," I said. "I thought . . . I even hoped that I might be the one."

"Don't be ridiculous," Xenobia said.

And as far as I know she's still a virgin.

Chapter 26

OU MUST KNOW YOU'RE GOING TO LOSE THIS wager," I said smugly to Miss Greenglass. "Why not give it up now and save time?" Miss Greenglass did not even bother to glance up from her keyboard at this provocation. I had not really expected her to.

"You have only a few weeks remaining, Mr. Walling, as I'm sure you realize," she said over the faint clicking of the keys. "The outcome is not yet certain."

"Just about," I said. "I've got Mrs. Burlesdon— Zelda—all ready and waiting. Raring to go. Champing at the bit, as it were."

"How elegantly you put it," Miss Greenglass murmured. "It is no wonder so many women find you so irresistibly charming."

I ignored the sarcasm. "And as for a Y," I went on, "it happens that I'm meeting with a lady this very evening whose name is, I understand, Yolanda. And who, with any luck, will provide the last link in the chain. Yolanda, and then Zelda—and then you."

Miss Greenglass gave that faint noise of hers which is far too ladylike to be called a sniff. "Even assuming that rather dubious name to be a real one," she said, "I'm sure you will understand, Mr. Walling, if I postpone my concession of our wager until it has actually been decided."

"Fine," I said. "And as for the name, I'll check it out all right. But the gentleman who told me about this lady assures me it is quite genuine."

I wasn't nearly as certain as I sounded, however, because what I didn't tell Miss Greenglass was that the gentleman in question was my brother Henry.

Those of you unfortunate enough to have read previous parts of this saga in which my brother Henry has appeared may be unsurprised at my reluctance to bring up his name in the presence of my lovely assistant, in whom he had once evinced an interest which, although evidently not returned, I found deplorable, to say the least. In fact, I deplored most things about Henry, and the only reason I am once again inflicting him, however briefly, on my patient readers is that he had been instrumental to the next step in that interesting wager which is the subject of this chronicle.

Henry had called me just after my session with Phyllis.

"Hey, Steve-O," he said. "How's it hanging, big brother? How's that sexy secretary of yours?"

"She's not a secretary," I said. "What do you want, Henry?"

"Listen, forget that lesbian bimbo." Henry had decided that Miss Greenglass was a lesbian because she had rejected his advances. "I got a real woman for you. She's dying to meet you."

"Is that right," I said. "And why is that?"

"I told her you had a big cock," Henry said.

"What?!"

"Not as big as mine, of course," Henry said. "See, she likes big cocks, okay? So of course she loved mine, and when she heard I had a brother, she wanted to know—"

"Henry," I said, "go to hell."

"She really wants to meet you," Henry said.

"Well, I'm not—wait a minute. What's her name?"

"Yolanda," Henry said.

"Yolanda? Are you sure? Is that real?"

"Sure, why not? About this girl . . ."

I wasn't listening any more. Though at that point I was really looking for a Q-lady, I was making slower progress generally than I had expected. It occurred to me that it might be a good idea not to throw away any possible future options.

"Give me her number," I said. "Maybe I'll call her sometime."

Which, when the time came, I did.

I suggested we meet at the Oak Room in the Plaza Hotel—which may not have been the ideal venue.

But the name Yolanda had led me to half-expect someone exotic, sophisticated and a bit mysterious, with an air of aloofness and a foreign accent.

This girl wasn't it.

She was in her mid-twenties, of medium height, with a figure whose charms were anything but hidden. She wore an orange pullover top which clung to her very substantial breasts and left no doubt that there was nothing underneath it. Her extremely shapely legs, covered by sheer white stockings, were enhanced by very high heels and almost completely revealed by her short blue skirt.

Her blond hair, obviously not its real color, was piled carelessly on top of her head, and her heavily lipsticked mouth moved almost constantly in the rhythmic process of gum-chewing.

This was the kind of woman I would expect Henry to be acquainted with. I had to admit, however, that in spite of her lack of refinement she made quite a libidinous picture, and since at the moment I had no other Y-lady in prospect, I was not about to be overly fastidious. I rose as the waiter led her to my table.

"You Henry's brother?"

"Unfortunately, I have that distinction," I said, "if such it can be called."

"Yeah, you're him," the woman said. "He said you talk like a fag."

I was nonplussed. "He said what?!"

"Yeah. He said you're straight, though. And you have a huge dick. Is that right?"

"Um . . ." I said. "Ah . . . why don't we sit down at this table, Miss . . ."

"Call me Yolanda," she said, as we seated ourselves. "So, do you?"

"Look," I said, "I don't know what Henry's told you, but—"

"I just told you what he told me. He said you got a schlong like a gorilla's. So is that right or not?"

"I assure you Henry is prone to exaggeration. Besides, he has no way of knowing—"

"Hey, I don't do this with just anybody, ya know," Yolanda said.

"I'm sure you don't," I said.

"But Henry says you got a really big one, ya know? Almost as big as his, he says. Jeez. I mean I wanna see that, for sure."

"Probably bigger," I said. "But tell me about your name, Yolanda."

"My name? What about it?"

"It's very pretty," I said. "Henry tells me it's your real name. Is that true?"

"Hah!" She gave a snort which would have done justice to a prize boar. "Shit, no. Who'd have a real name like Yolanda, for Christ's sake?"

I wasn't sure if I was disappointed or relieved. "What is it, then? Your real name."

She looked at me suspiciously. "What's the difference?"

"Just curious," I said.

"Well," she said. "If you must know. It's a stupid name. It's Yetta. It's an old Jewish-type name. I'm Jewish, okay? At least, my parents were. Why, you got something against Jews?"

"Not at all," I said hastily. "It's just an unusual name. And you kept your initial when you changed it."

Again I wasn't sure if I was glad or sorry about that.

"Big deal," she said. "So are we gonna do it or not?"

I hesitated, but not for long. "I suppose we are," I said. "Do you live close by? Or would you like to come to my house?"

"No," Yolanda/Yetta said. "We can just go upstairs. Henry's got a room here. He's waiting for us."

With some difficulty, I avoided choking on my drink. "He's what?"

"Yeah, he wants to watch. Actually, I think he wants both of you to do it to me at once. You know, like a sandwich. You ever do that?"

I put my glass down very carefully. "Yes, I have," I said. "Not with Henry, however. Nor do I intend to. Not ever. Not under any imaginable circumstances. Not even to win—well, not for anything. I'm sorry, Yett—ah, Yolanda. But if that is the only condition under which—"

"Hey, fuck Henry," Yolanda said. "I don't care. Just you and me is cool too, okay? Where's your house?"

In the taxi on the way to my house Yolanda put her hand on my thigh, then ran it up to my crotch.

But even as I was stiffening under her questing fingers, her attention was caught by something else.

"Hey," she said in what she probably thought was a whisper. "See that guy?"

"What guy?"

"The driver. He's got a towel around his head. See that?"

"Of course." Our driver was indeed wearing a turban, a not uncommon sight among New York cabdrivers, many of whom nowadays are natives of India or the Middle East.

"Those guys have enormous cocks!" Yolanda said. "Those Indian guys, especially the towelhead ones. Honest to God!"

"Is that right?" I said. "All of them?"

"Yeah."

Yolanda was checking out the driver's identification card posted on the back of the front seat as required by law. "Pravda Singh," she read. "Hey, cool!" Then suddenly she leaned forward and addressed the driver directly. "Hey Pravda! How you doin'? You're Indian, right?"

The driver turned his head slightly, but kept his eyes on the road. "I am from India, yes," he said, and his accent verified the statement.

"Great!" Yolanda said. "You got a big one, Pravda?"

He looked confused. "I'm sorry, what is the question, madam?"

"I said, do you have a big one? A big dick, you know? A cock, a nice big Indian cock. You know, like for fucking."

Pravda understood now. At first he looked surprised, and then a big smile came over his face. "Oh, yes!" he said. "For fucking, yes. Big, yes!"

He continued to grin at her, and then turned his head to include me in the merriment. I rather churlishly advised him to keep his eye on the road.

As he turned back around, much to my relief, I felt Yolanda's fingers moving again on my crotch.

"Hey, how about him?" she rasped into my ear. "Let's invite him in with us, okay? I mean two cocks are better than one, you know what I mean?"

"Ah . . . I don't think so," I replied. As she frowned I added quickly, "I'd prefer to have you all to myself—at least the first time. Okay?"

She looked mollified. "Well, okay. But hey, you don't mind waiting a few minutes, do you?"

"I—" But before I could answer she was leaning over to the driver again.

"Hey, Pravda! Pull over someplace, okay? Someplace nice and dark, know what I mean?"

"Yolanda—" I began.

"This won't take long," Yolanda said. "I just gotta take a look at that cock, you know? Don't worry—I'll make him so happy you won't have to tip him for the ride."

"I don't mind tipping him," I protested, but by now Pravda had turned into a quiet side street and found a spot to park, where an overhanging tree blocked the light of the corner lamppost. With a final pat to my crotch,

Yolanda swiftly opened the door and slid out. In a moment, she had joined our driver in the front seat.

"Okay, Prav, let's see it," she said.

Pravda seemed startled. He turned to look at me, but I couldn't help him. Yolanda recaptured his attention quickly by going for his crotch. I heard his zipper being opened. The meter was still running.

"I, ah . . . I think I'll get out here," I said.

"Oh, sweet Jesus!" Yolanda said. "That's a big one, all right!"

"I'm happy for you," I told her, and reached for my wallet, fully intending to pay the fare and get out of there. But at that point Yolanda crouched up on her knees on the seat, leaned over to Pravda, put her head down into his lap and, as far as I could tell, took the entire length of his presumably sizeable cock into her mouth at one gulp.

My planned departure was momentarily arrested by the spectacle of Yolanda crouched over on the seat that way, with her very shapely behind thrusting up and out, barely covered by the short skirt, and swaying back and forth with a deliciously erotic rhythm as her head began to move up and down on Pravda's tool while hungry whimpering sounds came from her busy mouth. I could also make out the swaying motion of her breasts under the tight blouse. I admit to thoughts of how pleasant it might be to move up there, flip up that skirt and take her from behind, a course of action I was certain Yolanda would not object to; but I preferred to wait until we were alone, and besides, the scene was a little too exposed for me, in spite of the fact that there seemed to be no traffic on the dim, quiet street. Still, I didn't leave, but sat there and watched as Yolanda's head moved faster, Pravda's groaning got louder, and my cock got stiffer.

Pravda appeared to be rapidly approaching a climax. My attention was fixed on the hypnotic gyrations of Yolanda's body as she worked on him, when I suddenly became aware that a car had moved up beside us and stopped. I had just time to turn my head and realize, to my great consternation, that it was a police car, when a spotlight flashed on and flooded the interior of our taxi. Just at that moment Pravda came, and as Yolanda lifted her head in surprise at the unexpected illumination, heavy jets of sperm spurted out of his convulsing phallus.

The spotlight stayed on as the car doors opened and two policemen emerged, with that deliberate, vaguely menacing manner that is endemic to cops the world over. Pravda's groans of passion turned into a frightened bleat, and he hastened to stuff himself back in his pants and zip up as the cops approached. Yolanda stayed as she was. So did I, not having much alternative.

One of the cops came up to the front window of the taxi and peered in. "What's going on here?" he inquired.

I cleared my throat. "Nothing, officer," I said as calmly as I could. "We were just—"

"Nothing, huh?" the cop said, his gaze on Yolanda, who was now trying to shade her eyes from the light with one hand. "Don't look like 'nothing' to me. Looks like something. How about it, lady?"

"How about what?" Yolanda said.

"How about telling me what the hell you're doin' here?" the cop said.

"Actually," I began, "we were only—"

"I was giving this guy a blowjob," Yolanda broke in. "So what?"

This silenced the questioner for a moment, but his partner was beside him now.

"Pretty public place for that kind of thing, isn't it?" the second cop said.

"If I could explain—" I said.

"Shut up," the first cop said. "We're talking to the lady here, okay?"

"You a hooker, honey?" the second cop asked.

"No!" Yolanda said indignantly. "I'm a respectable woman, for Chrissake!"

"Then how come you're giving blowjobs to two guys on the street?" the cop said.

"I wasn't—" I began.

"'Cause I like big dicks, okay?" Yolanda said. "What the fuck is wrong with that?"

"What's wrong with that is, you're under arrest, honey. All of you."

"Wait a minute, wait a minute," the first cop said. "Maybe she likes cop dick too."

"Do cops have big ones?" Yolanda asked interestedly.

"Are you kidding?" the second cop said. "Cops have the biggest!"

"I got one bigger than my billy club, baby," the first one said. "You wanna see it?"

"Hell yeah!" Yolanda said.

"Then get out of there and get in the car," the cop said. He looked at Pravda and then at me. "Okay, you guys can take off now. We'll take care of the lady."

Pravda, who had been trembling with fear, hastily turned on the engine. But Yolanda said, "Hey, wait—" indicating me. "Him and me got a date, okay? Let him stick around."

"That's all right," I said. "I'll call you another time."

"You heard the lady, bud," the second cop said. "She wants you to stay, you stay. Get in the damn car."

So both Yolanda and I got out of the taxi, barely getting clear of it before Pravda gunned the motor and roared away. Following the cops' instructions, I got into the front seat of the police car, while the two of them piled with Yolanda into the back.

Standing in the middle of the street, the police car was far more exposed than our taxi had been, but the cops didn't seem to mind. I heard the sound of two zippers being unzipped, and then a soft exclamation of delight from Yolanda. I deduced from this that their proportions met her standards.

At first I just faced straight ahead, looking out the windshield, but I couldn't help hearing, and soon the sounds coming from the back aroused my natural curiosity, as well as other things. So finally, I turned around to watch.

Yolanda was kneeling on the floor of the car while the two cops sat side by side on the seat, their flies open and their exposed phalluses sticking up in the air. Yolanda was sucking them alternately, leaning first one way, then the other, taking each in turn into her mouth and pumping her head a few times, then switching to the other one. Happy gurgling noises came from her throat as she did this, and the policemen didn't seem to be suffering either.

Finally Yolanda paused. "Oh Jesus," she gasped. "Big cocks, Jesus." And she pulled off her tight orange top, making her big breasts jiggle and bounce as she pulled it over her head. "I want them in me," she said.

Both cops leaned forward eagerly toward that naked bosom. Their heads bumped together, but that didn't stop them from each taking one of her breasts in his mouth. Yolanda groaned and opened her skirt. In a minute they were pulling her up onto the seat. They all tugged at each other, and Yolanda's panties got pulled off in the process. When things settled down, Yolanda was straddling one of cops, who was still seated, while the other knelt sideways on the seat beside them, so that as she moved wildly up and down on the cock that impaled her, she could lean over and take the other one into her voracious mouth.

But she still wasn't satisfied. "Both," she panted, her body still pumping rhythmically. "I want both of you in me. Both at once. Two big cop cocks in me, yeah!"

So they changed positions again. As the first cop lay down on the seat with Yolanda above him, the second one crouched behind her and worked himself gradually into her rear passage while she howled with delight. Then, slowly at first but soon picking up speed, the three of them found a rhythm, and Yolanda had two cocks moving in and out of her as her twisting body bucked ecstatically back and forth.

As I watched now, her glazed, wandering eyes came to rest on me. Her lustful face had a strange kind of passionate beauty in the dimness, which enhanced the provocative scene.

"Come on," she gasped, jerking her head at me. "Come on, let me suck you, come on!"

I can't explain why I succumbed to this temptation. My brain said no, but my body was moving, getting out of the car and into the back. It was very crowded back there, and I could barely squeeze myself into the space between the seats. I had to half-stand, half-lean over Yolanda, bracing myself as best I could.

I was surprised that she was able to take my whole member in at once, virtually swallowing it without in the least disturbing the rhythm of her movements; surprised and delighted, especially when her tongue and lips began to move in that same rhythm, until I would not have cared if a hundred cops had been in that car. I closed my eyes and there was only that mouth, that thirsty gulping throat. Soon I was gasping and the cops were groaning and Yolanda was moaning and swallowing.

I remember collapsing to the floor of the car as Yolanda said, "Shit! That was great! Let's do it again!" But we didn't. It took some time and awkwardness for us to get uncramped and untangled and into some semblance of decency. Finally we managed, to Yolanda's obvious disappointment. The cops were nice enough to drive us to my house and let us off with a warning against further public lewdness—but not before obtaining Yolanda's phone number.

I was prepared to take her home, but Yolanda was offended by this suggestion, protesting that she had expected to spend the night with me. After she graphically described a few of the things she thought we might do together, I could not but agree to that plan. Yolanda said she thought I damn well should. After all, she reminded me, she didn't do this with just anybody.

Chapter 27

ONKED OUT ALREADY?" YOLANDA (NÉE Yetta) said to me as I fell away from her for about the fifth time that night, and lay panting, sweating and exhausted on my back beside her. "Hey, shit, man, we got lots more stuff we can do yet!" Now I am hardly what any objective person would call inexperienced, but I have to confess that at that point I couldn't think of a single heterosexual act that she and I hadn't done that night, short of a few wild perversions at which I believe even Yolanda would have hesitated—although there I could be wrong.

"Dear God," I gasped. "Give me a break—I mean, let's take a break, okay? Get a little rest, a little sleep, maybe . . ."

"Sleep later," Yolanda said. Then she burrowed under the sheet. Her mouth searched and found the sweaty flesh of my stomach and then headed unerringly southward. I closed my eyes blissfully as her lips found their goal and worked in concert with that talented tongue to bring me to life again. It was a method that had worked more than once earlier, but this time I knew I was just too worn out to respond even to that warm, wet, wonderful clasping mouth, those soft, sensuously sliding lips, that busy, knowing, oh so sinuous tongue.

Well, maybe just once more . . .

Yolanda laughed with triumph as she swept the sheet aside and swung herself up and over to straddle me. She grasped my tired but once more alert phallus and lowered herself onto it. She gasped happily as she took it slowly but steadily inside her grasping pussy, and tossed her dyed blond hair back—the hair at her crotch was dark—and arched her back.

"Oh Christ," she moaned. "Ooh, your big sweet cock. God, it's so big." Yolanda, as readers of the previous chapter will recall, had a thing for big cocks. That was what had brought us together in the first place, through the good offices of my brother Henry.

"So big," Yolanda went on, twisting her body to take it in more easily, until she had it all. "Jesus," she panted. "Bigger than those cops, honest to God . . . bigger than that taxi guy."

"Bigger than Henry, right?"

Yolanda said nothing to that. Which might have disconcerted me if she hadn't just then begun to pump her squirming body up and down, making her large round breasts bounce enticingly, writhing her hips in a way that kept my battle-worn lance in a state of blissful arousal.

Come to think of it, she never did answer that question.

When I staggered down to the office the next morning, Miss Greenglass took one look at me and understood that my date with Yolanda had been successful, if hardly rest-

ful. Furthermore, she knew—and I knew that she knew—
that I would be spared the time and effort of searching for
the next and last woman in my alphabetical succession.
For weeks I had been cultivating the affections of an extremely attractive married lady named Zelda Burlesdon,
who by now was only too eager to consummate our mutual attraction. (Her husband seemed to be only a minor
inconvenience. She told me he trusted her implicitly. She
also said she had never been unfaithful to him before but
I, being less gullible than Mr. Burlesdon, took private
leave to doubt that.)

Thus, though I had only a matter of weeks remaining
of my allotted time, it seemed certain that I was about to
win our wager, and that I would soon be able to possess
the aforesaid Miss Greenglass in all her elegant loveliness. Miss Greenglass, however, showed no reaction to
this awareness but went about her duties with her accustomed cool competence. I was too depleted from the previous night to feel like teasing her about my incipient
victory. Let alone working. Halfway through the morning
I decided to take the rest of the day off. Miss Greenglass
disapproved. She pointed out that I had scheduled a couple of afternoon appointments which would have to be
canceled. But seeing that I was unmoved by this tragedy,
she gave up. She knew from long experience that it was
useless to try to keep me at my desk when I didn't want
to be there.

But as I prepared to leave, Miss Greenglass stopped
what she was doing, folded her hands (it was unusual to
see them idle) and turned her clear, direct gaze on me.

"Before you leave, Mr. Walling," she said, "may I
speak to you for a moment?"

I looked at her in surprise. "Of course."

She took a breath. "It is apparent," she said evenly, "that your, um, rendezvous with Miss—with this Yolanda person—"

"Actually, her real name is Yetta," I said. "But it's still a Y, so it counts. And yes, it was quite an evening. Let me tell you—"

"Please, Mr. Walling. If I may finish?"

I waved my hand deferentially.

"Since you have only one letter to go," she went on, "and since, as you pointed out yesterday, you have Mrs. Burlesdon, as you put it, chomping at the bit—"

"And a lovely mare she is, too," I put in. "Sorry. Go on."

"Therefore it would seem that you are about to win our wager," Miss Greenglass said. "And that you will have the right to claim my body—to have sex with me—as a result."

"That's what it's all been about," I said, grinning. "And may I say, Miss Greenglass, that sleeping with twenty-six women in order to win that right has been hard, grueling work, but I know that the prize will be worth it."

"I hope you're right, Mr. Walling. But if I may, I have a suggestion."

"Okay," I said. "Suggest away."

"As it seems inevitable," Miss Greenglass said, with no actual change in tone. "I suggest that you have sex with me now."

It took a moment for this to sink in. And when it did I just stared at her.

I cleared my throat. "Now?" I said.

"Now," Miss Greenglass said.

"Now?" I said again, stupidly. "Right now? Right here?"

"Here or upstairs in your apartment, whichever you choose," Miss Greenglass said, as if she were talking about where she was going to have lunch. "Upstairs might be more comfortable, but of course it may be that having me here in the office, where we have spent so much of our time together, might be particularly exciting for you. I leave that to you, Mr. Walling."

My brain was still spinning. Here she was—the elusive, unreachable Miss Greenglass—suddenly offering herself to me. Of course she was right, I had virtually won our bet, but . . .

"Let me get this straight," I said. "You're conceding the wager. I've won, right? And you're just offering me the prize a little early. Is that it?"

Miss Greenglass's eyebrows rose a fraction of a millimeter. "Not exactly," she said. "In order to actually win, you would have to completely fulfill the terms. Which you have not yet done."

I thought about that. "I see," I said. "So if I accept this sudden offer and make it with you before finishing the alphabet with Zelda—I will have won the prize but lost the bet!"

"That is correct," Miss Greenglass said.

"And having lost the bet," I continued, "I would then, I suppose, have to pay my forfeit and triple your salary."

"That is also correct."

"Very clever," I said. "But why would I do that? Attractive as you are, Miss Greenglass, why should I not simply wait until after my session with Zelda—which, as you say, is inevitable—and then claim the prize and the victory?"

There was a slight pause. "Perhaps, Mr. Walling," Miss Greenglass said then, "you might find a woman who freely offers herself to you to be a more . . . enthusiastic, perhaps a more . . . ardent partner than one who is simply discharging a debt, as it were." Her eyes never left mine.

I took a deep breath. "Tempting as that idea is, Miss Greenglass," I said, "I don't think I can take advantage of it at this point. For one thing, though your services are invaluable to me—and probably worth even more than triple your already considerable salary—having come so far in our wager, the fact of having lost it would discomfit me even more than the expense. And I suspect your winning it, even if only technically, would be more gratifying to you than the added income. Secondly, I further suspect that whatever the circumstances in which you give yourself to me, your innate integrity and sense of honor would not allow you to display any less enthusiasm or ardency (is that a word?) than seems called for by the occasion. I say nothing, Miss Greenglass, of your natural passion and sensuality, qualities which I have long believed to exist in abundance beneath that imperturbable facade." Miss Greenglass said nothing.

"And finally," I went on, "as strongly as I have lusted for your delightful body—and still do—and as much work, trouble and even sacrifice as I have put myself through to obtain it by winning this wager, it now occurs to me—belatedly, I admit—that if in giving yourself to me you will be doing so only to, as you put it, discharge a debt—if it is merely a duty which you would find unpleasant or onerous, or even one to which you would be indifferent, then the truth is that it would not, under those circumstances, afford me the kind of pleasure which I have so long been anticipating. I release you from your obligation, Miss Greenglass. I will go on to win our bet, but our platonic personal relationship will be unaltered. As, of course, will your salary."

Miss Greenglass's expression did not change. "You need not concern yourself, Mr. Walling," she said, "with my personal feelings in this matter. We have made a fair wager, you have—almost—won it, and I fully intend to honor it in every way. And my suggestion still stands. I will give myself to you right now, right here. Freely, and without reservation. Yes, you will have lost the wager. But I will match your gesture, Mr. Walling. I will give up the increase in salary. You are right; though the money would be useful, it is not my primary concern here. Like you, Mr. Walling, I want to win."

"And that, Miss Greenglass, is the one thing in the world that I would deny you," I said. "I intend to get together with Zelda as soon as possible; and after that, well, we'll just have to see, won't we?" I started to get up.

"One moment, Mr. Walling." Miss Greenglass stood up. "I have one more argument to present," she said. Then she began to unbutton her blouse.

I sat down again.

Miss Greenglass was calm as ever. Her gaze was level. Her fingers were steady. Before I could react or even think clearly, she had unbuttoned the blouse and slipped it off. She folded it neatly and laid it in her chair.

She wore a plain black brassiere that molded a high bosom which didn't appear to require its support and which made a stark contrast against the porcelain whiteness and smoothness of her torso. For a moment I couldn't breathe. Beyond the stunning loveliness of her body, there was the incredible fact that this was actually Miss

Greenglass, seminude in front of me—and about to get even nuder.

She stood thus for only a moment before reaching to unclasp the brassiere, still looking into my eyes.

"Wait," I said. And gathering my strength, I stood up. "Miss Greenglass," I said hoarsely, "I don't—"

Miss Greenglass took off the brassiere.

I took one quick look. And then—it may have been the hardest thing I ever did in my life—I closed my eyes.

"No," I croaked. "No. No no. No. I won't. I'm sorry, Miss Greenglass. No."

And I turned away and somehow got out of there.

As I made my way upstairs on unsteady legs, it occurred to me that I might not have been able to resist such temptation if I had not been so depleted by the previous night. I wasn't sure whether to feel grateful to Yolanda or angry with her.

I also wondered whether it was Miss Greenglass or I who had taken the more extreme leave of our senses.

I decided it was me.

Once in my private quarters, the first thing I did was take a long nap. Upon awakening I felt a lot better and ready to take on the world—or at least the female half of it. And the thought of the scrumptiously sensuous Zelda, whose voluptuous body promised so much delight, sent new fire through me and drove all vestiges of the night with Yolanda—if not the recollection of Miss Greenglass— from my mind. Well, almost.

I decided to call Zelda and set up a rendezvous as soon as possible. I had been putting off, with one excuse or another, the culmination of our lust until I had gotten through X and Y. Zelda had been getting impatient, and even a little suspicious. But now was the time.

"Zelda darling!" I said as soon as she got on the phone. "Great news! That deal has gone through and my schedule is finally all cleared. Let's get together. How about tonight? Or actually, maybe tomorrow would be—"

"Oh, Steven!" Zelda said, and her voice stopped me cold. It didn't sound overjoyed. "Oh, Steven, it's terrible!"

"It is?" I said. "What's terrible?"

"He's dead, Steven. Walter's dead. He—he had a heart attack last night and—and he . . ."

I had never met the guy, but naturally I was sorry for Zelda, though my impression was that their marriage had not been exactly compatible for some time. At the same time, I have to admit that along with those feelings of sympathy, what also leaped to my mind was the effect this would have on my immediate plans. Oh, we are all selfish, cold-hearted bastards at bottom, or somewhere. Or is it just me?

"Oh God," I said, as sincerely as I could. "I'm so sorry to hear that, Zelda. Is there anything I can do?"

"Yes," Zelda said. "Yes, there is, Steven. Get the hell over here and fuck my brains out."

Zelda opened the door at my ring. She was, as befits a new widow, all in black. Black brassiere, black panties, black stockings and black shoes. And that was all.

"Come upstairs," she said.

I followed her up the stairs. Zelda was in her mid-thirties, a sensuously graceful woman with shoulder-length auburn hair. The sight of her well-developed body swaying ahead of me in that outfit made me as ready as if I had never heard of Yolanda. But that was before we got to her bedroom.

The body of her husband was laid out on the bed.

At least I assumed it was her husband. It was a man—a middle-aged man dressed in a neat suit and tie.

"Jesus!" I said before I could stop myself.

Zelda smiled at me. "Don't worry, Steven," she said. "Walter won't stop us. He can't stop me from doing anything anymore. Maybe he can see us though. Wherever he is, I sure hope you can see us, Walter. And I hope you suffer, you filthy rotten bastard." And with that she took off her bra.

"Um," I said. Which was about all I could think of at that moment. It seemed to be my day for women offering themselves to me under less than ideal circumstances. This circumstance was a dilly. It is not often in life that one is presented simultaneously with a vision as exciting as Zelda's naked breasts and one as disconcerting as the body lying on the bed. Not in my life anyway.

The image of Zelda taking off her bra brought to mind the vision of Miss Greenglass doing the same thing a few hours before. The bras were even the same color. I saw Miss Greenglass's naked breasts in my mind's eye, the memory of that fleeting glimpse almost more vivid than the actual sight of Zelda's lovely red-tipped beauties.

"Come on, Steven," Zelda said. "Let's do it."

"Um, Zelda," I stammered. "You know, maybe—maybe this isn't exactly the right time—"

"It's the perfect time," Zelda said. "And the perfect place. Right in front of the son of a bitch. Right on his bed, with him still in it. Oh God, Steven, I need you now!" With that she twined her arms around my neck, pressing her body into mine. Her mouth found mine and clung to it, moist and open. Her tongue fluttered between my lips while those bare breasts jammed themselves into my chest so hard I could feel the nipples through my shirt.

By the time we broke the kiss I was hard as a rock. But when my eyes opened and fell upon the body on the bed, the rock swiftly melted. But only temporarily; Zelda slid down to her knees. Her hands were at my zipper, and then inside. Then her mouth was on my cock. I tried to concentrate on what she was doing—she was doing it quite well—but that figure on the bed kept getting in the way.

There was something else in the way, though I didn't want to acknowledge it. Since Zelda's removal of her bra had brought Miss Greenglass so vividly to my mind, she had stayed there, as she had a habit of doing lately. Maybe that wasn't fair to Zelda, who in spite of what seemed to be a seizure of giddiness due to her husband's passing, was basically a fine and intelligent woman. But she wasn't Miss Greenglass. Nobody was Miss Greenglass.

Zelda was moving now, backward on her knees toward the bed, clutching my thighs to pull me along with her while still keeping as much prick as possible in her mouth. Halfway there I stopped. "Zelda," I said. "Zelda, wait."

Zelda rose to her feet. "Come on, Steven." Facing me, her eyes blazing, she pushed her panties down and wriggled out of them, leaving only the garter belt and hose. Then she turned and climbed onto the bed. She crouched there on hands and knees, her buttocks thrusting up and out over the edge, her face practically hovering over that of her dead husband. "Take me this way," she breathed. "Just like this, so he can watch. I want the son of a bitch bastard to watch. Please, Steven. Take me now." It may have been the most bizarre situation I was ever in, but in the end I don't think that was what stopped me. I am not superstitious, and the presence of the dead husband, while off-putting at first, might not in itself have been enough to prevent my completing my task with the luscious, eager, exciting woman who knelt there so provocatively. It might even have been stimulating in a perverse way. But there was this other factor.

This was not like the time with Phyllis, when my conscience had troubled me—unnecessarily—with regard to Miss Greenglass's picky objections, and thus affected my performance. My body was more than ready for Zelda, her husband's corpse notwithstanding. It was something else entirely that held me back, and whatever it was, I wasn't sure I was happy about it. Not on any level.

I looked at Zelda's gorgeous thrusting ass. I moved closer to the bed, reaching out to touch it. It felt sensational. I was ready, I was there, she was there, she wanted me, I wanted—

"Damn," I said. "I can't."

Zelda turned her head to stare at me. "Oh, Steven," she panted. "You can. Look at you—"

"I can't," I repeated. "I don't—I'm sorry. I'm sorry, Zelda."

Zelda looked as if she were going to cry. Then she turned back to her husband, glaring at him in fury.

"This is your fault, Walter, you son of a bitch!" she yelled.

Whatever flaws Walter may have had as a husband, I thought that was a bit unjust. But Walter was in no position to object, so I let him take the blame. She was still cursing at him when I left.

So I had turned down two women in one day. Surely a new record for me. Hell, one would have been a record, if I hadn't entered into this ridiculous wager. And for different reasons I wasn't feeling very good about either of them. In fact I wasn't feeling very good about anything just at the moment. Women had always been my greatest joy. If my life wasn't about women, then what the hell was it about?

It was late afternoon when I got back, and Miss Greenglass was still in the office. There was nobody I wanted to see more at that moment, and yet the situation was awkward. I had last seen her that morning while running away from her as she bared her breasts to me. But she showed no sign as I came in that anything was out of the ordinary between us.

"Miss Greenglass," I said, before even sitting down, "I want to apologize for—for this morning. It was—it was just—"

"Please, Mr. Walling," she said evenly. "There's no need for that. We were both trying to win a bet, that's all. You have nothing to apologize for, and I hope I haven't either."

"Of course not." I sank into my chair. I felt a hundred years old. "Anyway, nothing happened with Zelda," I said. "Nothing's going to happen. That whole thing is a bust."

"Well," she said. "I'm sure you'll find someone else before the time is up, Mr. Walling."

"No," I said. "The hell with it. I'm tired of doing this. It's not fun any more. It's not—it's not what I want anymore." I shook my head. "You win, Miss Greenglass. Congratulations. Your salary increase is now in effect."

"But I made it clear that I was giving up the pay increase, Mr. Walling."

"Well I'm giving it to you anyway," I said. "I believe in paying off my bets, it's something my father taught me. Not that I remember ever losing one before. But there's a first time for everything."

Miss Greenglass said nothing. She kept on doing whatever she was doing at the filing cabinet. I sat and watched her, for no special reason except that there was nothing else I felt like doing just then.

After a few moments she stopped and turned to me. "Mr. Walling," she said, and she paused. It was strange to see her apparently at a loss for words. "Mr. Walling," she said finally, "the fact is, I haven't been completely honest with you."

I raised my eyebrows. "You haven't?"

"No." For the first time I could remember, Miss Greenglass avoided my eyes as she spoke to me. "I'm afraid I . . . I have misled you about my name. My real name."

"What do you mean?" I said. "You aren't Miss Greenglass? Anne Greenglass?"

"I am Miss Greenglass, of course," she said. "But Anne is actually my middle name. I never use my real first name. I've never liked it."

"I see." I looked at her closely, but she was pretending to look for something among the files. "And what is your real first name, Miss Greenglass?"

"It's . . . it's Zoe," she said.

There was a long silence.

"Zoe," I repeated.

"Yes," Miss Greenglass said. "Zoe. I'm sorry for having deceived you, Mr. Walling."

I cleared my throat. "Well," I said. "Ah-huh. So. Then if I had—had accepted your generous offer this morning, I guess I would have won the bet after all."

"That is correct," Miss Greenglass said.

"I see." I paused, and just waited, looking at her, until finally she raised her eyes to mine. "Then why did you do it?" I said.

"Why did I—"

"Yes. You were doing it because you wanted to win the bet, you said. But you wouldn't have. You would have lost it. So why did you offer?"

"I . . . well, I . . . you . . . you didn't know, of course. You thought my name was Anne. You wouldn't have—it would . . ."

"You mean you would have kept up the deception, slept with me under false pretenses, and then taken the salary raise for winning a bet you had actually lost?"

"I—Yes," Miss Greenglass said. She went back to searching the files.

I sighed.

"Miss Greenglass," I said, "you do many things well. You are a first-rate assistant and a fine businesswoman. I have never—till now—seen you attempt anything that you did not carry off with the highest skill and efficiency.

"But, Miss Greenglass, you are a terrible liar. Just terrible. Take it from one who is an expert in that area. In order to succeed in this world, Miss Greenglass, you have to be a great liar. That is no doubt why I am the head of this company and you are a mere assistant. Well, that and the fact that my father left me the business—but then, he was a great liar too." I was rambling on like that because I was having strange feelings that I perhaps wasn't ready to face just yet. But it didn't seem to do much good.

"Your name isn't Zoe at all," I said finally. "Is it?"

"No," Miss Greenglass said.

I couldn't figure out what I was feeling, and I wasn't at all sure I liked it. But whatever it was, there didn't seem to be anything I could do about it.

"Then why?" I said. "Why did you say that, Miss Greenglass?"

It seemed like an hour before she raised her eyes to me again. When she did, it was like there was nothing else in the world for me but those eyes and what was in them.

"I think you know why, Mr. Walling," she said evenly.

"Tell me," I said. "Please."

"Because I—I don't like to see you like this. It makes me sad to see you sad, Mr. Walling. I have—yes, I have feelings for you." Her eyes never left mine. "And I—I thought I wanted to win our wager, but now it—it seems I want you to win."

For a moment it was hard to breathe. "And suddenly I don't give a damn if I lose," I said.

"In that case," Miss Greenglass said, "my offer is still open, Mr. Walling."

I looked at her for a long time. I felt as if I had been on a difficult and exhausting journey and had unexpectedly come to a turn in the road, to discover the object of my search—at the bottom of a precipice. I wasn't sure if it was a good idea to jump onto that precipice, but something was already pushing me over the edge.

Finally I stood up and walked around my desk. She turned from the filing cabinet to face me as I moved toward her. I stopped a couple of feet away.

"Miss Greenglass," I said.

"Yes, Mr. Walling?"

"Do you think," I said, "that I might call you Anne now?"

And then an unprecedented, unexpected and most wonderful thing suddenly happened.

Miss Greenglass smiled.

She actually smiled.

"Yes," she said. "Yes, I think so, Steven."

And then I was kissing her.

As I held her in my arms I understood beyond any question that I had gone over the precipice now and that I would probably never be able to get back out again. And at that moment I didn't want to. It was as if every woman in the world had suddenly become Miss Greenglass—Anne—and she had become them. I neither needed nor wanted anybody else.

Her lips were soft and warm, and for a time I was conscious only of the sweetness of her mouth and my unaccustomed new feelings. But soon I became aware of her body pressed so tightly, intimately against mine as we clutched each other—the yielding firmness of her breasts, the soft pressure of her loins, the whole of her leaning into me as if in final surrender—and I began to get hard. At the same moment her mouth opened under mine, and the nature of the kiss changed swiftly for both of us. I slid my tongue between her lips and she met it unhesitatingly with hers, a small sound of something like release coming from her throat.

My hands moved on her body then, slid over curves and hollows, tugged blindly at clothes, thrilling at the touch of her even through the barriers of silk and cotton. As one hand found and caressed her shapely buttocks, she panted softly into my mouth, and I felt her hands moving downward on my back. Our tongues entwined and explored and probed, our bodies strained to get even closer, and I knew then that I had always been right about the inner fire that burned, banked and invisible but never extinguished, behind the calm beautiful eyes of this most extraordinary woman.

As if with one accord, still kissing, we sank together to the carpeted floor. We landed in a tangled heap, excited but confused, and after a moment we reluctantly broke the kiss and moved apart, both breathing heavily. I gazed at her lying there, more disheveled than I had ever seen her and more gorgeous, her dark hair mussed, her blouse awry, her skirt riding up over her lovely legs, and a passion in her eyes that I had only dreamed about till now. "Undress me," she whispered in a new, husky voice.

So I did.

I unbuttoned her blouse with one hand while with the other I stroked from her neck down over the swell of her breasts, tracing their shape through the soft material as she caught her breath. The blouse came open, and again I was struck by the pellucid quality of the smooth flesh above and below the black brassiere. I slid the blouse from her shoulders and in the same movement reached beneath her to unclasp the bra and pull it off.

Her breasts, which I had caught only a swift glimpse of that morning, were now displayed to my leisurely gaze, and my hasty impression was confirmed: they were perfect, round quivering hemispheres, large enough to stand out from her body even in her recumbent position, yet firm and solid. The pinkish-red nipples were stiff and almost pulsing as I kissed them. I kissed them for a long time, my hands moving on her, on her thighs, beneath her skirt, until she was moaning gently, and I felt her hands at the buttons of my shirt.

I helped her, and my clothes came off swiftly. I moved down to unfasten her skirt, and she arched her body for me as I pulled it down over those finely curved legs, and I took her panties with them.

I had seen bodies that were more voluptuous, probably more spectacular, but I had never seen one as exquisite as hers—never one so magnificently put together, one whose beautiful parts merged into such a surprisingly marvelous whole—or one which I wanted more than I did hers right now. She looked at me, too, and her hands touched me, too, bold and tentative at the same time. I gasped as I felt her moving fingers on my stiff, turgid phallus. My hands were on her silken thighs, and I looked into her eyes as I felt her widen her legs.

"Yes," she breathed. "Yes, Steven. Now."

I moved between those thighs, which widened to receive me. I found her soft moist entrance and paused, looking into those fine, steady brown eyes that gazed up at me with a new vulnerability, taking me inside her as surely, as willingly as her body was about to.

"Yes," she said again. "Please."

Our eyes still held as I slowly moved into her. We gasped simultaneously as the penetration was made and we were finally together. I held back, but she pushed forward to urge me on. When I was completely inside her, she tightened the clasp of her thighs and encircled me with her arms, moaning. I think I moaned too.

Then we moved together, beginning with a slow rhythm that was not much more than a gentle rocking, savoring the sensations of our naked bodies clinging to each other. I could hardly believe that this was really Miss Greenglass I was making love to, whose flesh I was caressing, whose body was moving beneath me; and yet there was no doubt of it, for I knew that no one else had ever or could ever make me feel what I was feeling now. I had made love with women who made me groan, made me scream, made me laugh or cry or go crazy, but never one who made me feel as if I was home. And strangely enough, that seemed to be the most exciting feeling of all.

Gradually our movements grew faster. I kissed her mouth, her neck, her shoulders, her breasts, stroked her straining body. I heard her beautiful gasps and whimpers and cries as she moved with me, taking and giving, matching my pace and urging me on. It was almost as if we were one person. After a while I slowed down a bit, conserving my strength and not wanting things to end too soon. Anne looked up at me, not saying a word, and with one accord we rolled over so that I was on my back with her astride me.

I let her set the pace now, watching her body rise and fall, her lovely breasts bouncing gently, until I had to put my hands on them. She panted softly as she worked herself up and down my straining pole. Then swiftly the panting became louder, turned into a series of sharp cries as her body arched backward and she convulsed in sudden unexpected climax. I let her ride it out and then, with a moan of completion, she collapsed on me, gasping into my mouth as she kissed me fervently.

I rolled her over again, maintaining our connection but lying still on top of her until she had recovered, smiling up at me and telling me with her eyes and body that she was ready for me to continue. I began slowly again, but very soon the passion between us had risen higher than before, and I was moving hard, harder, thrusting into her eager, pliant body as her cries mingled with my hoarse panting. Both of us now strained to get closer, to become one with each other in every way. I felt that we had done just that when at last I felt her tense and gather herself, shuddering for a long moment on the brink before exploding into orgasm once again—this time so strongly that she screamed and dug her hands into my back. When her climactic writhing and spasming brought me past the point of control, I released everything I had into that delicious and delightful and most wonderful body with a rasping shout of my own.

I don't know how long we lay there holding each other and getting our breath back. The carpet in the office wasn't that thick, but to me it felt like a cloud.

"Damn," I said finally. "That was the greatest bet I ever lost."

She laughed softly. "I think we both won."

"I'm sure as hell not complaining," I said, stroking her behind idly. "But the fact is you're the winner, and you are now probably the highest paid assistant in this country."

"I told you I don't want the money," she said. "Really, Steven."

"I know." I leaned over to kiss her. "But as I said, I always pay my debts." There was a pause. And then I said something I had no idea I was going to say. When I had said it, it surprised me as much as it did her. Maybe more.

"Of course," I said, "if we got married we could keep the money in the family."

And then I said, "Holy Christ!"

Anne laughed out loud, a sound I had never heard before. It was a wonderful sound. "Is that a proposal, Steven?" she asked.

"Damn," I said. "Well. Well, I—Jesus. I guess it is." I looked at her then, and suddenly I was sure. Well, almost sure. "Yes," I said. "Yes, it is. Will you marry me, Miss Greenglass?"

For answer she kissed me. For a long time.

"I intend to continue working, though," she said, during a pause for breath. "Regardless of salary."

"I think you'd better," I said. "The business would fall apart without you."

"That is quite true," Anne said. And then we resumed kissing.

"I'd better put a couch in here," I said at the next break. "We'll probably be having a lot of—ah—business conferences and so forth, and it would be more comfortable than this floor."

"Oh dear," she said. "We'd never get any work done that way. Perhaps we had better dedicate the office to business only. We'll have plenty of other time together, Steven."

"Mmm," I said noncommittally, and kissed her again.

"However," she said huskily, "we don't have to put that into effect immediately, do we? Tomorrow will do."

"Or the next day," I said.

"Steven," she whispered as she reached for my cock. "Let's have another conference right now."

"An excellent idea," I said. "But I may need just a few more minutes to recover from the last one."

Miss Greenglass smiled.

"Want to bet?" she asked.

What do Americans love almost as much as sex? Talking about it. Here, as told in their own, uninhibited words, is the state of the union between men and women today, in all its inventive, eccentric, energetic variety. The sex is unbelievable . . . and every word is true!

TWO TIMES THE PLEASURE...
A THOUSAND TIMES THE FUN!

Two classic collections of Letters to Penthouse come together in one extraordinary volume. See how the sizzle started. And discover what makes the fire burn even hotter than ever. Penthouse magazine dared to bring the voices of the sexual revolution to a world eager to listen. And its readers dared to bare it all—the good, the bad, and the very, very naughty—revealing, in their own inimitable words, just how free, just how fabulous, and just how sexy their lives (and yours!) can be. Now, in PENTHOUSE UNCENSORED, share the thrill all over again, page after scorching page.

(0-446-67735-3, $14.95 USA) ($21.95 CAN)